The Museum of Curiosities

John

Urbancik

The Museum of Curiosities

John Urbancik

ISBN: 978-1-951522-09-4

For more information, please visit www.darkfluidity.com

The Museum of Curiosities

John

Urbancik

TABLE OF CONTENTS

A MESSAGE FROM THE CURATOR

I have been a great many places. Walking through the air of a Tasmanian Nordic rainforest, inside an active volcano, under the Atlantic Ocean over the Bimini Road. In my travels, I have seen much and heard more. I collect keepsakes and memorials from some of the places I've gone. From others, I only keep memories.

And all of those places, all of the people I've met there, are reflected in the stories in this collection. The golden forest canopy was real. The apartment next to the elevated train tracks exists. Even the sign, *For your safety: please lock windows*, is attached to a hostel window.

You'll notice plenty of allusions and references to other stories — not only my own. A rich tapestry lines the walls of life, and it accompanies us through good times and bad. You might see reference to my City of Night, Midnight. You may recognize Cool-Eyes when she makes a brief and unnamed cameo. There are others. And if you miss all of these, that won't matter at all.

You might recognize places I've lived, not just the cities but the apartments and houses themselves. You might think you recognize people, but I assure you no one makes it into or out of my stories intact. You'll find recurrent themes and motifs because that's just the nature of an artistic life.

I have sought out mysteries and the unknown every day of my life, and in these stories I attempt to explore the most fantastical elements I've run across. Our lives are made up of the shadows, legends, and secrets around us. We record our sins in blood and stone. We dream of walking in the dark, and if you're anything like me, you've probably stained your fingers with ink more times than you can count.

I hope you find something magical and mystical within these pages. I hope you find hope and dreams but also nightmares and terrors. I hope you find something that inspires you. But most of all, I hope you enjoy this tour of the inner worlds I have been fortunate enough to travel.

When you visit some of the places I have visited, and places I've never been, I hope you recognize echoes of my stories and histories and dreams in the stones and in the statuary and in the streets. With luck, you'll also step through them still breathing, but you will undoubtedly emerge transformed.

JOHN URBANCIK

The Museum of Curiosities

FOR YOUR SAFETY:
PLEASE LOCK WINDOWS

I'm three stories up.

No one's going to simply walk by and try the window. No one's sneaking in without a great deal of effort.

And the size of the window precludes accidentally leaning out and tumbling to the ground below, which probably couldn't happen anyway because of architectural elements.

No, the window must be psychically or magically sealed, and the glass serves an important role in the protection from wandering spirits.

So I throw open the window for the duration of my stay despite the cold. There's a particular spirit I would love to see again. I hope she'll see this as an invitation.

Just in case, I am prepared for interlopers.

THE MUSEUM OF CURIOSITIES

PHOENIX FIRE

The wind howls like a dying banshee. The horrible sound cuts straight through Sarah's bones. She goes to the window to stare into the night, but can make out no shapes in the shadows, no faces watching her, not even the fluttering of nocturnal butterflies. She pushes open the window to invite the crying wind into her bedroom. "Everything will be fine," she whispers without voice to the wind, but she knows this is untrue. Everything will not be fine. Something, in fact, is terribly wrong, though at first disguised by the comforting aroma of a wood fire.

The town is made up mostly of wood houses pressed against each other—for protection or warmth or comfort, she can only guess. She didn't exist when they first built this place.

The wind increases its ferocity, banging her window all the way open and scattering the papers on her desk. In its bosom, the wind carries fresh embers. They're small, barely alive, winking at her and smiling, and covered with thin flakes of ash.

Someone is ringing the bell, as is always done when the fires start. She can hear its echoes finally reaching through the wind as the man runs down the street. She doesn't recognize him. It's too loud, and it's only getting louder as the orange glow of flames peeks over and around the houses. Pushed on by the wind, the fire grows and spreads and rages.

Sarah adjusts herself to see better. The odor is stronger now, unmistakable and inescapable. People run through the streets. Dogs. Horses.

In their panic, unsurprisingly, they ignore Sarah locked away in her little tower, with her long hair and combs, with one painting of a winged horse, with her books and her ivory-handled mirror. They forget about her as they flee. She smiles, briefly, when she spots someone familiar. The boy who fetches for the baker. The seamstress, with her needles and thimbles and curse-casting eye. The innkeeper, who stumbles, still laden with drink, in a different direction from most townsfolk but still away from the flames.

Sarah cannot run. Even if she climbed out the window, it's too long a drop. Her hair will never be long enough for that. She would break an ankle or leg or neck, and then the flames would simply consume her. The sound of the fire rises as the flames grow bolder. It sounds just like a rainstorm. When one of the nearby houses collapses, it mimics thunder.

Sarah picks up her mirror, the ivory cold to her touch, the quicksilver-backed surface equally cool. She strokes it, then looks into her eyes. Her gran always told her she had pretty eyes, powder blue things that seem too small to Sarah, too close together, too narrow.

Sarah doesn't call out to anyone because she has no voice. She's never had a voice. She's never uttered a word except to the wind and the woods and perhaps the godlings who sometimes frolic in the nearby stream. She can't hear the stream. The fire is everything. The flames. The heat.

She bends over her reflected face in the mirror and whispers, "The flames will burn this town to the ground, every scrap of wood, every yard of silken dress, every hummingbird's breath." Her reflection appears to agree. This is good. She smiles.

Outside, the flames have spread to engulf the entire town to the east, some fifty structures total. Sarah takes a deep breath, not liking the tang of the smoke. To the west, another fifty houses and shops await their doom. She doesn't laugh. That's not a thing she does. But she feels light inside, full of laughter, and checks the mirror to see if her eyes twinkle like stars.

Outside Sarah's tower, there's an elderly woman who has seen fire many times before. She stares at the tower, at the window, directly at Sarah. The woman's face twists into ugly shapes as she shouts accusations and blasphemies at the sky. She shakes her fist as though righteousness would make any difference. After a moment, Sarah remembers the old woman's name, but she doesn't really care. She flicks her fingers at the woman, a gesture that says go away, you're not wanted here.

The fire catches the woman before she finishes her unheard litany. It's a terrible thing to behold, but Sarah doesn't look away. The woman's flesh blackens, peels away like onion skin, and blackens again, all the layers of her until no hide remains, until her muscles have sizzled, until her bones are charred. The wind scatters those remnants. The old woman has seen her final fire.

In the west, the houses feed the fires eagerly. Sarah wonders if other people, like the old woman, choose not to flee the oncoming flames. She shakes her head sadly, but feels no pity. They're stupid to stay. Stupid or foolish or weak.

But if any hearts beat within that town, Sarah doesn't hear them. Only her own: fast and getting faster. Her tower is surrounded by flames now, the whole town afire. The tower is at the eye of the infernal storm, the winds whirling about it, screaming now, angry, agitated. They blow hot and thick. A funnel of smoke, not unlike a tornado from the old stories, encircles the tower, but it's short-lived. That smoky attempt at architecture collapses with a whoosh. Houses fall in sympathy. Shops have burned out, leaving only smoldering mounds of ash and soot. The fire has consumed the town, blackening every inch of what surrounded the white tower, now a sentinel in the midst of a charnel house. The wind settles down and the rains start.

Any embers still smoldering are doused by the cold rain. It's relentless and absurd, dropping an ocean onto the town, washing away every trace of burnt wood, every cinder, every smear of residue in its wake. Only the tower remains, brilliant at the center of a barren field in the middle of a thick green forest.

Sarah sighs. Dawn breaks in the east, a burgeoning sliver of red cutting the sky like an echo of the night's fire. When the sun rises and its first rays hit the blanched land where once the town stood, houses come again into view. Shops return and are sometimes replenished. Bathtubs slip into existence. Cradles. Leatherworks and tach for the horses. As the sun rays fall farther, the town returns from the ghosts of ash and charcoal powder.

Gradually, even reluctantly, the townsfolk return, trudging down the streets to their homes to reunite with loved ones scattered by the chaos of the night. All but the elderly woman. Only one child, practically an infant, looks up at Sarah in her tower. Sarah smiles. Waves. Blows the child a kiss. The child giggles, briefly, though the sound seems unnatural in an otherwise soundless world. "Of course I love you," Sarah whispers without a voice, delivering the message in the most direct way she can. The child looks away, clings to its mother, trembles.

And the town has risen. Again. As it does every time. Sarah sighs and flops back on her bed and closes her eyes. With every fire, with every purge, and with every rebirth, she's sure she's closer to escaping this damned prison.

The Museum of Curiosities

AS HE SLEPT

Under the warmth of a full moon, in the shade of a massive oak with gnarled, twisting limbs on a mountainside in the Catskills, he fell asleep. He slipped quickly into a dream world, where he was more than he'd ever been: a warrior, a pirate, and a barbarian; feared by his enemies and respected by his allies; talented with a sword and a cutlass and an epee; quick-witted and sharp enough to discern the truth from onion layers of lies. He went on adventures, joining Jason in his search for the Golden Fleece, though in this version the rivers of the moon ran with quicksilver and there was an inconceivable betrayal. He helped the detective solve a mystery concerning a killer hound in the moors of Devonshire—he hadn't, until slipping into dreams, even known what a moor was.

He wrestled an octopus some twenty thousand leagues under the sea and briefly joined the Baltimore Gun Club for a launch attempt to reach the moon and maybe beyond. He was locked in an iron mask and imprisoned in Paris. He swam through freezing, shark-infested waters to escape Alcatraz. He even ran point in an art heist; as his share of the take, he kept Rembrandt's only seascape.

Eventually, he realized the dreams ran long. He counted the days, then counted the months, but lost track of the years. He rode horseback on the Silk Road and fought Franco in the mountains of Spain—not every adventure ended with victory. Indeed, he might have lost a limb once or twice, but even in the dreams he slept and always woke perfectly whole, as if the loss of limb—and once or twice, life—was itself a dream.

He fought on both sides of the Crusades, later joined the crew of the Endurance for an ill-fated attempt to cross Antarctica, and failed to save Mary Jane Kelly, with whom he'd had a brief but tawdry affair—though it was distinctly possible his paramour was never who she claimed to be.

He also shared a night with a Marilyn Monroe lookalike in New Orleans, but he didn't dare mention it to the real Marilyn when they shared a box as her husband showed off during a spring training game in '54.

Cleopatra, apparently, had him buried him alive within a nest of asps.

The dreams continued over the course of numerous lifetimes until, inadvertently walking in on the set of *Duck Soup* during production, he received two fingers straight to the eyes. It was enough to jolt him back to reality. He woke with the liquor bottle still in hand but the Dutchman nowhere in sight. He vaguely remembered playing nine pins the night before; now, his beard was a foot long and his musket rusted to rot, and he had missed the Revolution entirely.

THE TRAIN, THE WOMAN IN RED, AND THE ROSES

The train rolls by right outside his window. It's the only window in his entire apartment. He can see commuters jammed shoulder to shoulder in their cheap suits and fancy ties, carrying briefcases and attaches, weighed down by the lifeless expressions of drones being moved to and fro to feed the gods of economics.

Those gods would never be caught dead in a train. They have fancy cars and drivers and security men making sure they can get into their backseats unaccosted.

When the train passes, the apartment, the whole building, shakes with its terrible unstoppable force. If one day the first cart of that train jumped the tracks and entered his living room, the rest of train would follow, dutifully and without interruption, until everyone in the train was dead and the bricks of the apartment building scattered for three blocks.

It's always raining when the train rolls by.

He sets his watch to its schedule. It's never early, and only late if there's been an accident somewhere down the line. The suits are drab, the faces bland, there's nothing of excitement inside—no murder, no betrayal, no steamy love affairs—and it wakes him most mornings. Every evening, it rumbles in the other direction on the same tracks.

He wonders if one day they'll try to drive trains in both directions simultaneously. That wouldn't end well. He doubts they have two trains with which to do it.

Some mornings, he's still awake from the night before, drinking cheap wine, maybe chatting with one of his lady friends online. They're always in another time zone so they don't know how late—early—it is for him. When the train comes, it's like thunder, like a storm, like a force of nature.

One of his lady friends says, "That is amazing. I must see it in person some time."

But she'll never see it.

Sometimes, he stares as the train goes by and tries to make eye contact with one of the passengers through the windows. It moves fairly slowly, but the people inside that steel snake are generally lost, gazing inward but seeing nothing. He's even displayed some of his paintings, waiting for someone's eyes to open, for life to creep into one of those cars.

Other days, he loses hope entirely.

This morning, the train grumbles as it wakes him. He fell asleep in his chair again, the one facing the window, the one from which he watches rain streak the glass and the factory smoke in the near-distance. Sometimes, he catches the reflection of the neon sign from the eatery across the street.

In one of the cars, wearing a brilliant ruby dress, a woman with blonde hair and dazzling eyes stares back at him. She sees him first, if that's possible. Her eyes lock with his. She's mysterious and alluring and damn beautiful, and she's the most colorful thing he's ever seen outside of his paintings. Her lips part as the train carries her past. She's got words to offer him. He wants to hear those words, her voice, her whispers. He wants to open a bottle of wine with her and discover all her secrets.

He puts aside his current canvas and works in reds and golds to create what might be an abstraction but might also be the most realistic thing he's ever rendered. It's the woman, of course, glimmering like the stars—what he remembers of stars from that one time when he was young and visited his uncle's country place—her lips as red as roses. He goes out and buys a dozen, and a bottle of burgundy wine; and he makes sure he's back before the train comes by in the other direction.

The train comes, and goes, but he sees no sign of the woman.

No one ever rides that train in a single direction.

He opens his window. He can't remember the last time he's opened that window. He's not even sure it's ever been opened. He's lived in the apartment three years. He lets in sticky wet air thick with city odors so he can lean out as far as possible to watch the train dwindle in the distance. It's mostly a straight line past his apartment until it curves, and there the train disappears, taking its noise with it.

There are still city noises. Everything's so much louder with the window open, louder and brighter and thicker, in ways that simply walking the streets never showed him. He takes a deep inhalation of the city and feels a smile stretch over his teeth. He hangs there for a long while, watching motionless tracks which carry the train twice every day. In his head, he searches for the right curse words, the proper epithets. Something must be appropriate, but his talents lie in colors and chiaroscuro, not in metaphors.

Eventually, he closes the window. He sets the roses in a vase. He opens the wine to let it breathe. He has two glasses on the table, and the painting facing the tracks so the passengers in the morning will see it. He sighs, and is just starting to pour a glass of wine when someone knocks on his window.

It's not a sound he's ever heard before.

The woman in the red dress stands on the tracks. She's angled precariously over the edge to reach his window. He opens it, and stares at her, and isn't sure if she's even real.

"Aren't you going to invite me in?" she asks, her voice more magnificent, deeper and more thoroughly soulful, than he'd hoped, and tinged with an exotic accent.

"Please, yes," he says. He extends a hand. She takes it, her fingers warm and nimble, and leaps over the abyss between tracks and apartment—just as the train might if, say, someone cracked the tracks in just the right place. In a frightening moment, she hovers, and from here she could drop three stories to dark asphalt and busy city traffic. She loses only one red shoe.

She lands in his arms. She smiles. She says, "Slow down, *Escamillo*." She stands back to examine the painting. "You made this today?"

"For you."

"Thank you," she says. "I feel the same."

They spend the night together drinking wine and telling each other stories, laughing and, at times, near tears. His lady friends in other time zones probably won't even miss him. He tries to present the roses to *la Roja* somewhere near midnight, but she says, "Best if we leave those. Something so they'll know we were here."

"And the painting?" he asks.

"And the painting," she says.

In the morning, the train, carrying its payload of office workers, drones, and zombies, hits a crack in the tracks exactly where *la Roja*'s heels had launched from. The train skips the rails and careens into the painter's apartment, shattering the bricks and the window, tearing apart the painted canvas. Each of the next seven cars follows the first blindly into oblivion.

Authorities count the dead and the wounded. Though they find no sign of *Escamillo* or *La Roja* aside from the tattered canvas, they piece together the scattered remnants of eleven roses.

Elsewhere, at the edge of the city where the sun glows golden on the horizon and the rain never falls, the painter and the woman in red — clutching one red rose in her free hand, her other clasped within his — never hear the train, even when it mewls and howls and shrieks. They hear only their own heartbeats, two syncopated rhythms circling each other and slowly becoming one.

DAY OF THE DRAGONS

1.

It is a well established fact: dragons are rare in the city of Madrid. But in the narrow lanes twisting through a section of the city called Malasaña, among the trendy vintage shops and cervecerías and tattoo parlors, you might find anything.

On a rainy Tuesday afternoon, Luis Diego walks under the gray streets. It is the middle of the day, so most of the shops are closed for lunch, but he isn't looking for something you'd find in a typical store. His hood protects him some from the rain and the cold. His hands are thrust firmly in his pockets. He glances with appreciation at the graffiti on the metal grates rolled down in front of shop doors. A cocktail glass here with a red liquid resembling a rose, a demonic face, a series of sloppy tags in half a dozen languages.

On a street just wide enough for a small car, he reaches his destination. Across the street, the white door has a red dragon curled around its edges. Luis smiles at it, but the door he wants is primarily glass, with iron bars, and an ornate 3 in the arch overhead.

He withdraws a key from his pocket. How he acquired the key is a tale he would rather not share. The old lock is stubborn, but finally acquiesces. Luis enters the vestibule and waits for the door to shut behind him.

Ahead, there are stairs on the left, and a hallway leading past them to an elevator. He walks toward the elevator, then around it. Two tiled steps down bring him to a courtyard between buildings. To the right and left, neighbors rise four or five stories, strings of laundry hang to dry in the rain, and small waterfalls cascade down the sloped roofs. Ahead, however, is another building, three stories, tucked between its neighbors so no side faces any street. Here, another hall ends at another elevator, the doors of which creak and rattle as they open.

Luis steps into the elevator. It's a long ascent. The machinery ticks and rattles as it rises.

The elevator opens, not on a hall or even a room, but a small landing with doors to the left and the right, and a staircase that coils around the elevator shaft as it descends. The identical doors appear reddish in the dark, thick and foreboding. He turns to the right. It's only one step away. He knocks three times on the door. The echo reaches down the stairs, returns as a whisper. From inside, someone disengages the locking mechanism, a series of key turns that moves the bolts and eventually opens the door.

He's an old man, short, stocky, with narrow eyes and solid shoulders. He looks like he's wrestled in the past, not in the Olympics but in darker pits, where the stakes are higher and the crowds rarified. The scars across his leather face and gnarled hands would tell a book of stories for someone interested in reading.

Luis says, "I'm interesting in a purchase."

The man asks, "What have you to trade?"

Luis reveals three coins. Each wears a difference face. Each is old as the moon, though not so old as the sun. They are pristine. Two have made long and probably arduous journeys to reach the Iberian peninsula. They glitter, even in the shadows, before Luis closes his hands over them.

"Fine," the man says, pulling the door further open. "Come in."

The first room in the apartment is a kitchen crowded with pots, some simmering on the stovetop, and numerous kitchen implements hanging from hooks. There's a birdcage, too, inside which a strange, featherless bird regards Luis with suspicion. Aromas strike him in waves: vanilla, then something rancid like sour milk, citrus, and finally an earthy cinnamon. The kitchen opens immediately onto a living room, where a window overlooks a hidden courtyard.

"They don't last long in captivity," the old man tells him.

Luis nods once in acknowledgement.

"Wait here."

The living room contains a couch, an array of books on shelves, a human-like skull full of pens, dice of brass and bone, and playing cards with mysterious suits and faces. A hall leads alongside another window onto that courtyard. Beyond that, another door leads to what may be a bedroom. Luis sees only the edge of a bed. In this room, the old man unlatches a window—Luis sees this through the window in the living room—and uses a pulley system to haul something up from the courtyard.

It's like a birdcage. The bird in the kitchen ruffles its featherless skin and issues a string of foreign curses.

The old man returns with the covered cage. He allows Luis a peek under the heavy cloth to see the small thing curled around itself inside, its scales golden and its eyes emerald. It looks up at Luis, yawning, and already looks tamed.

Luis hands over the three very special coins, takes the cage—it's lighter than he expects—and leaves the apartment. He leaves the street. He leaves Malasaña, and eventually leaves Madrid.

2.

Luis Diego, a young man now, in a studded leather coat, arrives in Malasaña on a Tuesday afternoon. He still has a key. The paint on the door opposite has faded and flaked, but still portrays that red dragon. He wonders, briefly, if it means more than he realized as a boy, but eventually unlocks the door to Number 3. He walks past the stairs, then around the elevator into the courtyard. Looking up, he cannot see the windows to the third floor apartments on either side, just the cracks in the walls, a line of clothes drying, and a Spanish flag hanging from the balcony of a neighboring structure.

Once again, Luis ascends to the third floor. The elevator takes its time, as though considering whether to deliver him at all. He uses his knuckles three times on the door, and again waits. After the old man disengages the locks and opens the door, he looks Luis up and down. His face has more tales to tell, some of them fresh. Luis repeats his words: "I'm interested in a purchase."

The old man twists his lips into something visceral and narrows his eyes, which causes the bushes of eyebrows to lower like shrouds. "With what?"

Luis shows him a notebook. It's handwritten, and not, strictly speaking, leather. It contains sketches and symbols the old man might recognize, and long paragraphs about the nature of unnatural things. The book comes from a distant land and a distant time, and has passed through the hands of people famous, infamous, and notorious, but only in secret. Luis allows the old man to look only with his eyes, and turns a few pages to display the legitimacy of the prize.

"Fine," the old man says, opening the door all the way. "Come in."

Luis enters the kitchen again. The odors this time are purely offensive and nearly overwhelming. The featherless bird gives Luis the evil eye and says, "You again. You again."

The old man ignores the bird. "Wait here." It takes longer for him to make his way down the hall and into that bedroom. It takes longer for him to operate the pulley, which requires some strength and, therefore, more effort for the aging old man. He returns with another covered cage.

"They don't live long, as you know," the old man says. "Not in captivity."

Luis nods. "I know." He peeks under the covering at the white dragon curled up inside. It looks up at him with brilliant crimson eyes still full of hope.

Luis hands over the book. He takes the cage and leaves the apartment, leaves Malasaña, and leaves Madrid.

3.

Luis Diego is older now. He reaches Madrid under cover of night. He wears a bespoken suit and sits in the back of a private car. His driver maneuvers through Malasaña like a professional, stopping between Number 3 and a door which barely shows the silhouette of a dragon anymore. It's still there after all these years.

Luis enters Number 3, passes stairs and elevator, walks through the courtyard, and doesn't take the elevator up this time. He no longer trusts it. The stairs creak as he walks, and strain to hold him, but they're safer. It's a long walk, those three flights winding around the elevator shaft. The shadows of the third floor landing are amazingly thick. Elsewhere in Madrid, the rising sun can probably be seen, but not here in a building hidden between and behind taller buildings.

Luis knocks three times on the door. He waits. He waits some more. He knocks again, and the old man mumbles from the other side, "Impatient, ungrateful," and a few other words swallowed by the wood. When he opens the door, he meets Luis's eyes and grimaces.

When Luis doesn't say anything, the old man eventually asks, "Interested in another purchase, are you? What have you got this time? An atlas? Starry jewels?"

Luis smiles, an echo of a long ago smile outside the door to Number 3, but shakes his head. "I'm here to end your trading days."

The old man narrows his eyes. He moves to shut the door, but Luis kicks it open, throwing the old man back and off his feet. Luis strides into the kitchen. The caged bird says, "Uh oh," and tucks his head under his featherless wing.

The old man looks up at him. The veins on his face reveal arcane secrets and hidden strengths. His fists tighten. His eyes glimmer despite the darkness. "They never survive long in captivity," the old man says. "I warned you. Don't make me kill you."

Luis smiles and bends over the old man. "You have spells and muscles and all manner of protections, I'm sure. I, however, have two dragons."

Golden and arctic, they crash up through the elevator shaft, destroying the device, shattering the stairs around them, scarring the walls and smashing windows as they rise. The size of baby and adult elephants, neither fits into the elevator, and neither fits easily through the door, so they splinter the wood and iron bolts as they enter.

"I'm just a trader," the old man tells Luis.

"Just a trader," the bird repeats.

"I know." Luis strides past the old man, down the hall, and into the bedroom. It's pathetic, crowded with relics the old man cannot utilize. He throws opens the window and peers down into the darkness of the second courtyard. It may as well be a bottomless pit. In the apartment, the dragons consume the featherless bird and its cage. They consume the old man. And they smash all the pots and shelves.

Dragons, in captivity, rarely live to the age of five, but Luis Diego never kept the dragons in cages.

The inner courtyard cannot be reached from the outside. It does not open between buildings. Luis rappels using the pulley ropes. The dragons shatter the bedroom window to descend after him.

Dragons, even infant dragons, are difficult to transport, especially in secret, so a trader illicitly selling them must be close to his source. The courtyard descends five or six floors, not merely three, into a subbasement below the basement, and leads to a tunnel. Luis lights a flashlight to follow the tunnel, the two dragons crouching as they follow. He feels the rumble of the metro not too distant and hears the thunder of automobiles on the street overhead. Finally, he reaches the chamber in which the mother dragon is detained.

She's chained, bound, tied, strapped in place, and hooked to a series of tubes delivering medicine meant to keep her meek and incoherent. She's a brilliant shade of russet, gleaming even in the darkness of this basement. There's a caretaker, but Luis isn't interested in him. He's just a young man in a lab coat thankful for employment. There's a series of cages, a dozen or more, in which infant dragons mewl and coo.

Luis says to the caretaker, "Release her."

"I can't do that."

"You can," Luis says, revealing his threat just with his eyes, "and you will."

The caretaker shakes his head and shows the palms of both hands. "No, really, I can't."

There are keys. Always keys. But these are dragons, and no mere iron chains can hold them. Luis says to the two young dragons, "Release your mom."

The chamber is hardly large enough for them to take flight, but they rise on enormous wings and spew plumes of white-hot fire on the chains, on the tubes, on all the things holding their mother down. The metals melt. The mother, being a dragon, is unharmed by the flames, and maybe even draws strength from the warmth.

Whatever the reason, she finds vigor enough to shred through the rest of whatever restricts her. She opens her mouth to scream, a thunderous sound that shakes the city as far away as the palace. Briefly, she eyes the caretaker. He wears fear like it's the ultimate fashion statement. She knows his sins. She swallows him whole.

Opening all the cages and releasing the infants, Luis pauses only long enough to tell the mother, "Up." These tunnels were never meant to house a fully grown dragon. There's no other direction to go.

She breaks through the ceiling. She crashes through basements and the tunnel of a metro line. She smashes through the base of a building, a structure four stories high, and brings the whole thing down. She spreads her wings for the first time in a hundred years and roars for the first time in a hundred years. The golden dragon lifts Luis through the new shaft behind its mother and deposits him next to his private car. Gold like sunlight and white like fire, the dragons follow their mother, as do all the babies freshly released: a formation of dragons like enormous birds across the Madrid dawn. Only a few thousand people in the city see the dragons fly.

His driver waits like a professional, leaning against the front of the car, just out of reach of the twisted red dragon door. Nothing else remains of the building across from Number 3.

No one has seen a dragon on the Iberian peninsula for a hundred years or more until that strange Tuesday morning, and maybe no one will see another. They call that day *El Diá de los Dragones*, and celebrate with feasts of roasted meats and wine. No one knows Luis Diego, or what else it is he's done, except perhaps a few hermits, wanderers, and practitioners who keep secrets both dark and wondrous.

The Poet

He wrote silly poetry for the woman he met online. He knew it was stupid to invest any hope in such a relationship. She sent him pictures, but could just as easily have been an aging plumber in Brooklyn nicking pictures off of Instagram.

He used to write poetry about landscapes and the human condition and existential atmospherics. He wove metaphor and meaning around evocative imagery until she waltzed into his life—no, she tangoed, and she led, and he was all in.

He told her he'd get a ticket to travel all the way to the other side of the country to visit. No, she said. Her living situation was precarious. There was an ex with a gun and a child and maybe a dog, an ultra-protective German Shepheard. I'll come to you, she said, when you least expect it.

Six eternal weeks, this had been going on. He'd stopped submitting to the national poetry rags, opting instead to send her sentimental verses about love and roses and poison and moonlight.

She sent a picture from the platform of an Oregon train station. Wind blowing her sunlit hair. Eyes practically gleaming. She said she was escaping.

Then: silence.

He wrote her poems of longing, of absence, of existential dramatic acrobatics. He evoked the carnival act of emotions shredding his guts. He didn't sleep. He drank twice his usual quantity of bourbon. He sent her lines about life on the road, about cosmic terrors, about the utter loneliness of a one bedroom apartment overlooking the Interstate.

Still silence.

He wrote about the ideals of poetic life, bards traveling from town to city, sleeping under bridges, making new friends and meeting new lovers in every new port. He even wrote a poem about repairing the engine in his twenty year old Toyota, twisting wrenches and cleaning grease from his jeans.

Nothing.

Then the morning came when the stupid day job that paid his bills told him they didn't need his services any longer. He could no longer pay the rent. No one in this city needed him to do anything. So he loaded his most precious belongings into his Toyota, left all the rest of it to the landlord, and hit the road.

He poeticized about the places he visited, the gunfire in Atlanta, the broken hearts in Tennessee, the windmills lining the pocked roads of Indiana, and cornfields in Peoria.

He drove through Iowa and called his mom from a gas station in Omaha. "I never thought I'd say this, but I'm in Nebraska."

His mom begged him to come home, or to be careful, or to at least keep in touch.

Through the Rockies, he wrestled with snow. In Utah, he stopped at a gas station welcoming green aliens in flying saucers. He turned north and got a baked potato in Boise, then crossed into Oregon without any fanfare.

That night, she wrote him. It was brief. It was quick. She said there had been no escape. That was it. Nothing more. No proclamations or declarations, no apologies, no explanations. He read the message repeatedly sitting on the foot of a neglected motel on the side of Highway 26.

"It's okay," he said aloud, forgetting to write this part in a poem. "I'm almost there."

He arrived the next day. Early afternoon. She was sitting on the porch. She must've recognized the Toyota from his poetry. She smiled, but did not get up. The German Shepheard growled. The ex with the gun actually had two, one in each hand, like a desperado in an old film, and smiled with crooked teeth.

The poet settled matters swiftly with a snub-nosed revolver he'd obtained on the road and one tug of the trigger.

The dog barked. The woman screamed. The child, inside the house, cried.

That night, sitting in a jail outside Bend, the poet received a visitor. The elderly gentleman leaned heavily on a cane. He called the poet by name, but insisted he was a hired deliveryman. The envelope had been opened and the letter read by the policeman up front.

I'm sorry, the note said, and was signed *A Plumber in Brooklyn.*

The Ghost Writer

If we sneak into the ghost writer's laboratory, we can get an idea of what it's really like to work with words. Because he doesn't merely spin words into the kinds of phrases you'll remember forever. He works in mists.

Look at him now, dipping that sharp fountain pen into a jar of ectoplasmic shadow. You can feel the ghosts scream—they don't make any noise that can be heard by human ears, but it rattles the bones and plays hell with your vision. If you're prone to migraines, you probably shouldn't have come this far.

He doesn't just reach into that jar casually. It's like he's fishing. He has a particular ghost he wants, and he can see the lines that differentiate one from another. There may be a thousand and one ghosts in that jar, but I've never known him to miss. He's been writing these kinds of tales for quite a while now.

He spreads that phantasmagorical ink on the page and can almost just sit back and let the stories tell themselves. But he's a cruel taskmaster. He leans in and whispers. He tells the ghosts the stories he wants: not just about their lives, but about their souls. He wants to reveal the kinds of truths those ghosts were unable to reveal when they were alive.

That's why they end up in his jar: because they were insufficiently brave and failed to live their truths.

You'd be shocked at how many ghosts end up in jars just like this one. There's a packing plant in Ithaca, New York, with a huge warehouse, and some ghost writers will simply order them wholesale.

But this guy, he's quite particular. He spends time in bars, crossing countries, riding on subways and airplanes, listening to the stories of real, living people and deciding if theirs is a soul that would give him the right kind of tale.

Most souls are only good for one story. We all have one that's the story of us, the essential core of who we are and what we were meant to do. We don't all live that.

He picks his marks, he follows them into alleys and hotel rooms and bathrooms, wherever he finds it's most appropriate, and collects the ghosts in little glass vials he carries in an antique apothecary's case.

Don't look so surprised. How did you think ghost writers worked?

All the best of them collect their own. To be honest, true geniuses will groom their ghosts, but that takes the kind of time and effort that doesn't allow for prolific production. If you spend five years working on a single soul, it's a long stretch between stories.

And this guy, he's damn prolific. Although I hear he sometimes special orders his ghosts, one at a time, from specialty shops in Prague and São Paulo. And he's got a cousin in Brooklyn who haunts the darkest crevices of Coney Island to pick off some sweet stories of heartbreak and genuine pain.

Oh, and you, you weren't brought here simply to be a spectator. Sorry. I misled you a little bit. You're to be the star of the next epic. You've got a broken soul—everyone's soul is cracked and chipped apart—but yours is exquisite, and our ghost writer has been waiting for you to come round and let him use your deepest sorrows, your most crippling fears, the fading memories of your greatest joys.

Oh, it'll be mostly painless, don't worry about that. And we'll take good care of your body. We'll just deposit your soul and your heart in this glass mason jar—I'll seal it tight—and when he's ready, when you've gestated enough, when the juices of your story are thick and viscous, he'll use that sharp fountain pen and give your tale a stab.

WINTER TRAVELERS

A traveler arrived despite the snow, despite the wind, despite the blinding sunlight reflecting off every surface. He was a grizzled man, leathery of face, his limbs moving stiffly, but his cracked lips smiled generously.

The innkeeper took the traveler in, sat him at the fire, gave him hot chocolate. "I wasn't expected anyone today," the innkeeper admitted.

That was when the innkeeper noticed the traveler's eyes. One was light brown, almost amber, almost golden. The other was gray and lifeless and did not move. Perhaps glass, the innkeeper thought, but he didn't ask.

"I appreciate the hospitality," the traveler said. "It's been a long many miles on this endless day."

They were far enough north that each day lasted days. The sun was low on the horizon, but already rising again, never having actually set. The moon was nowhere to be seen.

"Where might you be headed?" the innkeeper asked, a common enough question.

"South."

"Out of the snow?"

The traveler's smile faltered. "No, no, not that." He sighed heavily, as though the weight of the sky rested on his shoulders, as though he was all that prevented the blue from smothering the world. "There's a poet, south of here, I need to find."

"A poet?" the innkeeper asked, intrigued. "I know of several, all far from here, and some of those may be dead."

"And all of them," the traveler added with a little laugh, "are mad."

"Do you seek a particular poet?"

The traveler nodded. "He's an adventurer of the soul, a self-proclaimed wordsmith, who has had hard and easy times in his life, but he's at the end of a big project."

"I don't understand."

"The world is a sphere," the traveler said. "When you start here in any direction and proceed, never stopping despite the obstacles, you come back around again to here."

"That seems unlikely," the innkeeper said. The world, he knew, was enormous, and no one could walk so straight a line as that. There were oceans, volcanoes, deserts, everything.

"It's illustrative," the traveler said, sipping the chocolate. "This is quite delicious."

"I borrowed the recipe from the memories of a woman I once knew in Barcelona," the innkeeper confessed.

The traveler nodded. Finishing the last of the drink, he put the mug down and leaned back. "I'll be leaving again soon. I have many more miles to travel."

"Can I ask something?"

"You may ask."

"Who are you?"

The traveler smiled. He looked away, as if searching for an easy explanation in the ceiling or from the spiders who must surely spin their webs in the corners — or maybe some crevice within his mind. "I am but a traveler," he said, "and a patron of poets."

This excited the innkeeper. "Like a muse?"

"You might say that."

"I do," the innkeeper said. "You're going to show this poet that the end of one project means the beginning of another?"

"I'm going to show this poet endings are never truly final," the traveler said. He shook his head. "I'll do so by giving him an ending."

"My favorite tales always end with a happily ever after," the innkeeper said, ignoring the big knife in its sheath on the traveler's hip. "But I know they don't always."

"His won't," the traveler said.

The innkeeper did not pursue that line of conversation. "More hot chocolate?"

"That would be lovely."

The innkeeper refilled the traveler's mug and one for himself. They sat for a while at the fire, listening to its crackle, though it really did little to keep back the arctic. The traveler was a hefty man, a burly man, and quite content sitting staring into the flames, but the innkeeper's curiosity had been aroused. "What's the name of the poet you seek?"

The traveler shook his head. "Just a poet," he said. "His name is unimportant. No one will remember him."

"That's sad," the innkeeper said. "I would think a poet should be remembered."

"Some people think that," the traveler said. "A great many more simply do not care."

"And what will happen with this project he's finishing?"

"He'll leave the pages for his heirs."

"Will they do something with it?"

"Who can say? But I doubt it. So if you're meaning to ask if you might see the poet's project, I suspect no. But I am no fortuneteller."

"I happen to know a fortuneteller," the innkeeper said, "though she's far from here."

"Yes," the traveler said. "She's a poet, too, isn't she? I may visit her, too, if only to share a drink."

"I didn't tell you her name."

"You don't need to."

At that, the innkeeper nodded and excused himself to do a bit of unnecessary bookkeeping and housekeeping. The traveler leaned back in his chair and closed his eyes, and for all the world looked to be sleeping when he suddenly said, "I know something of you, too, innkeeper."

"What do you mean?"

"That little black book you keep in your room."

The innkeeper put down his pen and stared, horrified, from his desk. "I haven't shown that to anyone since my wife passed..."

"She told me."

"When?"

"More recently than you'd care to know," the traveler said. "Might I make a suggestion?"

The innkeeper took a breath. Held it. He didn't quite know what to do. He looked down at the pen, a nice little fountain pen, and the brilliant ink it left on the page. The same ink he'd used to scratch in his little black book. Reluctantly, he said, "You might."

The traveler never turned his gaze from the fire. "You might show it to someone."

Another traveler knocked at the door just then. The innkeeper appreciated the interruption.

At the door, shivering in the cold, stood a woman with powerful green eyes and trembling lips and an insufficient coat for the climate. "Come in, come in," he said, ushering her toward the fire. "I'll have a room ready for you straight away. In the meantime, there's the fire in the hearth, and I'll have a mug full of hot chocolate for you to warm your bones."

The traveler, the poetic muse, had gone—not to his rooms, as no bed had been prepared yet. He'd simply vanished, leaving an empty mug of chocolate and a little black book the innkeeper was sure he'd kept well hidden in his room.

The woman picked it up, turned it over as she sat, and said, "Thank you." Without asking, she opened the book, turned to the first page, found the words he'd scribbled in the darkest of long nights, and began to read.

The innkeeper made no move to prevent her. After simply staring for a moment, less at the woman than at his own book of poems in her hands, he noticed the trace of a smile forming on her lips. Without looking up, she asked, "Are these yours?"

The GREAT ESCAPE

They planned the great escape poorly.

The people with money—not intelligence or skills—made all the arrangements. They didn't consider, as the earth broke around them, the "masses" would insist, quite strongly, on their own salvation. Not nearly enough ships were constructed. Their spacious living quarters were, quite forcibly, subdivided.

This meant the resources, food and oxygen supplies, were insufficient for the long, long journey. Even before takeoff, there were numerous betrayals, poisonings, shootings, and morally questionable machinations. The scientists most qualified to handle the logistics had been excluded by both the elite as inferior and the masses as elitists; it didn't require a deep, penetrating understanding of omens, portents, tea leaves, or tarot to foresee what was likely to happen.

Further, though the wealthy had arranged to bring their favorite pianos and assorted family heirlooms, no allowance had been made for the personal items of the crew, never mind the masses that joined them. Some of those people brought pots and pans, which displayed a certain level of an otherwise absent foresight. Others brought books, videos (but no machines to play them), boards for draughts and backgammon, an insufficient supply of playing cards and bottle caps (for betting, of course), fancy bowls, and family photo albums.

Thus, fuel was insufficient, and at launch they would barely reach the velocity required to break the atmosphere. The scientists, in their secret vessels launched from remote sites in the red centre of Australia and South America's Amazon, could observe the faltered trajectories from their porthole windows.

Politics, of course, interfered, as well as uncomfortable family dynamics, an excessive degree of ignorance and arrogance, and enough abuse and bigotry to fuel the collapse of empires.

On the day the ships broke the clouds—ninety gleaming silver rocket ships in total, including the secret scientific vessels, the *Kepler* and the *Jump Cannon*—more than seven billion people watched with anger and animosity, shaking fists and shouting curses.

After that, a quiet fell across the earth.

After the quiet, an unforeseen level of peace erupted. It took a few days, weeks really, for most people to realize maybe things would be better without those who had so desperately sought to escape the problems they and their ilk had spent generations creating. Perhaps the worst seeds of humanity had constructed the ships or forced their way onto them.

It took a while longer for the earth itself to calm down, for the volcanoes to begin cooling and the hurricanes to stop spinning, for the earth to cease its quaking and the fires to burn themselves out. After all that, brothers divided by centuries of conflict tore down the walls and barbed wire and went to work clearing minefields and cleaning beaches.

On the ships, as they passed the orbit of Jupiter, a new problem arose. The masses had refused to allow the elite to escape without them, and the ships had become battlegrounds. Lines were drawn, sides chosen, feuds ignited; then something worse happened, something unimagined.

The gods, the little petty gods, the wicked gods, the minor deities and false idols and all manner of spirits, emerged from hiding. They, too, especially those who were immortal, refused to remain on a dying planet. They'd stowed away, and now they squabbled like meaningless but powerful gods had always squabbled, dominating sections of ships, driving one straight into the oceans of Ganymede, where it sank and was never heard from again.

The little gods divided and conquered and ruled over the refugees like little gods always had. Eventually, quite quickly in fact, the ships went to war with each other as the gods rekindled long-held grudges and hostilities. Only about three dozen ships reached the heliopause — a fact recognized only by the scientists on the *Jump Cannon*, but even they were beset by river nymphs and gods of twilight struggling for relevance.

When the final three ships collided, some years after beginning their exodus, it took less than twenty hours for the light from that explosion to be visible in earth's night sky. Around the world, a memorial was held, a kind of wake, with an appropriate moment of silence, a mourning period of almost a full week, and a jazz revival that went on for a year.

ThE ENDLESS DANCE ENDS

We dance at midnight and we dance at dawn. The musicians, when they tire, are replaced; there's a steady supply of clarinetists and trombonists. The dim lights are just enough to not call it dark, but shadows enshroud the ballroom. The only reason you can see anything is because the colors are so damn violent.

I mean vibrant.

Surely I meant vibrant.

We dance, whether we wear red shoes or brown. Melodies melt seamlessly into the next, giving us barely enough time to switch partners, if you want to switch, if your partner will let you.

My legs ache. My smile aches. It's not much of a smile, but it's pasted on, and I keep it on, because otherwise someone will ask questions. Smile too much, and you're not taking the dance seriously. The chaperones will remove you. The chaperones remove you utterly from existence.

Or maybe they expel you from the dream, because that's all this is: an endless, shifting dream where the players are all imagined, not actual people suffering at the end of another day of ceaseless dancing.

You can always escape, but survival in the hellscape outside the dancehall seems unlikely. Molten red skies stretch thinly from horizon to horizon. Yellow birds screech. You can see the scars from their razor beaks on the brick columns visible through the dancehall windows.

There aren't many windows. Just enough to dissuade us.

So we dance. The musicians play. The chaperones enforce frivolity.

Inside, we die a little every measure, every beat.

My partner now, she's a weight, heavy in my arms, unable to hold herself up. If I let go, she'll drop. She pleads with her eyes for me to support her, to keep her going, to give her a chance to catch a second or twentieth wind.

I do what I can.

My feet are leaden. My heart aches. That pain stretches through my veins to my eyes, my fingers, my back. I lean on her as much as she leans on me. I whisper, "Wake up."

My partner's eyes go wide. The chaperones seem to notice. They stir, agitated, scanning the hundreds of dancers for the one who spoke. They have their batons and their knives and their nasty little grins.

Someone else says it. "Wake up." Like a ripple reaching across the calmest of lakes. "Wake up." "*Despierta.*" "*Vaknaðu.*"

The chaperones move through the dancers, weaving between us with arrhythmic staccato. One of the clarinets falters. The chaperones get him first. Slices his hands off at the wrists, then the gut, the throat, fillets the musician even as the others redouble their efforts. But the beat is lost. It becomes too quick. Too frantic. Dancers start to falter.

The chaperones act without mercy, without compassion, and without hesitancy, slicing their way through the fallen dancers, taking shoes as souvenir keepsakes. But soon, there's too much blood on the floor for anyone to maintain their footing.

The chaperones are busy.

This is the chance for some to run. Out into the red world, the dreamscape hellscape of scorched rocks and petrified trees like skeletal hands reaching out from the earth. The birds swoop in, worms burst from the ground, tumbleweeds ensnare fleeing dancers.

One man stands in the middle of the dancefloor, his brogues still shiny and new, his arms extended in a permanent questioning shrug, saying, "What's all the hurry?"

The chaperones don't trust him. Two, in tangent, remove his arms. He looks horrified. Mortified. Confused.

My partner and I, we're not so stupid or rash as the others. There's no hope on the outside. We retreat into an alcove. Luck, and the diversion, saves us from the eyes of the chaperones. The dancehall is a warzone. We stand cheek to cheek, pressed against the brick walls, listening to the ongoing carnage, pressing our eyes closed as though we can possibly hide from what's happening.

Then it goes quiet.

The quiet spreads like a disease. We're uneasy as we open our eyes and gaze about. Limbs scattered in the congealing blood, but no faces. There's a quivering body on the stage still clinging to an upright bass.

"Is that it?" my partner asks. "Can we rest?"

"We can rest," I say, though of course I don't know. The chaperones are gone. Is it because no other dancers remain, or have they gone to hunt down those who slipped past the wildebeests and wolves?

We slump to the tiled floor. The pool of blood hasn't reached us, not yet, but it will. There's no escape. The chaperones will likely return.

My partner closes her eyes. She's asleep almost immediately. It's a blessing, I'm sure. The weariness is overwhelming. I can't, and won't, resist the same fate.

Sleep.

It's like a myth.

I wake with a start in a sweat, the sheets an abstraction around me, my hands stained with the blood of dancers. I blink several times, unsure if I've really escaped. My legs are weak, but they carry me down the hall to the kitchen, where my dance partner drinks a glass of milk. She's beautiful in the golden light of dawn streaming through the kitchen window, even with dried blood in her hair and under her ragged fingernails. She's poured me a glass, too, and indicates it on the table with a nod of her head.

"Are we free?" I ask.

She giggles. She tries not to, but the choked sound builds and erupts from her and she can't stop it. She looks out the kitchen window. Down the street. All those other houses, all those other dancers, and the fairy folk—the chaperones—driving from house to house in their big black vans—is the answer I didn't want.

the museum of curiosities

ELECTRIC GODS

That small crackle of electricity underneath the lamp: it seems to wait. Frenetic, never still, it undulates and vibrates and hums, and at some certain moment, it slips along the wires to spread through the apartment. Every line in the wall glows blue, visible through plaster and sheet rock like an alien skeleton in x-ray. The digital clock in the bedroom flickers and goes dark. The light on the Blu-Ray winks out. The smoke alarm releases a quiet, high-pitched sigh as its batteries pop, fizzle, and melt. The computer hums briefly, and a trickle of smoke seeps from the vents at the back of the monitor. The dark television screen glows iridescent blue, shows a face even, like a newscaster at her desk in Atlanta, but the image disappears with a single flicker—just one of the odd colors and lights and sounds.

The moment after it begins, it ends, leaving Eden alone on her couch in an utterly dark and unnaturally silent apartment, accompanied by the faint odor of charred rubber and copper.

Eden puts down her book and goes to the window to draw open the shade. The blackout ripples across the city, led by a jagged wave of brightness that stretches almost organically, and quite swiftly, past the edges of the horizon. Streetlights die. Headlights, too, and the cars themselves. Brakes screech and cars crash. Fires erupt in seemingly random quarters.

As the glow leaves the city, it seems momentarily brighter, and the darkness in its wake darker. Flashes of distant light highlight the textured clouds overhead, like the wires snaking through Eden's apartment, like the outline of streets on a map over other streets over older streets until not a spot remains unlit and only texture separates one layer from another.

There's a moment of stillness, of silence, of nothing at all, and then a flash on the horizon as bright as an exploding sun. Blinding. Eden doesn't see what happens next, but she hears the thunder. It's deafening. Two senses, gone in an instant. The last thing Eden hears before the concussive force of the thunder knocks her off her feet is a distant, muted shower as every window, every bowl and vase, every mirror, every piece of glass in the city shatters.

Eden smells the ozone. Energy builds. Rises. She uses the wood frame of her coffee table—the glass top is in shards on the rug—to pull herself to her feet. She's shaky. Unsteady. She sees the afterglow of the lightning ball, little else. Outlines and silhouettes. Shadows in darkness. There's no sound, not yet, not through her ears. The whole apartment trembles, or it's her fragile bones. Her mouth tastes like pennies. Her vision returns slowly.

There's little to see. What was once a nighttime skyline dominated by glowing office windows and the lights of the distant bridge and the constant stream of traffic appears now to be an abandoned monument to some long-dead era. Towers of dark. The slight luminescent cloud cover only amplifies the fact that not a single star shines through, nor the moon. She sees no sign of airplanes in the sky, no blinking red lights or moving white dots.

Scattered fires provide the only light. They're hot. And they spread. Fires burn in her apartment building, though not in her flat. She'd had only the one light going, no television, no microwave, not even the computer. She'd meant to spend the night alone with a paperback. It had fallen to the floor when the coffee table shattered. She leaves it there, and leaves her apartment, and takes the time to lock the door though she doesn't expect to return.

Smoke wafts along the ceiling. Eden hurries to the stairs, not yet needing to hold her breath. The building still seems to tremble. She isn't sure how much longer it will stand.

There are others in the stairs, descending in nearly complete darkness. Someone cries. Someone curses their flashlight, which refuses to cooperate. Someone recites the Hail Mary over and over again, just loudly enough to be heard. No one speaks to anyone else. They are a sea of lonely survivors moving together: stunned, bewildered, frightened.

"It was the magnets," someone is saying, while someone else says, without panic, "It's an invasion." Too much shock for panic.

On the street, crowds gather around burn barrels, people of every social strata and race and religion seeking warmth and solace and companionship.

Eden walks. Far enough in any direction, you leave the city. She passes churches overstuffed with people, not worshippers. She watches a man climb a milk crate and preach about the known evils of electromagnetic generators stealing all their electricity, about the particle accelerators hidden under the mountain, about quarks and anti-electrons and Tesla and Franklin and other prophets of doom.

She finds it hard to focus her thoughts. Her internal energies, too, are out of whack. The electricity had seemed sentient in that final moment. It had gathered. It had formulated some sort of plan. And when it vacated the premises, it took every spark of its brethren with it.

There is fighting, and looting, and hollering on some streets and in some alleys. She ignores them, and they ignore her. Gunfire, distant and near, crack the night at random intervals.

The air feels like it might rain.

A boy runs up to her, a teenager of perhaps fifteen, his eyes glazed as though on some sort of drug. He grabs her by the shoulders, barely having to reach up at all, and asks, quietly, "Will there be phantoms to save us? Spirits?"

Eden shakes her head. "I don't know."

Every trace of hope vanishes from the boy's face. He lets go and drops away, reuniting with the city, becoming part of the background and the atmosphere, giving himself up to whatever comes next.

Eden walks.

She realizes, later, as the buildings around her reach less dizzyingly into the sky, as the clouds hang closer to the earth, as the surrounding chaos ebbs and flows in waves, that people walk behind her. She doesn't look back. She hears the steps of a thousand feet, their hushed voices, the weight of five hundred pairs of eyes. Eden follows no one. The road hasn't cleared, but strangers—some of them—wait to join her crowd.

Ozone builds in the atmosphere.

"The government did it," one old man is telling another, sitting on their stoop, watching Eden but not getting up.

"We're too old," the other says. "We can't blame the government anymore."

"Well," the first says, "they did nothing to stop it."

The road Eden walks leads to a bridge which would carry her out of the city proper. More city waits on the other side, of course, and suburbs beyond, then long tracts of land split by narrow lanes of asphalt, until finally the valleys where orchards grow the grapes to make their wine. It is a long trip by car, longer still by foot, and it isn't actually a destination. Eden barely has a direction, never mind a purpose.

They cross the bridge like an army. Underneath, sailboats wind their way downriver, toward the ocean, weaving through rafts and drifting motorboats. Though weak, the wind persists.

Crowds had gathered at the river's edge, in prayer groups or suicide pacts, some hoping to swim to safety or hijack a sailing yacht or confront their god. There is singing, from one group, voices carrying through the night and echoing as though the whole of the city has become their amphitheater.

The suspension bridge sways gently under a thousand pairs of feet. Children are dragged in red wagons or pushed in carriages and shopping carts, and a few elderly or disabled are in wheelchairs. Eden hears them all behind her, but does not look back.

Most cars on the roads had simply stopped working, causing some to careen without brakes or steering into the railings or other vehicles, and again a few little fires litter the roadway. The heat of the city on Eden's back, however, and the heat of a thousand fellow walkers, is greater.

Storm breaks. It brings rain. It brings wind. It had threatened, it had lingered, and as quickly as it starts, it stops, leaving a thousand suddenly drenched people on the bridge, thousands more on city streets behind and ahead of them. The momentary downpour leaves nothing unwashed.

The air crackles. The electricity had been drawn, had gathered and accumulated, and now is ready to strike. Eden feels it. She tastes it. The air reeks of its stink. Around them, thick steel cables stretch into the sky. Lightning rods might offer some protection, but Eden doesn't think this will be regular lightning.

Around them, a thousand autos have been abandoned, all with rubber tires and Faraday cages and, even if there's no truth in any of that, at least a sense of relative safety. Eden turns to the multitudes. She climbs onto the hood of a nearby car. She yells, "Get inside!"

At first, it seems like no one will respond. They stare at her, and they listen, and maybe they hear her, but no one moves. Nobody reacts. Eden looks to the sky, to the clouds brimming with static charges. The sky glows and bristles and, at some certain moment, rains down its lightning.

Jagged bolts connect the clouds to the ground like anchors. They land closely enough to see colors. They come thick and fast and constant. They strike up and down the streets ahead of them, the strike points moving like a wave until they reach the bridge. They progress along the bridge's cables, bolt after bolt after bolt climbing one side, striking, exploding.

The sky cracks. The air cracks.

Around Eden, some fifteen hundred fellow walkers tug open car doors and climb into abandoned buses and fight to get into the beds of pick-ups. Some are struck. They char and smoke and their bones become briefly iridescent. The afterimages of their bodies hang in the air as burnt flesh drops to the asphalt.

But most make it into the cars. Most find protection as the lightning deluge falls, seeking the path of least resistance, moving along vehicle frames and the water on the tires, spurning the air inside and the rubber and the plastic and the cowering people.

Eden, however, never manages to move.

She stands atop someone else's car, near enough to consider it the very center of the bridge, and when the lightning reaches her it comes from a dozen directions at once. She sees individual colors in the bolts, reds and greens and blues, all oversaturated and unstable. She hears the roils of thunder as a single, vibrating note, a resonating frequency that hardens the hollow of her bones. Her eyes glow, and also her vision, so that she sees the bridge and the city behind her as if every shadow and silhouette has been accented with veins of electric. Beneath her, the tires explode; the plastic and rubber inside melt. The car quivers, or the bridge trembles, or the lightning shakes Eden from her core to the tips of her fingernails.

Perhaps she should have died.

Perhaps she should have burned.

Perhaps her heart stopped, in that moment, and something else started in its place.

Eden feels like she should collapse, but her body refuses to falter. She thinks her bones might burst, but they hold. Her muscles contract and expand and pulse and somehow keep her perfectly still. She sheds tears of steam. Her blood vessels crackle. The thunder dies, or her ears fail, and the ozone sticks in her nostrils. She closes her eyes, or thinks she does, but still sees the strange outlines to every shape, the whole world in distinct, sharp shades of blue. For what seems like a long time, she can't move.

The lightning shower has ceased. The crowds alongside the bridge have scattered or been quick-broiled or have somehow been spared. Eden's fellow walkers emerge from their sanctuaries. They stare at her. They whisper. They sigh. One man falls to his knees, then another, and more after that. They bow their heads. They refuse to meet her gaze. Or they stare in awe and fear and astonishment. She sees the bones beneath their flesh, and their lips, their fingernails, the shape of them under their clothes and the textures of those fabrics. She sees more than she should see, and she can't shut it off. Phantoms and spirits surround her.

Her followers clear the area, putting cars into neutral and pushing them down the bridge or over the side. Eden watches the sky, waiting for the next sign of storm, but the heavy clouds only send an occasional sprinkle. It's enough to keep the ground wet. It's enough to force everyone to keep their distance.

They talk about divine retribution, positrons and quarks, ancient Greek and Norse deities, singularities, neutron bombs, shifts of the magnetic poles. They talk around Eden, and about her, but never to her. Not anymore. They worship her. They bring flowers, and the dead, and ask for blessings she cannot give. The sick and injured beg cures, as if she were some benevolent god thing who performed such miracles.

Eden crackles.

Eden cries. Her tears evaporate.

The sky has assumed an indigo hue, day or night. The clouds churn, ever changing, ever shifting, dropping hints of rain but never anything substantial. Not anymore. No lightning lights the sky; it's all in Eden now.

As the days pass—and days do pass, despite that Eden cannot sleep and cannot eat and breathes only out of habit—stories of others like her reach the bridge. By now, they're three thousand strong, encamped along the shores on either side. Tents house the oracles and priests who claim some right to Eden's presence. Gifts are brought to her. The holy men take their share. Strangers tell Eden stories, but there's nothing new in them. "I survived the storm," says one woman. "The hall lit up like some science fiction ray gun. I thought I was gonna die."

We all thought we were doomed, she wants to say, but she is doomed, and they can no more bring comfort to Eden than take any away.

"I prayed," one says. And then, those stories: "The god on the southern pass, he says it's over, the world is ended, there's no mercy. But you, Eden, you are mercy, are you not?"

"No," she tells them.

"The expressway god says to bring him oranges, but we can find no more oranges. Do you want oranges, Eden?"

"No," she tells them.

"The bank god rants and raves. She tells everyone to go, and she lashes out at everyone she can reach. She's insane. Are all gods mad?"

When she finally answers that one, Eden tells them, "Yes."

Days run together. She doesn't sleep. She doesn't dream. The holy men take shifts, assuring Eden they'll do all they can to protect her, that the self-proclaimed God Killers have thus far failed in every attempt. She no longer sees them as real people. She sees the electricity flowing within them like blood. She sees shades of blue and silver and white. She sees as if through prisms, as if through a kaleidoscope, as if all the world has been tie-dyed in a neon wash. Her focus drifts. Even when she doesn't listen, they go about their prayers and their offerings and their requests and their pleadings. They think she can do something. They think she can act. She stands, and she crackles, and she sheds no more tears, but she does absolutely nothing. What is there to do?

"Is there hope?" someone asks.

"No," she tells him.

"Are we doomed?"

Again: "No." She doesn't know truth or lies or fiction or opinion anymore. She spends her time staring at the shores, afraid to finish crossing the bridge and afraid to start back. No life waits for her.

She's not the only one. She likes that idea. Perhaps someone cursed with this gift can understand, can maybe change the course of the world. Again. The lightning brought no wisdom. She doesn't know what happened any better than the scientists or mystics or alchemists or philosophers. Still, they come.

One man has a black notebook, and though he watches her and records her responses, he never asks questions. He's there for days, perhaps. It's hard to say. When she notices him, he knows it. Her holy men know it. Her followers know it, too. They gather around her in a protective circle.

"Who are you?" they ask. "Why are you here?" "What are you doing?" "What other gods have you seen?"

"I have seen six gods before Eden," says the man, brandishing the little black book like a weapon.

Murmurings ripple through the crowds.

"I have seen storm gods and lightning wranglers and sentient carbon electrodes. I have recorded the words of these gods, and I have discovered something."

Eden, no less so than anyone else, awaits his revelation.

"These gods," he says, "know nothing."

Sparks drip from Eden's grin. "I could've told you that."

"You never have," says the man.

Silence.

Silence stretches a long time. It breaks with a word spat like a curse. *"Heretic."*

They pounce on him. They tear away his notebook. It goes into the river. They drag him close to their god, to Eden. When he protests, they beat him, then drag him closer. His blood appears royal to Eden's electric eyes. Cheering and jeering and cursing and praying, they throw him at Eden—not at her feet but into her arms. They demand punishment, and she's in no position to refuse them.

He can't take her charge. She doesn't care. She embraces him. Whispers apologies. Whispers adulation. Thanks him for his courage, his strength, his wisdom. She kisses him. It's her first kiss since the storm. He returns the kiss for as long as he's able, but in the end he's a charred husk, a collection of burnt bones, and she pushes him away.

She misses touching.

She misses the taste of chocolate and the smell of cinnamon and the sound of traffic. She misses life. She doesn't know what she's got now. She exhales one last time. She has to concentrate to not inhale. She's spent a whole life building that automatic response. She doesn't go dizzy or weak.

She moves.

Her muscles protest. She leaves a trail of sizzling embers behind her. Every step hurts. Eden returns to the city. To the place where she loved and had her heart broken. Where she lost her innocence. Where she once upon a time sipped wine and bought flowers and read sappy paperbacks and flirted with whomever she pleased. The pain might not be physical. No one stops her. No one dares. The holy men protest. They make promises. One falls to his knees and begs. Eden puts a hand on his shoulder. The electricity flows through him, lightning up the veins under his skin, then his bones, and burning his flesh. He tries to pull away, but the power of the surge holds him.

At the end of the bridge, Eden pauses. She says goodbye to the lives she's lived. Something new awaits. Something different. Something unheard of.

Time means nothing. Hours or days pass. Eden walks. Her followers stay as close as they dare. Six thousand strong now, they are a parade behind her as she makes her way through the heart of the city. Power draws her forward. Energy. Something like her. Another so-called god.

She wonders if they're right. Maybe she is a god. Can she die? Can a God Killer put a bullet through her brain with an honest hope of stopping her? She hasn't done anything, but she can kill at a whim.

For fun, and as a test, she focuses her attention on a streetlamp. They haven't burned in weeks or months or years. There's little left. The casing is gone, but the bulb, somehow, survives. Eden projects. The bulb flickers, and lights, and explodes.

Her followers don't follow so closely anymore.

At an intersection, a man like her walks toward her. They're drawn to each other. Electricity pulls like gravity. Irresistible. They step closer. They crackle and sparkle and hiss.

"We're like gods," he says.

"But we're not."

"No," he agrees. "Not gods. Something like gods."

"But you don't know," she says.

"I know a great many things," he admits, "but nothing that matters."

"Do you know your name?"

"I was called Adam. I was outside the circus tent when the storm came. The lightning converged on me and I lived. No one calls me Adam anymore. They call me the god of the circus."

"They think I'm the god of the bridge," Eden says. "As if you could pass only with my blessing."

"No one guards the bridge now," Adam says.

"I was Eden. Before."

All the while, they circle around each other, moving closer, afraid to get too close but unable to do anything but delay it. Six thousand behind her, six thousand behind him, and another three thousand pairs of eyes spying from cubbyholes in the windowless buildings and alleys all around them.

"Do you have holy men?" Adam asks.

"They think they are. I killed one whilst walking."

"So did I."

"Do you breathe?" Eden asks. "Do you eat or sleep?"

Adam shakes his head. Sparks drift from his hair. "I do nothing human."

"Let's do something human, Adam," she says. She reaches out. He reaches out. The static between them pulsates and glows. Their fingertips touch with a sonic boom. The buildings vibrate around them. Witnesses cower and cringe.

They embrace. They kiss. Every lightbulb for a mile around them goes nova and bursts. Whatever was left of their clothes is easily shed. Neither dies because of the touch. Their consummation, in the city center, is electric. Bolts of lightning connect their writhing bodies to the sky and burn the eyes of holy men who stand too close. Their touch is unlike anything they have ever known. Their minds entwine as much as their bodies. Secrets are laid bare. His fetishes. Her weaknesses. His shattered dreams. Her lost loves. His hopes. Her wishes. His self. Herself. Their selves. Their single self, in the end. She knows his history, his experiences. He knows hers. Both drift. Extraneous knowledge is lost. Bits of the past fade. Shared experiences are magnified. The act of love becomes a final union.

Eden/Adam rises from the asphalt. S/he surveys fifteen thousand pieces of meat. S/he reaches toward one and draws his personal electricity. The body falls, unburnt but lifeless. His knowledge joins Adam/Eden's bubbling reservoir. There are no secrets. There are no individuals. S/he is the child of false gods, erroneous acts of supernature. Other sources of power exist, pulsating, drawn to each other. S/he pulls from a hundred followers at once, reveling in the taste of them, the surplus energy. There's more to be had, more and more, and next there is the so-called god of the bank, then the god of the park, then the god of the subways. Her/his followers know of gods beyond the city. They must all be drawn together, united, merged with the very earth itself, then with the sun—and with the sudden shift of gravity, other stars as well. There's a galaxy to consume, a universe, and others beyond.

Adam/Eden has never felt so alive. Or hungry.

STEPHANIE AT THE SOIREE

Magic isn't a real thing.

She's been told this a thousand times just since Tuesday. Get your head out of the clouds. Real results require real work.

But magic requires real work, doesn't it? Nobody understands. Especially not her mother.

Real results require real work, now work on tidying your room before company arrives. Because company is always arriving. And Stephanie must adhere to the rules and regulations of proper children at all times. Proper children don't mix potions in their laboratory, especially when the lab is actually just the bathroom under the stairs.

But other children mix things all the time, and you call the results *cake*.

That's real work, of course, involving flour and eggs and beating and baking.

Stephanie's wearing her pretty dress, the one her mom always insists she pull out when there's company to be trotted in front of, even if they won't be here for hours or weeks or years.

The staff is busy, everyone running this way and that, twirling around her as if she's not actually in the way. But she knows better. The kitchen maid gives her a sprig of grapes and suggests she go out into the garden.

Flowers are a kind of magic, aren't they? No one understands that, either.

In the garden, she sits under the shade of one of the big statues, some goddess whose name she's never been able to pronounce. I'll be like you one day, she thinks. Big and strong and full of magic.

In the dirt, she's got to be careful not to mess her dress. She doesn't want to disappoint her mom. She just wishes someone would listen to her.

Just once.

She bows her head and stares at the spot of dirt between her knees. She wiggles her toes. If no one will listen, then she'll just have to make some magic. She concentrates on the moist soil, sending all her best vibrations into the earth. She whispers a word, one word, with all the power of a spell: *Grow*.

Nothing happens. She sighs. Her shoulders drop. She tries to smile, but it takes some effort.

But then there's movement.

A crumb of soil trembles. A piece of the dirt tumbles aside. A tiny little unobtrusive green stem pops its head out of the earth.

Oh, she thinks. I did that.

See? There is such a thing as magic.

But nobody listens, and now they're calling her. So she thanks the stem, and promises to return as soon as she's able, and runs inside because company is beginning to arrive.

It's one of those big soirees, which is a fancy name for a party they use when it's fancy people in fancy dresses and so many sparkling jewels. She runs from place to place, listening to men talking figures, women talking fashions, staff talking gossip.

These things go on forever. Hours and hours. They get boring. She sits for a while in front of the hearth, but it's too warm outside for anyone to light a fire. She wants to ignite a spark with the magic inside her. Just one little spark.

And that's all it takes to create one little spark. A tendril of smoke that looks almost identical to the stem outside.

She smiles. She almost giggles. That would attract her mom's attention, wouldn't it? It might be okay to giggle at a party, but certainly not at a soiree.

From another room, someone screams. Stephanie goes running to see why. No one's supposed to be screaming at soirees, either.

In the big room, tendrils of vines thick as elephant trunks snake in through all the windows. The lush green grabs people, squeezes them, drags them screaming through the windows.

Stephanie runs outside. It's her stem. It's still growing. It's a tangle of vines as big as the house now, a hundred of them probing every window, reaching into the cars out front, knocking over all the champagne.

One of the servants comes out with an axe like some sort of heroic adventurer. He hacks at the base of the plant. Every cut he makes just adds to the number of heads. It's like a hydra.

That makes Stephanie giggle, despite that she's at a soiree instead of a party.

Then she realizes something. Inside, there's a little bit of fire in the fireplace, no bigger than the stem was when she left it, and if that also grows out of control...

It's too late. The house is already burning. The fire meets the plant in some places, and very quickly the air outside fills with rolling, choking black smoke.

She tells them to stop. She tells them to recede and retreat. She begs them not to hurt her family or her family's friends or the staff or anyone else. She begs them not to hurt her.

When her mom finds Stephanie, she's furious. You did this, you and your magic, you and all the things I told you not to do.

But it's not my fault. You never listen. You never, never listen.

Her mom kneels in front of her, wipes a tear from Stephanie's cheek, and says I'll always listen. But we're going to have to put this all away now. Then she waves her fingers, and the tentacles of the plant wither. She waves her fingers, and the flames snuff themselves. She waves her fingers, and lightning cracks the sky to release a deluge of rain. She waves her fingers, and magics everything back to the way it was.

She waves her fingers one last time, and the society pages won't mention the vines or the flames or anything else.

One of the guests, leaving, glances down at Stephanie, acknowledges her in a way most the guests never do. Watch her, she says. She's a power. She's a girl who will be able to do anything.

And her mother asks, watch her? I've been waiting for her to find her way.

Wait. Stephanie's confused. You mean magic is a real thing and always has been?

Yes, dear. And magic courses through your veins.

The Museum of Curiosities

THE KING IN BLUE

This platform could work as an amphitheater. Remove those stairs, put a stage there—an honest stage, with an entrance left and right—it wouldn't take much effort to hollow out the back wall behind the inside of the loop. The only issue, really, would be getting the MTA to stop running that damned 6 train through here for the duration of the show. It would be spectacular. It's already pretty damn steampunk. Look at the tiles on those arches and tell me they aren't gears. Lose the plaques. I appreciate the work all those men did to make this thing—the whole thing, this station and the subway and maybe all of New York City—but they aren't here today. Move them back to Brooklyn Bridge or up to Grand Central. No one sees them in this godforsaken golden chamber.

Look at those chandeliers. I think that's brass. Nice job there. Why can't they turn them on? There's the tinted sun filtering in through skylights on either side, when there's daylight, and the cacophonous squeals accompanying railroad headlights. Seems like every fifteen minutes, there's a flood of subway light and sharp shadows. It's disruptive. What kind of show can we stage with that? That's the problem with the world today. All that extraneous noise.

Anyway, it's just me tonight. I assume. Sometimes, it's hard to say. I don't see anyone lingering on the stairs or under the arches, and the powers-that-be haven't been kind enough to install a bench good for laying out. Truth is, down here on the platform itself, there ain't all that many cubbyholes and corners. It's a curved track, and the track is active. A good way to get yourself killed, looking for a spot to sleep down there. A good way to discover that the enemy was, is, and will always be those damned rats.

Behind the stage, up those stairs, that's where you'll find crevices and pits and I don't know what else. That room ain't right. It's like a dome. Arches across all sides and topped by a round window—a rose window, I think they'd call it, if this was a church, though there ain't nothing rosy about it if you ask me. They've got a bench there, something like a bench, a wood thing that's flat but has got speed bumps to make it awfully uncomfortable. And walls of bricks, lots of bricks, creamy golden bricks that shouldn't be there. Knock through those bricks, there's tunnels to all sorts of places—unimaginable places, faraway lands you can't normally find except in wardrobes and looking glasses and the like. I don't like it up there. Don't like what else might come down through that window in the dark. I look out that window, through all that ironwork—it looks like a clock, if you ask me, not keeping its time anymore—and I see blue, so much blue, the blue of the sky. But it ain't the New York sky. It can't be. I've seen the sky over New York. It's gray. It's gray like its buildings are gray and its streets are gray. The rest of everything down here, all in shades of gold and brown and— let's be frank, cocoa and burgundy and saffron and other frou-frou flavors—it all fits together, a forgotten world under the city, a ghostly remnant of a New York from a time when Rockefellers and Astors gathered at the Cotton Club to decide our fates. The blue, it just doesn't belong there. It makes me nervous. And what makes me nervous, I leave alone.

I know all the tales, the old stories, the histories and legends. I know for a fact the king should be in yellow—but there are others. He comes down in blue, that very same blue, even in the middle of the night, from that dome-like room with the rose window. He wears a crown, or something like a crown. It's dark, how can I be sure? He carries a scepter, and everyone around him—and I mean everyone, even the rats with their yellow and red eyes twitching, the crazies who roam the tracks as though on quests, the bats hanging off the chandeliers, and the damned shadow things with their biting teeth and vicious claws— everyone and everything bows to this king in blue. He walks tall and straight, like a god would walk, like one of those Greek gods coming down to rut with mortal beauties.

One night, when he comes down, I sneak around behind him and into that domed room with the clock-like window. Though there are other stairs from here, they lead to nowhere. It's nighttime. The window is dark. The window glimmers with outside lights, but those reflections are like eyes in the ceiling, as though more things wait to descend. He says to me—this king, this king in blue who doesn't even look at me but knows I'm there—he says, "There are thunders in these mountains."

I know nothing of thunder or mountains. I know better than to acknowledge him. He could be speaking just to hear his own voice. I might not be the target. "There are glories in these stars," he says. I do what I can to stay invisible. I'm not invisible. I'm not anything like invisible. I only need to remain unseen. So many things and people are unseen in this subterranean world, why can't I be one of them?

"There is fire in my blood this night," he says. He's coming back up the stairs. Rising from the depths, from the platform itself, to this backstage area where there should be cardboard sceneries and lighting rigs and a chaos of actors and stagehands; but there's no place to hide, not really, not from a man who is not a man. I feel the heat of him, the razor sharp edges of his teeth, the stone calluses in his regal hands that crush coal into diamonds and skulls into jelly.

At the center of the room, directly beneath the window, he raises his head to look straight up into what's supposedly New York City's night sky, but I know you cannot see stars from there, and you cannot see clouds, and you cannot see the edifices we mere mortals have built to cut the heavens. You can see the blue, only the blue—and at night, only the dark and the twinkling eyes, and maybe they are his audience instead of me. He states, "We shall reclaim what is ours!"

The whole station trembles at his words. Or maybe it's the 6 coming through, another fifteen minutes, give or take, since the last. Down here, you get confused about the truth of thunder. There's so much of it.

I sneak away. Whatever this king intends to make happen, I want no part of it. But even now, I can think of little else. Even now, after all this time—and a tremendous amount of time, it may have been—

I sneak away. Down to the platform again. Under the tiles that say *City Hall*. They offer no protection. The shadows are thick, and I suspect they're half alive. There are snakes amongst the rats, and blood drips from the chandeliers. There's fire, somewhere, down the ends of the subway tunnel, beyond the curve, as though Brooklyn Bridge station burns, but I know it doesn't.

I remember the good people—there must have been some good people, don't you think?—who used this platform, caught their train and went home to Harlem or switched out at Grand Central. Some must have detrained here, ascending to the city at its southernmost heart. If I can draw on the good of them, I think—the intentions if not the actions, the beliefs if not the truths—maybe I can shield myself from the shadow things and the gaze of the king in blue and that damned rose window.

It shatters.

There's no mistaking it. The glass explodes and falls. Shards cascade down the stairs, reaching my feet. Reaching me. Cutting my soles through the bottom of my shoes. I never should've let the leather get so worn. I never should've found myself in this place at any time, any time at all, much less here and now. I think these things and I think it's over. The rush of rats and bats and shadows carry me back up the stairs against my will. I'm helpless to resist. I'm caught in the tide. I rise through the air, not backstage but at its center, beneath the hole where once there was a window. The twisted remnants of clock-like ironwork await me. The jagged ends glow redly.

I do not see the king in blue rise from the station. I do not see if he went north or south or west. I do not see where his followers followed. As I rise through the window, the iron pierces me, and it sears my wounds. Glass seeps into my blood. Near as I am to death, I am dropped on asphalt, and the things rising from the subway, the rats and snakes and wolves and dragons, trod over me. Every footfall shoves glass or iron or claw deeper into my flesh, but what does it matter now if I die? Who will mourn my untimely passing?

After an untold age, the parade is done. There's no trace of it but the blood on my back and face, the trails they've tattooed upon me with scars instead of ink. My eyes, when I open them, burn and bleed, and they are never to be like eyes again, because I have seen a thing, in the shape of a man, no man was ever meant to see.

There are, as he said, thunders in these mountains.

Later, the light of day hurts me, and though I want to retreat through the shattered window it is whole and unharmed. I find another way down, a secret way, as I know many secret ways. I return to the platform that has become my home, though I must scurry and hide when the self-proclaimed authorities make their rounds. No one from any train has ever seen me or ever will. I've become quite adept at making myself invisible. I ain't the man I was. I practice with discarded newsprint, shifting the ink, burning it in my palms. I catch the rats and I feed them and I eat them. I'm not who I was and I'll never be again. No one mourns my death. But some, perhaps many, will mourn my reawakening.

I know I'm close. I know how the play is supposed to end. I know a great many things I never knew, and I've forgotten a great many things as well. But my king, when he returns, when he's reconnoitered this mortal world and settled upon a strategy, when he knows the weaknesses and exploits, when he's determined that we shall reclaim what was, is, and always will be ours—I will be ready. I will fight at his side.

If it's a good day, if I'm more the man I was than the man I am, if I'm as aware as I am today, maybe I will fight *against* the king in blue. But I fear, as I get stronger—and I have become extraordinarily strong— I lose more of who I was. I know how the play ends. In madness.

GARDEN OF
POISONOUS DELIGHTS

She shows him the garden. He thinks the date is going well.

The garden is filled with pretty flowers: purple rolls, bright blue bulbs, little white petals like popcorn, and finally one he recognizes.

"Is that wolf's bane?"

"What need would I have for wolf's bane?" she asks. "There are no werewolves within thirteen miles of here."

That's quite specific, actually.

"And these white ones...?" He reaches for the small sprays of white at the end of long stems, but she swats his hand away.

"Mustn't touch the hemlock," she says. "You'll spoil the tea."

"Will everything in this garden kill you?"

She laughs. Playfully, even flirtatiously, she touches his arm. "Oh, nothing in this garden will kill *me*."

"Those mushrooms," he says. "Those are death caps, aren't they?"

"My, my," she says, "but you are well versed in your poisons."

"I told you, during the day..."

She shakes her head and jams her palm against his mouth. "I don't even want to know your name."

He's told her his name. He knows hers. Through her hand, he asks, "Do you mean to kill me?"

She smiles. Chuckles. "I never *mean* to kill anyone, silly."

That doesn't reassure him.

They continue the tour. There are statues, and stone pillars, and spider webs between some of the cherubic faces. "Are they venomous?"

"All spiders are venomous, don't you know?" she says. "Not all spider venoms will *kill* you."

"Not all spider venoms won't," he points out.

"You do know how hard it is to milk a spider, don't you? Nearly impossible. And if you try to create a spider farm, it turns out they're quite territorial. They won't abide another in their domain."

He stops when he hears the all-too-familiar rattle of a snake's tail. He doesn't see the source, but he knows it's close. "How many snakes..."

He doesn't complete the sentence before she's smooshing his lips together under her fingers. "You ask too many question. Do you know that?"

Her eyes bore into him. It's not rhetorical. He nods one time. She removes her fingers. Cautiously, he says, "You present a lot of questions to be asked."

"This is supposed to be a *date,*" she says. "A fun time. Dinner. Dancing. And maybe making out for an hour by the pond. Wouldn't you like that?"

They haven't kissed yet. Dinner, however, was magnificent: roasted vegetables, an amazingly light sauce, seared scallops and sautéed sausages, two shared bottle of red wine so he's a little light-headed.

They haven't actually done any dancing yet, either.

She sees it in his eyes. "Yes, you were meant to *dance* with me tonight, silly." She grabs one of his hands, pulls it up as though they're about to waltz. "There's supposed to be a violinist out here somewhere."

As if on cue, the unseen violinist begins to play something classic and Italian.

They dance. She leads.

His head swims. "Oh," he says.

"Quiet."

"No, let me speak."

She doesn't pause the dance, but she does give a little shrug: permission to speak.

"You've already poisoned me." It's not a question.

She's close to him. She presses her lips to his throat, kisses him briefly—he can feel lingering lipstick—and breathes into his ear: *Yes.*

"You've poisoned my body," he says.

Still a whisper: *Yes.*

"You've poisoned my heart."

She stops the dance to take one step back. "Have I?"

"How did you do it?" he asks.

This time, it's a full-bodied shrug. "It was easy. You're so very trusting."

His vision is blurring and his legs feel leaden. "Why?"

"Oh, there's an antidote," she says, ignoring the question, "but you haven't found it yet, and I've given you so many opportunities."

He lifts his arms. It's a struggle. He reaches for her. She slaps his hands away and steps back. "Oh, no. Not like that. You're sluggish now."

"One kiss," he says, his voice pleading but also slurring.

She smiles. Almost giggles again. "Well, okay. *One* kiss for dying."

He stumbles into her, kisses her sloppily—but it's a delicious kiss, a taste he'll remember till his dying breath. It lasts for as long as he's got the strength, which isn't long enough, and soon he's dropped to his knees.

"Well, that wasn't awful," she admits. "But did you really think I'd keep the antidote in my *lipstick*? Do you think I'm mad?"

He does, in fact, think she's mad, but it's the last thing he ever thinks.

CHE CRADE CONCLUDED

He returns to the apartment.

It's an Airbnb, so he only has to wait—now that he's waited this long—until it comes available. He walked past the dragon painted on the gate three years ago, and he walks past it now. The red paint has faded some, but it's the same dragon, and the ice cream place up the road still serves fish-shaped waffle cones.

In the apartment, the dishes are the same. The shower curtain still displays Batman. The same hall leads to the same bed. He can't be sure of the sheets.

The windows in the hall look down a shaft to a small courtyard. No one ever seems to use it, though there are chairs down there, and a table—but no grass, no shrubbery.

He wanders the streets of Madrid, drinking cheap *vino* and sampling *tapas* throughout the district. It's a late city. All he has to do is stay up later than most everyone else. Some of the bars start to close. The noise at street level ebbs. He returns to his apartment, the same apartment they had shared just three years ago.

He remembers all too vividly the way Ana had smiled and laughed.

He unrolls his bag, revealing a rope ladder and a grappling hook. He attaches it inside the window and descends the shaft to the courtyard, careful not to hit the windows of the two apartments below his.

It's a stormy night, but he's afraid the thunder might be insufficient. Still, he cannot be easily dissuaded, not even by his own doubts.

With a pickaxe purchased locally, after he got off the plane and through customs, he cracks open the concrete floor of the courtyard. He times each strike of the axe to the tempest's rhythm. He feels the ghosts are sympathetic to his intentions; they seem to rile up the storm, to increase its velocity, its volume, its ferocity.

Breaking through the thin layer of concrete, he digs, and this only requires a few more inches before he finds his treasure: an ornate wooden box with a red dragon painted on it. The dragon curls around the sides and shows it profile on the lid. It's locked.

He wears the key on a chain around his throat where he's worn it for three years.

He opens the jewelry box.

It contains assorted dime store necklaces and rings, dangling earrings that might be real diamonds, and a coin.

He presses the coin to his palm. Squeezes it. Turns his face up to the rain and smiles and thanks whatever gods might be listening. After three years, he had no reason to expect it would still be here, but he was hopeful.

He closes the box, loads it into his pack, and ascends the rope ladder back to his apartment. He leaves the equipment on the floor of the courtyard: a mystery for someone else to puzzle over.

He leaves the apartment.

The Metro, a familiar series of snakes twisting through the veins and bones of the city, brings him near the center, near the temple and the palace, where the darkness seems particularly dense and the rain extraordinarily heavy. He walks downhill to an underpass. There are buses and taxis and cars and even mopeds, despite the hour and despite the weather. A manhole cover near the northeast corner opens rather easily. It's not as heavy as it looks.

He slips beneath the city.

The tunnels are damp, lit weakly by orange and yellow bulbs. He navigates to a throne room unimagined by most of the five million residents of the city above. There, they greet him in another language, but he says the right words to the right people to get an audience with the king himself.

Not the King of Spain.

"I remember you," the king says.

"I'm honored."

"You are here to reclaim your good faith?"

"It's been three years."

"So it has."

For a moment, it seems nothing else will be said. He produces the coin. It's big, heavy, solid gold, possibly mined in a distant, difficult to access netherland. He tosses it to the king. The guards surround him, spears and swords raised and ready. The king catches the coin, examines it, turns it over in his hands, and bites down to test the metal. He's satisfied. He says, "You have kept your end of the bargain. Let us conclude this ugly business."

Ana emerges from a dark alcove, head bowed, all servile and quiet. The laughter has been stolen from her. She might be someone else entirely, but she still looks and sounds and smells like Ana.

He leads her back the way he came, witnessed by the members of the court, the guards, even the king. Eventually, he brings her back to the surface, to the rain, to the garden behind the palace. The storm has abated some and the clouds have thinned in places. A hint of the moon glows low against the horizon.

She asks, "What took you so long?"

"I had to wait," he says. "And then, well, a lot has happened since you were gone."

"A lot," she admits.

He never sees the blade. He barely feels it slide between his ribs. She's good. Well-taught. She hadn't spent the past three years imprisoned, but in training. She whispers, her breath tickling his ear, "You should have come sooner."

He dies at the edge of the garden, a stranger in a foreign country, another mystery for others to puzzle over. Ana walks away, free but haunted, maybe disturbed. Whatever he'd traded her for, it couldn't have been worth it.

the museum of curiosities

HE TALKS TO THE
GODDESS IN THE MOON

He finds a key on the street.

It's a toothed key, old-fashioned, iron, solid and heavy and just like the kind of key he's always wanted to find. It's a special key that must unlock a special treasure, though he doesn't yet know where.

The key gleams in the moonlight. It's shiny and clean and couldn't have been there long. When he bends to pick it up, he looks around. There's no one who might have dropped it, no one searching for a lost or missing anything, no one anywhere near him at all. The park is dark and quiet and cool.

It certainly won't open any ordinary door, nor even a safety deposit box.

He runs his finger along the key's edge. It's smooth, except at the edge, which might be useful in a self-defense situation.

There's no one nearby to defend himself from, either. So he speaks to the moon. "Was I meant to find this?" he asks. "Does this mean I'm meant for something?"

He doesn't bother talking to the key. Keys are inanimate objects. But the moon, as everyone knows, is a goddess of the hunt; he's always giving her smiles and hoping for her favors. She never responds, never shines any brighter on him than anyone else, and never brings him gifts. Tonight is no different.

"Still," he says, tightening his fist around it, "now I have a key."

And keys are important. There's always something to be unlocked later, a treasure to be discovered, piles of gold or maybe other magical items. Amulets. Potions. Spells.

He looks around the park for anything he might never have noticed before. There's the big statue in the middle. The wide paths cutting between the flowers. Soda stands all shut down for the night. They closed about the same time the sun set. It's not a nighttime park, though it never closes. He cuts through the park to get from the metro station to his apartment.

He's about halfway between them now and he doesn't know what to do.

It's almost midnight. Tomorrow is close to beginning. Is the key something he'll need then? Is it important to rest well tonight? He's had some wine, but that won't prevent him from sleeping.

He pockets the key. "Okay," he tells the moon, because she must be listening. "I'll just go home, but I'll keep my eyes open."

It's downhill from the metro station, but he tries not to walk too fast. He could be home in five minutes, but he stretches it to almost ten before reaching his apartment building. It's just around the corner from a fruit seller and newsstand, both closed for the night. There's no one and nothing. Even the vestibule is empty; he checks the corners for spiders, in case one has written him a message. He reaches the small elevator without incident, walks in, notes again how dim the light is inside, and presses the button for the fifth floor.

Home.

It's a good thing he's keeping his eyes open, because he almost misses it. There, at the bottom of the panel, where the numbers range from one to eight and there's a call button he doesn't know who would answer, there's also a keyhole.

Yes, there's the key for the fire department. This is different. This is new. He's never noticed this keyhole before. It looks to be about the right size, shape, and age for the smooth silvery key in his pocket.

So he tries it.

He inserts the key. Turns it. Hears a mechanism responding inside, the click and clack of cogs and sprockets. When the elevator stops on the fifth floor and the door opens, the mirrored panel behind him also slides open.

That's new.

There should be a brick wall there and the building next door. Instead, there's a hallway that looks a lot like his hallway. He pokes his head out, glances up and down, confirms that it is, in fact, a mirror image of his hall. It's otherwise identical. He walks down to what should be his apartment. His own key opens it.

He enters.

It's dark. Cold. Quiet. He says, "Hello?"

No one answers.

He says, "If this is some sort of trick." But he can't complete the thought. He has no threat to make, and no one to direct it at. The apartment looks like his, although everything's inverted. The furniture is the same that came with his place. The window, when he goes to it, looks out onto the same street and the same park.

"That's confusing," he says aloud.

He retreats down the hall. The elevator waits there. He can walk through the paneled mirror door, through the elevator which has never opened in such a way before, and back into his regular apartment where everything faces the right directions.

But tomorrow will be a new adventure, and he's sure the moon will be disappointed if he simply gives up on it.

He returns, instead, to his new apartment. He locks the door behind him, turns on the light, pours a glass of water, even brushes his teeth with the same toothbrush he's been using for months.

Before going to bed, he opens the window, looks up at the moon, and smiles. She doesn't respond. He's only slightly disappointed. "I don't know what will happen," he tells her, "but I'm ready for it."

He's always wanted the life of an adventurer.

He undresses and climbs into bed, shuts his eyes, and falls quickly into dreaming. Outside the window, high in the sky, the hunter goddess in the moon smiles and winks at him and whispers, unheard, "You're not ready, but you'll figure it out."

ONE NIGHT IN BROOKLYN

The barbarian, with his intense blue eyes and sinewy thews...

No, that's not the place to start. With the librarian, not the barbarian, although her eyes are also blue like crystal skies; like cotton candy or fairy floss or ghost's breath, whatever you call it; like sapphire dreams, although you and I both know sapphires come in so many colors, they had to call the red ones rubies just to make them seem special.

And I never knew her as The Librarian. I always thought of her as the Book Master. Like a Dungeon Master, or so my teenaged mind had wanted to believe. But let's be fair: at that age, I had absolutely no idea what that really meant.

Anyway, the librarian, with her intense blue eyes and...

See, I can't really go there without objectifying her body, and I'm not the teenager I once was, and the thing that most impressed me was her vast knowledge of all the worlds. All of them. She knew Oz and Narnia and Middle Earth as well as anyone alive knew London or Shanghai. She had met Dumas and Homer and Hemingway at a dive bar somewhere in Brooklyn before I was even a child...

Yes, Brooklyn. Of course Brooklyn. She's a mermaid. Did I forget to mention that? You got hung up on the Book Master thing, didn't you?

I realize not all mermaids come from Brooklyn. But these days, many of them, at least the ones that can withstand the cold of the North Atlantic, get there at least once. For the parade. For the sideshows. To ride the Cyclone. Last time I was there, it was still only five bucks, and even if it isn't the fastest, loopiest, scariest roller coaster on earth, it's probably the most famous.

Yes, so, at that dive bar, there were artists, too, like Vermeer and Da Vinci and El Greco. I bet they talked about perspective and light, but I bet they also talked about how the world had moved on in the strangest of ways, Picasso laughing over his absinthe.

I remember this one solitary day, before I knew the librarian or the barbarian—he hangs out at the gym to laugh at the muscle heads—I opened a box. You know Pandora had seven of them, right? All the evils, that's the one everyone remembers. Another carried all the dreams; apparently, no one's ever opened this, but the seal isn't strong so they seep out like mists to get scattered by the wind. Anyway, she gave me this box. I was a just a kid but I had seen some things, I knew the blues, I was a deeply scarred soul already, and she told me only open it if I needed the time.

Needed the time. I didn't even know what she meant.

I think we shared drinks, bourbon or something—it definitely felt and sounded like New Orleans, though I don't remember if it smelled like New Orleans. She said something about dancing with ghosts, I know that, but you can dance with ghosts in any house built before they knocked down Rockaway Playland to make room for a housing development.

That was my first roller coaster, by the way. The Atom Smasher at Rockaway Playland. So close yet so far from the Cyclone. I was just tall enough to ride. So the coaster jockey let me ride twice.

I opened that box, yeah, and the librarian told me I'd been foolish but I didn't necessarily believe her. She brought me to that bar in Brooklyn, but Hugo refused to talk to me, turned his back on me, uttered French curses just loudly enough for me to hear. Apparently, I'll never learn French. The chrononaut at the bar kept downing Old Fashioned after Old Fashioned and told me he could feel the cracks in his blood.

Also, I got the Beatle's thirtieth album on vinyl. Score!

Anyway—this is where the barbarian comes in—right into the bar like he owns the place, but he walks that way into everyplace he's ever been. He goes up to the librarian. She's smiled at me and kissed me once, but it was all an act, a ruse, a lure—she got me here so the barbarian and I could have our little talk.

The things he said—I don't remember, I really don't. Maybe there weren't many words. Something about serpents, about his distaste for magicians, about a proper order to things. He'd met Pandora once or twice, he admitted, maybe yesterday and maybe tomorrow, and then told me I had to close the box or he would open my skull.

That, I think, is an exact quote.

So I closed the box. You don't argue with blue eyes or sinewy thews. Now I'm in this dive bar in Brooklyn, all alone, me and the woman tending bar, and maybe she's Clara Bow but the lighting in here is horrible and she won't talk to me, just casts those big eyes in my direction and pouts. I don't think she likes me.

phanTom island

At the edge of the map, the wind took hold. The *Phantom* shuddered. The sailors struggled, heaving with all their might, certain they could win this struggle against the daughters of rainbows and thunderers. The ocean sprayed around them, the captain shouted commands in his pirate's language, and the "mild mannered" studious woman on deck, who should be below and safe from the tumult, stood on the steadiest legs, compass in one hand, sextant in the other, parchment map folded raggedly in her pocket and fluttering in its attempts to escape her.

I should have known by her eyes: nebulous, unfathomable, shifting their hue like prisms in the sun. I should have known by her lack of a foreign accent, though clearly she had never before been in Moon's Hollow. I should have known by the grin, the paper butterfly folded into her hair, or the way hardened sailors withered under her unspoken threats.

I was in love.

I'd been in love or something like it before, but this was newer and inescapable; and as the only other passenger on this ill-fated voyage, an unverifiable mystery in my own right, I know deeply of these things. I daresay I'd written a volume of poetry exploring the edges and mists of love in all its numerous permutations. Yet here I was, smitten like a schoolchild.

So if I can't explain exactly what happened to the crew, know I'm telling only the truth when I say we reached land with more force than could possibly have been intended, and the ship came apart in the sand.

It was a special day, she told me later, the coalescing of celestial objects, a certain phase of the moon, of the sun, and of Venus low in the sky. There might even have been a comet lending its influence, who can be certain?

When I came to, she was already awake and aware, picking through the wreckage, tossing random bits of wood and iron aside with wanton disgust. I watched for a while before clearing my throat and asking, "Can I help?"

She looked at me. Clearly, she hadn't meant to arrive on this island—thus far, I'd seen only the sand and the tree line—with company. There was no sign of the captain or the ship's crew, and this couldn't be all the wood that had made up our ship.

She looked at me at angles, shifting her head and narrowing her eyes, and said, "I must need you here for something."

"Are you mad?" I asked. "Or is it only me?"

"We've made it," she said, smiling, holding out her arms to take in the whole of the island and all the now calm ocean, all the sky, all those varied blues sparkling also in her eyes.

"Where's the crew?"

"Where's your sense of adventure?"

To be fair, I've been an adventurer a long many years, and I have found my inquisitive nature to be rather advantageous, but I didn't ask again because already I was beginning to get an idea of the truth behind the answer. Instead, I asked, "We made it where?" And this is where I told my first lie, because I felt compelled to manage her expectations of me. "I'm merely a student of the sea. What island is this?"

She whipped the map out of her pocket. She didn't have to unfold it; the parchment sprang to life as if it had been wound up and made to wait impatiently. She pointed at the edge of the map—where we'd been—and said, "We've flipped over to the other side."

That, I'm sure, I would have remembered.

"We've reached the Emerald Island."

I laughed. It was partly her infectious joy at the prospect and partly the preposterous nature of the claim. The Emerald Island lay off the southern coast of Australia, if it could be found anywhere at all, a great many miles distant. She misunderstood my laughter as a good sign and took me by the hand to lead me into the woods.

The Emerald Island, as I've nothing else to call it, was filled with greenery: shrubs and trees with large, lazy fronds offering shade and catching fresh rainwater. Over time, we built a kind of shelter around the convoluted base of a live oak tree centuries old.

From the ship, we salvaged only a small amount of food and no medicine to speak of, but a chest of hers filled with clothes and books—I wasn't in love with her merely because she was the most beautiful, graceful, and extraordinary woman on the Emerald Island—but not what she had been wanting to find. When I asked, she told me cartography instruments, and I never had reason to disbelieve her, but I doubt that was all to it. She had a natural way with the herbs and flowers growing wild on the island, and seemed almost to commune with the fish in the ocean. One time, though I admit I may have dreamed it, I saw her whispering with an octopus.

We made a home on the Emerald Island, and there we lived for seven long months, through summer and the hotter summer, and the heat of whatever followed. The ocean breezes were a salvation, and the rains were often icy. Sometimes, we could sit on the beach at night with a bonfire burning behind us and watch the stars while listening to whalesong, maybe holding hands, breathing so shallowly a stranger might mistake us for ghosts.

We hunted boar on the island, but nothing hunted us. Sometimes, she looked wistfully toward the sunrise, but when I asked what she longed for, she would say something like "Spices" or "A good knife" or "Only you."

I never believed she loved me. And we had a knife, albeit a small one, which I'd had on me when we wrecked.

She told me stories about the island: how Captain William Elliot, who first saw it in 1821, had been an idiot in the wrong ocean; how its original inhabitants disappeared before a volcanic eruption that reshaped it; how the sands were once pure white and once thickly black and once finer than confectioners' sugar; how the winters would bring snow and ice but for the dragons living beneath the shore.

Some nights, we walked the beach together, but sometimes we each went on our own. When I didn't have her lightness next to me illuminating the whole of my world and my heart, I once or twice saw the lights of phantom vessels against the horizon. When I told her about them, she laughed and said she enjoyed my stories, and sometimes she kissed me to stop me talking.

We didn't seek or even hope for rescue. It was an adventure. We ate fish and pork and berries and flowers. She knew instinctively which would taste like honey and which would taste like almond paste and which might ease an upset stomach, headache, or bruise. She told me stories about the fairy folk from her home, or gods, or mothers—her stories melted together and it wasn't always easy to keep them straight, especially after she started making sweet wines from berries she found in a secret place she refused to tell me about.

We spoke often in whispers about magic, and about mysteries, but we never spoke of our pasts. I never told her where I'd been and what I'd seen or why I'd been on that ship with her. I never told her of my first wife who had died or how I'd quested into the depths of Hades for one final kiss. She never named her previous lovers, the roads she'd traveled, the spells she could cast.

I assumed, then and now, she'd cast some sort of spell over me. I never understood why, not until my last night on the island, when I got only a hint of why she might need to keep me ensorcelled. In an unguarded moment, I overheard her speaking with the stars—the depth and breadth of their voices echoing like choirs. And I saw her eyes reflected in the clouds, reflected not by the clouds themselves but by something in the clouds, a kind of snake or serpent winding through the air, shifting in and out of sight in the darkness and the ocean mists.

When she saw me, when she found my spying on her—which is not what I was doing; this was a small island that never offered any true semblance of privacy—I saw her teeth, rows of sharp, jagged teeth that I had never before seen or imagined, and for a moment—though it might have been the wine—I thought her body curled into the darkness like the dragon's.

She said my name then, rushing toward me as though I'd stumbled wounded into her arms. She caught me, though I shouldn't have been falling or fainting. I wasn't drunk, but the warmth of the wine coursed through me. She shook her head and wiped tears from her cheek and said, "You shouldn't have seen that."

"But, my love," I said, meaning it with all my heart and all my sense of adventure, "I didn't see anything..."

It was a lie. I had just seen my love and life slip away from me but hadn't realized it yet. She kissed me, there on the shore that last night, brushed the hair from my face, held me close, and whispered secrets I won't share here or ever. I drifted to sleep, to dreams, to fantasies and fancies I will forever treasure though they remain hidden in the recesses of my mind—I remember the feel of them, the warmth, the beauty—

After that, I don't know how long I drifted on the ocean, supported by the last plank remaining of the captain's lady, his *Phantom*, with the face of the masthead staring sightlessly and lifelessly into the night sky, before I was rescued. Brought to the surface, to a barge filled with shipping containers, I learned the *Phantom* had vanished without a trace on an entirely different ocean.

But I had the compass, and a parchment map, the edge of which was once promised to me, and I have money to book passage on another ship. I don't care where they think they're destined to dock.

STORAGE UNIT TALES #42

Another item I found in the storage unit had never belonged to me or to anyone else. The bowl had manifested itself, slipped across a dimensional rift, or been deposited as some sort of *joke* by a creature with more mischief than brains in its head.

It was a small bowl, not ornate, green in color but smooth in texture, and it might have been made of glass. It was dreadfully smooth, and if you held it up to your eye—its diameter wasn't much more than that—it distorted everything you saw. It must've done more than that, too; it had been wrapped in packing paper, and ink had started seeping in from the edges of that blank newsprint.

I tried to read it, or discern the picture, but it too faded, not yet intact, and the edges looked and smelled like they'd been burnt.

Inside that bowl sitting in storage and hiding on a shelf in plain sight was the lingering acrid scent on the air that brought my attention to it.

I unwrapped it, looked through it, held it to my ear as though it might tell me secrets, and asked it, out loud, where it had come from. But that little piece of almost-glass offered no answers.

One of my ghosts, who once upon a time had sprawled across grand pianos and sang torch songs in smoky bars, whispered, "Put a little sugar in my bowl." Every chance to be suggestive, she ran with it. But, I'm game for a lot of things, and it seemed like a decent and relatively safe way to run a test on the bowl. So I took it home. I put two tablespoons worth of sugar into the bowl and watched.

While I watched, of course, nothing happened. My torch singing ghost laughed and said it was my fault. One of the other ghosts shushed her. They argue like that sometimes. It's usually all in fun.

I washed up, and opened a bottle of wine—I was expecting company of the romantic sort—and put the bowl of sugar to the back of my mind. My friend arrived. We drank and laughed and discussed possible futures and drew cards to commemorate the evening. She brought me a rose. That would prove to be important at a later date; I include it here only to point out that we're always involved in multiple stories simultaneously.

After she left—sometime between one witching hour and another—depends on who's counting—I put out the candles and was washing up the dishes when I noticed the green bowl had shifted to something red enough to be considered angry. The sugar inside had become caramel. Burnt caramel. Again, it was the odor that alerted me.

I wouldn't trust the caramel to eat. I wouldn't trust it to feed my enemies or put in a dish. I had to obliterate it entirely, which took quite a bit of effort, and wasn't something I'd been prepared to do. I washed the bowl thoroughly with hot water and sage.

The bowl didn't like that. It cracked in half. Each of those halves tried to cut me. I asked, again, where it had come from, and I asked my torch singer ghost what I should do with it.

"How should I know?" she asked. She called me *sugar*, but I thought it was a joke.

"You suggested the sugar."

"And now you know what it is."

"What is that?" I asked.

She stayed quiet. She didn't know. The ghosts trusted me to be smart about these things. In truth, I kept so many ghosts because each had a certain set of knowledge and experiences that might prove useful one day.

I put the two halves of the bowl into a container and sealed it. It was a waste, I thought, but too much of a risk to allow the bowl to remain loose. Despite the time, I went back to the storage unit.

Even with the full strength of the moon behind me, the storage unit was not an easy place to walk through. Its angles were sharp, its shadows deep, its echoes threatening.

One of my ghosts chuckled in the background. Then my phone rang.

I often don't answer the phone. I often ignore it. Leave the ringer off. Everything. But it was my friend, from earlier, and I always answer her calls. She makes so few. "What's wrong?"

"I lost something," she said.

"What?"

She tried to explain. "A thought. A memory. An echo of what we do and did. Maybe a color, a sound, like the tinkling of bells in the corners of my mind. A song I used to sing when I was a child."

I cursed. I reserve those for only the most appropriate occasions. I had just stowed that container in a distant corner. I retrieved it. I took it out of the storage unit, out of the building, a mile down the road into the woods, and crossed the river via a footbridge. I wanted the distance, the water, all of it. There were too many other dangers inside the storage unit.

I drew a circle in the dirt with an obsidian knife. I recited ancient poetics, and unsealed the container.

The bowl was whole, almost back to green, radiating and even pulsating with joy.

"You took something," I told the bowl.

It didn't answer me. Even if possessed—which this bowl was not—it was still an inanimate object. It wouldn't talk to me, it wasn't going to grow legs and run away, it was just a piece of—something like glass, like obsidian, maybe a kind of mirror.

That's what I looked at. What was reflected inside. I saw echoes of songs, I saw rainbows obscured and sounds fluttering in darkness.

Without ceremony—the walk was ceremony enough—I brought the knife down on the bowl.

It shattered.

It shattered into a thousand and one pieces that fell into the dirt, drifted on the wind, would have floated in the river if not for the circle. It shattered well beyond the strength of me. Whispers and glooms escaped as the bowl screamed.

It was a scream born of hellfire and brimstone. It scratched at souls, it charred the grass in the dirt around me—only within the circle—and very nearly sent me reeling.

I rang my friend. "Are you okay?" I asked.

"It's back, if that's what you meant."

"It is," I said. "Of course."

I gathered each of those pieces and returned it, the dust of it, the shattered remnants of the bowl, into the container and resealed it. I sealed it a second way, too, just to be sure. I was meticulous about collecting. I counted the pieces. Counting has its purposes. Some were not more than dust. I was still working when the sun rose, and I continued working in the light of day.

Though the pieces were small, I was reasonable sure I'd gotten them all. But I'd admit, lacking real knowledge of the bowl, its origins, or its purpose, I cannot be sure one fleck of its powdered remains didn't escape my attention.

As to what else I might have released—I wouldn't have to wait long.

The Museum of Curiosities

WOLVES OF THE MOON

The sickle moon provides little light.

He runs down the alley, the narrowest of canyons, over asphalt and under fire escapes, in places where the moon can barely see him. He doesn't feel safe. He's exposed in ways he's never been, and the wolves are at his heels.

He works his fingers and recites specialized poetics under his breath. He can't spare much. He needs it all for his feet, his muscles, his speed. He's disconnected from the magic here.

Wolves howl.

In the city, the buildings are tall art deco nightmares. He rounds another corner in this maze of backstreets and courtyards to face a mural.

It's a wall, so he has to stop.

The image is of him running through hills, wolves at his heels, the moon high—full, in all her glory—and moonbeams radiating like lightning bolts to strike him and the wolves.

He places a hand on the painting. It's solid, dusty brick. Paint falls away in flakes under his fingers.

He turns to face the wolves.

There are seven of them. Jagged teeth. Vicious grins. Eyes like fire opals, milky white shot through with greens and reds. Such violence. Such potential.

"Heel," he commands.

They don't listen. They're beyond obedience. They're wild. Feral. Hungry.

It's his fault. They're not supposed to be here—wherever here is. He's out of breath, out of time, out of hope. He looks up, but there's hardly any moon to be seen, just a sickle blade hanging in the sky.

He draws that from her: the weapon, like a scythe, a hook, yellowed like the moon tonight, like the wolves' fangs.

He can't fight them all. But he doesn't have to go down docilely.

He counts them again. Seven. That's bad. Twelve had followed him through the portal. Twelve had chased him across the wild country. Twelve had followed him to this city. Wolves hunt in packs. They're probably all around him now.

Surrounded, he takes a breath of resignation. Closes his eyes. Sight can be deceptive. He won't trust it, not in this garish place, not when the shadows are thick and soupy. He hears movement to his right, and strikes with the sickle.

Its weight and momentum push him back. The rush of blood is pungent. The wolf whimpers, but others move in.

In another place, another time, these were the supreme predators. In another place, another time, he was. He had dominated the favors of the huntress. This is a retribution. She'd opened the first portal. Allowed in her wolves from another place. Vengeance for sleights unintended.

He cuts another of the wolves.

One of the wolves buries its teeth deep into the meat of his shoulder.

Another bites under his ribs.

He drops to his knees. The name of his moon—not this moon, not the one shining so weakly upon him now—on his lips. He opens his to eyes his fate. He drops the sickle.

That was the last of his weapons. He's out of magic, out of plans, out of breath, and out of ideas. He hasn't got strength enough to face a single wolf. Twelve, even if two are wounded, are more than enough to take him down.

There's a lesson to learn here. He's sure of it. Maybe he'll get it right in the next life. If, in this world, there even is a next life.

The alpha takes him by the throat.

He wakes with a start. A new body. A new place under the same sickle moon. He takes a deep breath, sighs heavily, thrills that he's got all his fingers this time, all his toes. He walks to the window, to the fire escape, briefly uncertain of where he is.

He looks down on the mural. A past version of himself running from the wolves. In the alley, the wolves still tear his most recent body apart.

He smiles. No time wasted this time. That's good. He checks the room, searches for weapons, spell books, anything he might use; but the weapons are butter knives and the books are fictions.

In that time, the wolves have abandoned the alley. He descends the fire escape. He ignores the blood. Looks instead at the mural, the field, a version of him eight, nine lifetimes back. None of the wolves died down here. None of their corpses remain. They even took the sickle—or the moon did.

He looks up. She's thin, ragged, dim. He says, "I do this for you."

She says, "You did it for someone like me."

That's true. That's the lesson. He takes a breath, turns to the mural—that familiar field—toward the rendition of his moon. He curls his fingers, pulling at the ethereal and the invisible threads that hold universes together. He lifts the veil between realms—something he could not have done before the wolves started chasing him—and steps into the mural.

The wolves, of course, follow him.

He finds himself facing the moon, his moon, whose favors he had dominated. He bows his head, drops to a knee, says, "I never meant to offend you."

She smiles sadly. "You still haven't learned." She bends down to whisper. "You're just another wolf."

And the pack surrounds him again.

The Museum of Curiosities

ELK GOD OF THE FOREST

There were things that simply could not be real. They spoke of a massive deer or elk or moose, something that stepped through winter with antlers like spears—and it breathed fire, or so the stories said. They also passed around stories of fairies who stole teeth, goddesses of night lingering in the necropolis, and wolves with amber eyes and crimson fur.

Damon didn't believe such stories.

He was a very practical man of thirteen. Late one afternoon, in an effort to prove how much he knew and how little he feared, he told Diana to wait for him by the church steps at midnight. "I'm gonna venture deep into the forest," he said, "after twilight, and I bet I find no trace of the elk god."

"What do you mean by trace?" she asked.

"I won't see it," he said. "I won't find its tracks in the mud by the river, I won't hear it breathing, I won't feel its fire, I won't even find its leavings."

Diana made an exaggerated face to show her disgust.

"And I'll return a hero," Damon said.

"But not seeing something doesn't prove anything."

Despite her protests, he set off, armed with only his imagination and courage—no different from the boy in the story about the squid and the ocean—and left the village.

The woods around the village were dark, and home to more creatures than Damon could name. He had seen foxes he suspected were really beautiful and beguiling women. He had seen dragonflies on patrol. He had seen snakes, which were actually quite scary, especially the ones with the gold stripes between red and black scales. They were like dragons, and he'd seen them spit acid.

But an elk god breathing fire? That was impossible.

Cold crept through the woods. The first snows hadn't yet come. They'd be here soon, but not tonight. The stars would be visible if he could see the sky through the prismatic canopy of leaves overhead.

As a boy, he had run through these woods. He had even gone with his father once on a hunt. They hadn't caught anything. His father spent most the time telling Damon stories about all his most exciting hunts, but Damon never believed jaguars roamed this forest. No one had ever seen a jaguar. No one had ever taken home a jaguar's pelt. It was true that his father had once found a large stray cat, but its fur had been smoky and it purred a lot. They named her Minx. She still wandered in and out of the village today.

Damon followed a deer path through the woods. He knew all about deer paths, and he couldn't think of a better way to find the elk god. Brambles reached into the path to scratch his shins. Hard roots jutted from the earth and tried to trip him. When night fell, the iridescent colors in the leaves all went dark in an instant.

Damon marched forward undeterred.

The chill nibbled at his bones and scratched the back of his neck. Night birds sang their nighttime songs, all ominous in their minor keys. Rabbits and other critters raced through the underbrush around him, crunching through the layer of fallen leaves, but nothing would stop him.

He intended to walk halfway to midnight, maybe to the fabled lake, or he would come upon the elk god. Until then, he kept walking, marching, exploring.

The woods in the night were, in fact, darker than he'd expected. He had long ago left the lights of the village. He wanted to move faster, but he didn't want to poke out an eye on a low-hanging tree limb.

He heard the snakes slithering. He felt the whisper breath of whippoorwills and ravens. He smelled the forest, earthy, green, mossy, and pungent all around him.

He heard the gentle movement of a stream.

It wasn't much, and it wasn't loud, but no one told stories about streams or creeks or rivers in the forest. There was the lake where all the animals came to quench their thirst and brag about their day's conquests to the other animals that would listen. There was the lake with its waterfall and its deep, dark denizens and its deep, deep waters. It was bottomless, or it connected underground to other lakes, or it had covered a lost city of men. There were plenty of stories, but no one had ever seen the lake—not the magical lake deep in the forest. He couldn't have gotten that deep. He wasn't sure he'd gone in the right direction.

He found the stream easily. He would've stumbled into it if he hadn't heard it. His were a hunter's ears. The stream was in a gully, but it wasn't deep, and something—a red fox—probably a fairy woman spying on him—lapped water from the other side of the stream, pausing briefly only to look at him and decide he wasn't a threat.

"But I *am* a threat," he said to the fox.

She paused again and bent her ears to listen.

"I'm a big bad man from the village," Damon said, "and a hunter, and I could've been carrying a spear or a bow or a rifle, and then what would you be, little fox?"

She returned to the water, drank her fill, then slowly walked away. She was genuinely unimpressed. Or she disguised her fear well. That seemed more probable.

Damon bent at the stream, cupped his hand, and took a few mouthfuls of water himself. Even hunters got thirsty. The water ran cold down his throat. But it was forest water, obviously enchanted, and it would have given him the power to see the elk god if such a thing had ever existed.

It exhaled loudly behind him.

Damon turned slowly. He looked up, trying to see its face. In the dark, he couldn't see much more than the points of those spear-antlers and the amber glow of its eyes and the plume of smoke it had just released.

The elk god was real.

Damon took a step backwards, which put him perilously close to the edge of the gully. The creature—it was a god, no doubt about it, ten times his size, a hulking shadow in the dark, bending its head to look into Damon's eyes.

"I didn't mean anything by it," he said to the elk god.

It struck him anyway. One of those antlers pierced his shoulder. It threw him clear across the gully. He landed on the slope on the other side and slid into the stream, banging his shoulder, splashing and crying out, fighting to get his feet under him again.

When he did, the forest was still, quiet but for the water which oozed like ribbons of ice into his legs almost up to his knees. The elk god was gone. Nothing remained but the animal smell of it, and he couldn't take that back as a trophy.

He heard a sound, like a step in the dark, and scrambled up the side of the gully. He ran through the forest, able to see now because of the enchanted river water he'd ingested. He dodged the violent tree limbs, hopped over roots, burst through brambles when they tried to snag him. He ran all the way back. Hours of running. Through the woods, his legs freezing beneath him, the chill of the air biting into him, he ran until, out of breath, he broke out of the forest and into to the village. He was still panting when he reached the church steps.

Diana waited there. She smiled. She said, "You're early."

"I saw it," Damon said between gulps of breath. "I saw the elk god."

Diana laughed.

"I'm serious," he said. "Look, it gored me." He showed her his shoulder. The wound still bled, though not badly. He felt lightheaded, like maybe he had lost too much blood. He refused to faint, and instead sat on the steps. "It's real."

"That doesn't look so bad," Diana said, though she couldn't see the gaping hole in his flesh underneath his shirt. "You could've done that to yourself with a stick."

"It's real," he said again.

She kissed his cheek. "Thank you," she said. "It's a lovely little story." Then she walked away, back to her home, where her father never liked Damon and never would, and where it was warm. It was warm in his house, too. He could dry off there and catch his breath. When he saw the wound in a mirror, it wasn't much more than a scratch. But over the next few days, his bruises spread and yellowed. For at least a little while, he'd be able to count those as hunting trophies.

FLORAL APOCALYPSE

Palm trees outside the window are yellow and red. I don't think that's normal. They're getting closer to the house, and I don't think that's normal, either. When they said an apocalypse was coming, they didn't say it would be the trees.

But I know what the trees are doing. Without green leaves—I mean, even the firs and pines up north have changed—there'll be no photosynthesis. They intend to suffocate us. But even that, for some of the trees, won't be quick enough.

Look, the palm trees are practically brushing against the windows. I heard tap dancing on the roof last night. I look up and down the street, and I wonder how much longer I've got. All the while, of course, eating strawberries and citrus and any other fruit I can get my hands on. It feels a little bit like fighting back.

I'm probably only making them mad.

Do trees get mad? Or is it me?

Anyway, they're closer. I heard a window shatter in another room. I closed the door. What else can I do? The golden ivy will wind its way into my home, force open the doors, snake in through the ventilation.

I wonder what the snakes think of all this. Don't they need oxygen, too?

Anyway, the experts on the Internet have advised me to stay home, to keep my doors locked, to live off the food I've got, to take what I can without getting too close.

I would've gotten out of here, but on what they call Day 2, the tires in my car had been overrun by brush, and at least two of them were flat, punctured by roots suddenly protruding through the driveway.

Through the windows, I watch the tall grass sway in the wind.

I wonder, too, if the wind has thought, but I assume it's against me, against us.

When I opened the door the other day, my cat ran out. Decided he didn't trust me to protect him. He's probably right. I've got guns, but they don't seem to slow down the advancing trees. I think the leaves are yellow, but the red is blood. I don't know what they're eating, but they're suddenly all carnivorous. Probably to make up for the fact that they're not consuming sunlight.

And what does the sun think?

Nothing. I doubt the sun cares. It's not a god or something. It's just—the source of all light and heat, no small thing, sure, but not all the things.

I can only afford to think that for as long as the sun provides light and heat.

Last night, I tried to call an old girlfriend. She didn't answer. Her voicemail was full. I haven't talked to another person in eleven days. I haven't talked to the cat since he left me. I can watch the videos on YouTube, but social media has been vacant. I'm beginning to wonder if I'm the only one left, but that makes no sense. I wasn't the best prepared. I'm not the smartest, strongest, bravest, nothing like that. I'm just a guy living a mile or two from the ocean in the Florida peninsula trying to avoid the vengeful trees.

I think they built a glasshouse around me and my neighborhood. That's got to be it. Keeps the Internet out, kills the phone lines. It's why the cable news networks are all buzzing rainbows.

I have a machete. I'm not completely helpless. But the palm trees, they keep getting closer. And while the bamboo might fall to my blade, I'm afraid of the oaks. The cypresses might just drag me into the swamps and feed me to the gators.

I'm almost out of food. I'm going to have to venture out there, at least to the neighbor's house. If I can break in, if they're not there, I can eat their food, and maybe I don't have to die right away.

But it's a forest, now, between me and the neighbors, and I can't really be sure the trees haven't already overrun those houses, too.

I don't know what to do anymore.

Another window shattered in another room. I'm running out of places to retreat to. There may be nothing else to do. I keep waiting for a helicopter rescue, a rope ladder dropped down to lift me over this encroaching forest. I hear animal sounds, and see movement in the leaves, serpents but also jungle cats and boars and bears and maybe even sharks walking upright. It could be sharks. It might as well be sharks. I'm careful not to cut myself. I'd rather avoid a feeding frenzy.

The palm trees, yellow and red, pressed tight against the house, laugh at me now. There are fewer windows unbroken. I'm out of strawberries. I'm out of citrus. I finished the last box of pasta. It was full of seeds. I ate them anyway, and now I fear the trees are growing inside me, taking root in my intestines and spreading through my lymphatic system.

I can hear them whispering. I don't understand the words, but I realize I'm not moving anymore, I'm consuming the sunlight myself. Even without photosynthesis. I don't know how I'm still alive, or why, or what they plan to use me for—food, I assume, because that makes the most sense—nourishment—vengeance—or maybe they'll lift me up and display me as an example to any others—if there are any others—if there's anything else left. Last time I was able to turn my head, the skin of my legs had gone to bark. I cut myself in an attempt to lure the sharks, but maybe I was wrong about them. I tried to use the machete on my own limbs, but there were too many now, and branches coming off of them, and leaves of yellow, red, and even orange. Ultimately, I couldn't bring myself to harm the blue flowers dripping from my fingertips.

the museum of curiosities

MEASURE OF SILENCE

The stars fell out of alignment. Across the earth, repercussions rippled throughout the animal kingdom. Jaguars retreated to their temples. Mosquitoes went still all along the equator. Whales beached themselves. Criminals turned on each other.

But the jazz played on.

The bass kept an easy heartbeat. The drummer brushed the skins. The piano drove the melody and the atmosphere: something melancholic, something human.

The stars fell, and they were noticed all across the galaxy. On one distant planet, bells tolled, Russian Orthodox bells — replicas, actually — in lamentation. On a battle-riven battle cruiser orbiting a binary singularity, a temporary cease fire occurred organically.

On a distant gleaming rocket ship, hurtling through the vast void to a mysterious destination, a man named Hooker broke out his saxophone for the first time in an age. His song entwined with the jazz piano so many, many astronomical units away.

From the earth's oceans, great old beasts arose. From the earth's seas, ancient creatures emerged. Dark figures crawled out of the rivers. Shapes crept loose of creeks. Shadows overtook the atmosphere and hid the sun from cities. Military arsenals were let loose with a collective effect of nil.

But soon, on ancient wings not meant for seas or skies, the old, ancient, and alien gods abandoned the earth and sailed toward unknown and unknowable universes, parallel, perpendicular, close, distant, and impossible.

On his gleaming rocketship, Hooker reached a measure of silence. In a bar on Esplanade in New Orleans, the piano reached the same and the bass paused. Only the drums brushed through the next moment. Only the sweep of rhythm.

When the earth's core cracked, they heard it in New Orleans and they heard it in New Haven. They heard it in Wales and New South Wales. They heard the crack in Tibet, and they heard the crack in Tierra del Fuego.

Hooker also heard the crack, despite the distance, despite the years, despite the laws of physics and metaphysics alike.

The measure of silence ceased, and Hooker played on, solo and unaccompanied, his saxophone talents unmatched in all the universe.

the museum of curiosities

The Sanders Haunting

A ghost haunted the apartment.

It was a new apartment, built maybe three years ago, occupied briefly by the Sanders family when they believed it couldn't possibly be haunted. They'd paid a premium for a spirit-less joint, and ended up taking the complex to court.

The ghost did the typical ghost things: hiding steak knives, scratching threatening messages into mirrors, screaming incoherently when Orion's belt could be seen through the sliding glass doors to the balcony.

The place had granite countertops and a washer/dryer hookup. It wasn't supposed to have a ghost.

The apartment remained empty during litigation, but if you sat in a car on the street outside sometime after midnight, you might catch the lights flickering or hear the ghost playing Nina Simone records.

The ghost also did this thing where it changed the color of Mr. Sander's eyes. That was probably why the complex eventually settled out of court for an undisclosed sum presumably in the six or seven figures.

The complex declared bankruptcy shortly after that. The court appointed someone to continue operations, as a hundred other families lived in the other apartments, everything from studios to three bedroom cribs with cathedral ceilings and jetted tubs.

The designated operations manager hired a historian to learn who the ghost was and why they lingered in the brand new apartment. She arrived on a Tuesday with a suitcase, an air mattress, a laptop computer, and a book.

She read in the living room until dinner time. She ordered delivery. She turned the pages in her book for hours after finishing off the General Tso, but the ghost never made an appearance.

The next day, under the historian's instructions, an apartment's worth of furniture was delivered, including dishes and cooking implements, steak knives, even laundry detergent. She finished her book before dinner, so when she ordered pizza she also requested any random paperback if one happened to be available.

She tipped the driver excessively since it wasn't her money anyhow, then stayed up reading until well past midnight.

The third night, she made a fancy omelet on the stove, with cheese and bacon and mushrooms and an assortment of spices. She'd picked up another book in case she finished this one, but sometime near 3am fell asleep twenty pages from the end.

In the morning, nearly noon, she showered and made a phone call.

Her associate arrived in the early evening with homemade lasagna and garlic bread. They opened a bottle of red wine. They talked and laughed and, at midnight, broke out special cards and incense and crystals. They invoked the ghost.

When her associate's eyes changed from blue to green, the historian knew she had him. She spoke plainly to the ghost, as she doubted it had been lingering here since the eighteenth century. "Dude," she said. "What the hell?"

The ghost shrugged her associate's shoulders. "They paid me."

"They paid you?"

"A percentage of the settlement," the ghost said with her associate's voice.

"Do me a favor," the historian said, since there wasn't a record player in the apartment. "Play me some Nina Simone."

"Why?"

"Verification purposes."

So the ghost briefly abandoned her associate's body and "I Put a Spell on You" drifted through the apartment, followed by "My Baby Just Cares for Me."

The historian found herself singing along. "There," the ghost said, speaking with her associate's lips.

"Thank you," the historian said. "But what would you listen to, if it was up to you?"

Her associate's lips smiled.

The Spice Girls' "Wannabe" came on next.

"That's better," the ghost said, though her associate's throat constricted in resistance to the suggestion.

"Okay," the historian said. "I have been authorized to deal on behalf of the owners of this complex. First, you'll have to leave."

"But..."

"We'll make other arrangements," the historian said. "It'll be okay. Second, you can keep the money, and in fact we'll double it."

"That sounds reasonable."

"It is," the historian agreed. "But you'll have to testify."

"In court?"

"If it comes to that, yes."

The ghost considered this, and finally said, "I don't really like the Sanders, anyhow."

The historian smiled. "Nobody does."

THE MUSEUM OF CURIOSITIES

THE LAZARUS BELLS

The bells atop St. Lazarus Cathedral do not move when tolled. Their tongues swing every dawn and dusk by a series of ropes. There is no melody. The rhythm resounds throughout the city. People set clocks to the bells. People wake in the morning, or begin their evening dalliances, by the bells.

The lettering on the iron bells is primarily old Slavonic, with some Latin interspersed amongst the images of saints and martyrs. The twenty-two bells range from twenty pounds to thirteen tons, and each retains a secret name. The master Fyodor Matorin cast the bells in the late seventeenth century. The bells escaped St. Petersburg before the Bolsheviks had a chance to melt them down into cannonballs like so many of their kin.

Some Russian bells resisted that purge, and sometimes people died. Others fled to Western Europe or Asia. The Lazarus Bells escaped over the Atlantic, eventually being restored to glory in the towers of St. Lazarus, and later came with the church to Midnight.

Midnight: a city of a million living souls tucked between two mountains in such a way that the sun never shines on it; a city where its own legends walk the streets; a city as much underground as beneath the naked stars.

Peter helps the bells sing. Perhaps, in another time and another place, he was called Petrov, or Pytor, when his beard still had some black, when his eyes could discern more than just shadows. He hadn't arrived with the bells, but the moment he came to the church they became his duty. It was only natural; he speaks their language. He cleans them and caresses them and makes certain they have, not a tone or a chord, but a voice. "Representative of the very voice of God," someone had once said, describing similar bells in a similar belfry in some other corner of the globe.

Thirty minutes before the bells ring, Peter drags his bones up one hundred and three steps. He moves between the soprano bells, touching each, whispering to them, perhaps breathing their names. Patient, are the bells. Watchful. They have witnessed centuries to our decades. They have seen peace and wars, and communions both sacred and blasphemous. They have transformed the stone hearts of criminals to beating flesh.

Such are the stories, anyhow, which Peter relates to any visitor.

Months ago, during twilight, the Wandering Reverend had asked to bear witness. He climbed behind Peter in darkness and silence. The twilight sky caught the red of an unseen setting sun. The bells moved Peter to a momentous performance. After it was over, whilst still the bells vibrated, and also his bones, the Wandering Reverend stayed in the tower. He said nothing.

Peter is never too ill to perform his duties. He never wearies. One hundred and three steps, twice daily, perhaps one for every year of his life. People have stopped asking Peter his age. He doesn't know. He doesn't want people to realize he has no idea, so he makes up birthdates. There's often something significant about the dates. January 22, 1905 he once said, and June 28, 1914, and September 16, 1925, the day physicist Alexander Friedman succumbed to Typhoid Fever. He will tell you he drinks only vodka, then drink whiskey instead. He claims he doesn't smoke, but most days spends an hour or more in the courtyard with a Maduro.

One priest at St. Lazarus believes as much about the bells as Peter. Father O'Leary has witnessed visions and miracles, and horrors, that bind him to this church. The church is home to other relics, some hidden, some forgotten; Father O'Leary knows more than most, and he gives the bells a great deal of respect.

Midnight is a city that refuses to let its legends die. People still believe they mined sapphires in this very valley, though no one admits they've ever seen any indication or photograph or painting of any mines. They say ghosts stalk the theatres, all of them, except perhaps the multiplex which stands neglected. They say the city was settled by its founders two—or perhaps four—centuries ago; or they say the city was settled by a man named Midnight who merely paused for a last glass of scotch.

They say the ghosts of St. Lazarus Cathedral came to the city with the church. The building once stood in the heart of New York, or London, or perhaps Rome, and even now has doors that sometimes open onto other basilicas, mosques, synagogues, and bingo halls. They say a cardinal was buried alive in its crypt during the Inquisition. They say the reliquary holds Mary Magdalene's funerary garments.

They say, too, that the bells, when they are ready, will find their way home.

Dawn paints the sky blood as Peter entices the bells to sing. It's a clear morning, so he can see the faces of both mountains, City Hall, the

Museum of Curiosities, and the sea of treetops stretching south of the city. He has no time to spend with the cityscape, however. With some effort, he hears the distinct voices of each bell. They resonate. Despite the volume, and despite his proximity to them over the past ten or twenty years, his sense of hearing remains sharp.

The cacophonous rhythm echoes to the highest reaches of the mountains, and as far as the nearest unseen shore. At this moment, not one of the million souls of Midnight sleeps, and the restless souls pause in their hauntings. Something sounds different. Mournful. The bells toll a lamentation.

Father O'Leary leaves his breakfast, scrambled eggs and toast on a bare wooden table, and races to the bell tower. It's a long ascent, one hundred and three steps spiraling around a stone column poorly lit by ensconced candles. The flames flicker as he rushes by, as fast as a man his age can rush up steps such as these. The higher he climbs, the louder the bells sound. They practically scream as he emerges in the bell tower.

There's a transfixed raven watching the mother bell.

There's the slightest breeze.

There's an impossibly ancient Peter clutching the ropes, his arms still moving with the motion of tongues on the bells, but they've ceased striking. They've stopped singing.

Peter slumps to one side, his arms in rhythm with the ropes, all color washed from his face.

Father O'Leary calls to him anyhow, knowing Peter will not answer, will never again. As they say, he's given up the ghost—and he's given that ghost to the bells.

For the first time since St. Lazarus Cathedral opened its doors in Midnight, the bells are silent at dusk. Indeed, the entire city seems quiet. Traffic stops. Children cease their wailing. A blind girl on Fox Street, they say, was suddenly able to see, and three babies were born at the very moment the clouds were most brilliantly red. In a small church, St. Francis Cabrini, a mere series of rooms seventy feet below the surface of the city, the saint's statue cries. Such stories will later grow to be legends. The tears will be recalled as blood, and the girl will go on to heal hundreds with her breath as though she were a mistress of the moon itself.

The Wandering Reverend attends Peter's funeral. It is arranged quickly, as per instructions in the will. Though intended to be a small affair, the cathedral overflows with mourners. The mass is at dawn, and for a second time the bells remain soundless.

There are no provisions in Peter's Last Will and Testament as to the duties of the bells, and there is little enough already in those papers. Peter leaves a ring bearing, presumably, his initials, *PAR*, to Father O'Leary. No one is quite sure what other names belonged to Peter. He leaves a locked box for his daughter, but does not name the girl and no one steps forward. The box will be held in the reliquary until the unknown daughter comes to substantiate her claim, perhaps by possession of its key. He leaves a small bit of money, crumpled dollars and rubles and koruna and yuan, not amounting to much, to the church.

A thousand people follow Peter's casket to the cemetery. They move with hushed tones. Magpies and crows bear witness. The gravediggers had done their job, and the graveside rites are handled by the cardinal himself. After, whispers wind through the crowd, suggestions that no soul in Midnight had ever grown to such an age. Even the founder, Carlton Midnight, legend says, died at one hundred and two.

The Wandering Reverend speaks to Father O'Leary. "He will be missed," the Wandering Reverend says. "He was a good, dependable man."

Father O'Leary can only say, "Yes."

The day's shadows stretch long. The police find little to occupy them. Early dinners are quiet affairs, though here and there a child may break the silence. This isn't everywhere in the city. This isn't everyone. But it is so pervasive, one believes even the forest magicians pay respects in their own ways.

It is an hour before the day's end when blood is again spilt on the streets, the victim stabbed seven times by a drunk and jealous lover. His, the first death in Midnight since Peter's, somehow eases the tension. In his room at St. Lazarus, Father O'Leary finds he can breathe more easily. He still feels the weight of death on his chest. To look at him, you would believe he's witnessed the last breath of angels. He's an old man, getting older, and he's tired of seeing friends die.

Thirty minutes before dusk, Father O'Leary goes to climb one hundred and three steps to the bell tower. The Wandering Reverend awaits him at the bottom of the stairs.

"The bells will become somebody's responsibility," the Wandering Reverend says.

"Tonight," O'Leary tells him, "they are mine."

The Wandering Reverend follows the priest up the dark stone stairs. They ascend without words, with barely even the echo of their footfalls. In the tower, the iron bells watch over Midnight like sentinels, big and small arranged in lines issuing from the thirteen ton Mother Bell. The ropes and pulleys and pedals contrive to make a labyrinth, a man-sized cat's cradle, an indecipherable mystery. There is that single bird again, silent, waiting for the music.

"He would speak to them," Father O'Leary says.

"He knew their names," the Wandering Reverend says, perhaps not aware of this truth until that very moment.

"These bells have been at this church longer than I," Father O'Leary says, sliding his hand across the bottom of the unmoving Mother Bell. "And I came with the church to Midnight." He's not saying anything the other man doesn't already know. "Perhaps it would be best if they remain silent."

"No," the Wandering Reverend says. His voice carries authority.

"I don't remember the man who rang the bells before Peter. He was old, I recall that much, but nothing else. He didn't die so much as fade."

After a silence, the Wandering Reverend asks, "Do you believe in ghosts, Father O'Leary?"

"Yes." Without deliberation, without hesitation; this is not the answer of conviction or faith, but of knowledge and experience.

"Do the ghosts of the bell ringers stay with the bells?"

Father O'Leary's smile is weak, and perhaps a bit sad. "Would that be a reward or a punishment, Joshua?" Few ever call the Wandering Reverend by his given name.

The silence between them is palpable, and the sky above reddens. "It's time."

Father O'Leary grabs hold of the Mother Bell's rope and swings, and swings again, and a third time before the tongue strikes the side of the bell. The sound is hollow, without resonance, and the priest loses his will to continue. The rope slips from his fingers. The bell's tongue, however, continues to move, and the next strike sounds like the bell ought to sound. Loud. Full. The other bells add to its joyful noise. Sadness tempers the joy.

There's no ghost. No hand rings the bells, either living or dead. The bells themselves announce their grief, and their resolution. The twenty-two Lazarus Bells, without harmony, united in rhythm and purpose and intent, scream their pain into the dusk. Perhaps they call a new bell ringer from one of the corners of the earth. Perhaps they dream of past glories, the mother country, the faces of friends and even their brothers who did not make the journey to St. Lazarus. Perhaps they need no hand to guide them. The bells have seen cities fall to plague and war and intrigue, and they may very well witness the death of Midnight itself. Perhaps they are more than merely representing the Voice of God.

Downstairs, one of the other priests greets Pietra, newly arrived in Midnight and inquiring about a position, any position, perhaps as a cook or a maid. She's come a long way. She's cold. Weary.

The priest asks her to wait in a stone room with dark wood chairs and a bench around a thick wood table. When Father O'Leary returns from the bells with the Wandering Reverend, the priest whispers into his ear. "I think she's come because of the bells. I think she's Peter's daughter."

"Has she made such a claim?" Father O'Leary asks.

"No," the priest says. "She may not know it. But she has his accent and some of his words."

"I'd love to meet her," the Wandering Reverend says.

Father O'Leary hesitates, but the moment is brief. He nods, and the two enter the room where Pietra waits. Hugging her knees to her chest, she sits on the bench. Her eyes are closed; she rocks gently back and forth, too slowly to match the chaotic rhythm of the Lazarus Bells.

Father O'Leary turns harshly on the young priest. "Have you brought her no food? No blanket. Quick now!" His volume is low, his tone rare.

The Wandering Reverend steps forward and bows graciously. "Miss Pietra," he says. "I am Joshua, the Wandering Reverend. This is Father O'Leary. He has been with this church for longer than I can remember. How long have you been in this City of Night?"

"Two nights," she says, a whisper, a breath.

"Two nights," the Wandering Reverend repeats. "And during that time, have you eaten anything? Have you had water?"

"Some water, yes." She chooses each word before pronouncing it; she is uncomfortable with the language. "Bread. I have no money."

"Money is often overrated," the Wandering Reverend says, withdrawing some from a pocket hidden in his robes. "And often underrated, too." He puts it on the table, within her reach, but makes no effort to give it to her. "This will help, I think, for a short while. You've come to a good place. I am sure Father O'Leary will find you some honest work, and make certain you have a soft bed this night."

She glances at the priest. "Thank you."

"Should you ever need me," the Wandering Reverend tells her, "I can be found on the streets most nights. Dream well tonight, Pietra. *Bazhayu garnykh synif.*"

The Wandering Reverend pauses at the door to whisper to Father O'Leary. "Look at her eyes. She's seen much. This city will not easily break her."

"Good," Father O'Leary says. "The asylum is crowded."

The Wandering Reverend leaves as the young priest returns, wool blanket in hand. Without a word, he gives it to Father O'Leary and then rushes away again.

Father O'Leary puts the blanket over the girl's shoulders, allowing her to pull it tight over her knees. He sits in one of the chairs. He appraises her for some time, her dark hair, close-set eyes, the nearly invisible scar at the corner of her lips. "We do not normally have women staying in the church rooms," he begins, "though we will make an exception, at least for tonight. We can worry about finding you your own place in the morning. We haven't got much to offer by way of work, not here, but I'm sure we can find you something."

"I can cook," she says. "I can clean." Then she adds, "I am pious."

"Do you wish to confess?"

"No, *Otche*. Thank you, *Otche*."

The young priest returns with a plate of sandwiches cut into halves and a pitcher of water. He sets them on the table, leaves for a moment to fetch a napkin, glass, and plate, and says, "Don't eat it all too quickly. Don't want to bring it back up right away." He glances at Father O'Leary, bows nervously, and leaves.

"He..." She has trouble finding the word. "He fears you?"

"He's young," Father O'Leary says. "When he walks through the church, he thinks of the bodies in the crypt, and the huge empty spaces candlelight cannot reach. He's almost as young as you."

"I'm older than I look."

Father O'Leary smiles. "So is he. Eat."

She does. Her first bite is huge, too big for her mouth, but she chews it up and swallows it in two gulps and washes it down with the water. Subsequent bites are not so zealous. She finishes three of the sandwich halves before wiping her mouth with the napkin and meeting Father O'Leary's gaze. The food is bland, and half of it is gone, but she says, "Will you eat?"

"I'll eat later," Father O'Leary tells her.

"I will be hard worker," she says.

"I'm sure you will."

"I will be worth...effort."

Father O'Leary nods. "Yes."

"But I don't think I am what you think I am."

"And what is it I think you are?"

Pietra shakes her head. She stuffs more food into her mouth before answering. She finishes the first glass of water, refills it. Her hands do not tremble. "Answer. You think I'm the answer to a riddle. I'm not. I'm just a girl from Kiev." She frowns. "*Bloudnaya dyivcheena.* Lost girl."

Father O'Leary nods. "No more, Pietra. You have been found." He stands. "Come, I'll show you to your room."

"I can wake early," she says. "For work."

"What sort of work would you do, early?"

"I make eggs. I polish pews. I light candles. I fold linen. I make music."

"Ah," Father O'Leary says, smiling as he turns to lead her to her new home. "What do you play?"

"Piano," the girl says. "I play piano and organ and a little violin. And some flute, when I was young."

"You're still young."

"More young," she says. "Saint Andrews had no bells. But your bells, they call me here. They sound like home."

"Do they speak to you?" Father O'Leary asks.

When she doesn't immediately answer, he pauses, turns, and asks again. "Do they speak to you, Pietra?"

She lowers her eyes. "Yes."

"What did they say tonight?"

She shakes her head. "Sad. They say they are sad. They cry. They say they want someone from their home. But they can find no one else. Sad, because they lost someone they loved."

"We all did," Father O'Leary said. "Can you ring bells?"

"I ring bells," Pietra says. "I ring bells at Saint Sofia once. They sound younger than your bells."

They reach the room where she'll be staying. It's small, sparse, containing nothing more than a bed and a small desk. It's warm, if not overly comfortable, but the bed is soft and the pillow filled with down.

"They ring at dawn," Father O'Leary tells her. "Do not oversleep."

In the morning, Pietra finds her way to the bell tower and climbs the hundred and three steps. She wanders among the bells, touching them, introducing herself in whispers, promises to use all her strength and weight and faith when she pulls their ropes. Shadows conceal Father O'Leary; if she notices him, she does not acknowledge him. She knows no sun will rise, but feels dawn's arrival as if by instinct. She works the ropes.

At first, the bells seem hesitant. They find a different rhythm than Peter's hand ever guided them toward, and finally sing out proud and strong. She works up a sweat, her muscles strain, and as the Lazarus Bells echo into silence, she is breathless. Tears stream down her face. She makes no sound. Even after their song falls to silence, the bells still vibrate; she waits until the last of those unheard tones pass through her bones before trying to find her feet again. As beautiful as the bells sounded, as clear and vibrant and discordant, one was off its voice. Not the Mother Bell, but not one of the small ones, either. She climbs under it, sticks up her head, slides her hands along the insides. The iron, smooth and rough and cold and sharp, still sings to itself. Near the top, above the tongue, she finds something attached to the bell. Something that shouldn't be there. Something that requires all her strength to be dislodged.

In the weak light of Midnight's dawn, she withdraws a key.

CRYSTAL FAIRY

She's made of crystal.

The light shines through her as through a prism, reflecting and refracting, throwing rainbows and spotlights across the hallway. She walks carefully, attempting stealth, but she's unaware she's already been seen.

Little Jenny sits on the floor next to her door, which is opened just a crack, so she sees the crystal fairy. She smiles, and reaches up for the doorknob, because she wants to say hi.

The house is dark. It's night. Jenny is too young to understand night. She doesn't yet know about the phases of the moon, though she's seen them. She doesn't know shadows or the things that lurk within them. She knows lollipops, but those aren't of the night; and she knows clowns, but only as the creators of balloon menageries.

She knows the word menagerie because, despite being slightly less than three, she's incredibly smart. Everybody says so.

But the doorknob is quite a reach. She has to stretch on her toes, so she inadvertently pushes the door all the way shut. That makes it harder. She doesn't just need to pull the door now, she needs to open it again, and she's got all the strength of a two year old.

It takes effort, but she's persistent.

Jenny opens the door.

The crystal fairy is nowhere to be seen, so she pouts. She was there a moment ago, all radiant and light, smiling and sneaking.

Jenny ventures into the hall.

In the night, in the dark, the hall is full of shadows, but Jenny hasn't yet mastered the art of fear. She's felt it, yes, when mommy left her alone that one time in the car, and when mommy left her alone that one time in the living room, and the night when mommy cried because of something on the television. But there are nuances to fear far beyond her ken, so she feels no threat in the darkened hallway.

The banister doesn't allow her to slip through. She'd have to climb over. But that wouldn't help her. The crystal fairy had been prancing toward the stairs, so she probably went down to the living room, to the kitchen, or maybe out the front door.

Jenny goes down the stairs.

She has to take them one at a time. She climbs each step, scooting over to the edge, tottering once or twice, swaying, barely able to keep herself upright. She feels no fear, but she knows it'll hurt if she tumbles. She'd roll all the way down and into the living room—and maybe crash into the big wood coffee table with all its edges. She doesn't want to do that, so she's careful and she moves slowly. Halfway down, she pauses because she sees the lights of the crystal fairy shining into the living room from the kitchen.

She can't see the kitchen.

But she hears the twinkling of bells. Clashing and smashing. They're louder than any bells she's heard, high pitched enough so that only Jenny and maybe the dog—asleep in her room—can hear them, but no one else. She knows this because she's smart.

"Fairy," she says.

It's not loud, but the sound echoes through the living room, into the kitchen, maybe even upstairs toward her parents' room. She doesn't care. She has no need for stealth. She's giggling.

The bells go suddenly silent.

It's a brief pause, and then there's a wolf at the kitchen door.

It's not really a wolf. It has wolfish teeth, but it's bigger than a wolf, and it stands upright on two feet like people, not like wolves at all. It's got claws instead of fingers, and teeth that gleam even in the night.

She stares a moment, and opens her mouth to say *oh*, but no sound escapes. Her little heart skips a beat, maybe two; it's something her little heart has never done before, not ever, not even once. The hairs on her neck rise. She doesn't even know if she's got hair there, but they're like goosebumps, except there were never any geese involved, and she wonders if she's seeing something she was never meant to see.

The light of the crystal fairy moves behind the wolf/not-wolf, but the creature launches forward, up toward the middle of the staircase, straight at Little Jenny. She rocks back, banging the side of one of the steps, and ends up tumbling exactly how she didn't want to be tumbling.

She rolls to the bottom of the stairs. She spills into the living room, but does not smash the wood coffee table or any of its edges. The wolf lands where she had been sitting. Its claws shatter the banister. The sound wakes the house, but everyone is upstairs—her mommy, her daddy, her doggo—everyone. The only thing between her and the wolf is its claws, and it's turned and leaping through the air.

And it would've reached her, too, if the crystal fairy wasn't there. But the crystal fairy is there, and her arms were crystals, and the crystal arms end in sharp crystal spears. So the wolf, when it leaps, lands right on those crystal spear arms. The wolf cries out like a wolf cries out: horribly, terribly, incredibly.

The doggo and the parents arrive too late. All that is left is the dead wolf, and a blood-soaked crystal fairy, and Little Jenny giggling on the living room floor.

The crystal fairy is gone before her mommy gets down the stairs. Her doggo, however, follows the crystal fairy into the kitchen. But apparently the fairy gets out of the house because the dog just barks and barks at nothing, and all that is left for her parents to do is clean up after the big bad dead wolf.

MENAGERIE

It's Florida. There shouldn't be a basement, a cellar, anything at all underground. Denise has been in the house for a year, more than a year, and only today discovers a hidden doorway? To be fair, it was well hidden, in the back of the laundry closet behind the washer. She wouldn't have found it at all if the hose hadn't come loose from the machine.

But now she's found the door, the half door, a thin piece of drywall she can shift aside. It moves easily, without extraordinary effort, but not smoothly. At first, she thought it was simply a loose piece of wall, behind which might be two by fours framing the house, electrical wires, maybe a cigar box with a small piece of worthless treasure. She'd get a story out of it, nothing more, and she'd have to bang in some drywall and that would probably require a trip to the hardware store.

But no. It's narrow, but it's a staircase.

Logistically, on the other side of this wall is the deepest corner of her little walk-in closet, which must end just a couple of feet more briefly than she'd imagined. But below the house, below the crawl space, below the ductwork and raccoon nests—she has no idea what to expect.

She ignites the flashlight function on her phone and tests the first step. Not all her weight, not immediately. It might be rotten. Soft. Broken. But it's sturdy, strong, unwavering in its support. The steps are deep and small, with little headspace. It's almost a ladder to a lower section of a submarine. She descends into the basement that shouldn't exist.

It's vast, beneath the whole house, almost twelve hundred square feet. The walls are concrete—and amazingly, dry, unsullied by mold or mildew or even spider's webs. It's kept dry by a dehumidifier that's not only been running the entire time she's lived here, but is emptying its water directly into the sewage pipes.

The ceiling of the basement is reinforced, and is not in fact the floor of her house. There is the crawl space.

Along one wall, there are bottles of wine, a hundred or more, a reading chair and table, and a man sitting unmoving with a pipe in hand. It's not lit, not emitting any smoke, and there's no sign of breath in the body. He doesn't belong to this age. He's stepped out of a past century. There's a glass of wine beside him, an open bottle, and not even a suggestion of dust.

"Lovely, isn't he?" a voice asks. The long, sillowy woman slips out of the shadows. "I rather like the cheekbones, and the color of his eyes are the most amazing shade of auburn, don't you think?"

"Who are you?" Denise asks.

The woman tsk tsks and shakes her head. "Such manners. I would have thought by now...ah, well, no matter. Call me—I don't know, how about Lucy? Would you like that?"

"Who are you, really?"

"Don't ask questions when you can't accept the answers," Lucy tells her. "So, where are we now, anyhow?"

"What do you mean?"

"I captured this specimen outside Dartford," Lucy says. "I've been wanting another to place beside him. In a kind of dance, you might say. Do you dance, Denise?"

"You know my name?"

"I know everything about you."

"Then why don't you know where we are?"

Lucy smiles narrowly. It's disconcerting. "You believe that's a good question, don't you? I know your eyes are green, more like emeralds than jade, and I know your hair is—not that color by birth, but that's okay. I can wash the dyes out."

"I like my hair the way it is."

"I'm sure you do," Lucy says. "It must be the fashion of the day. But I'm not so interested in your days. Would you like to see other rooms of my menagerie?"

"I think I've seen enough."

"The walls," Lucy says, shrugging her shoulders in a way meant to mimic human shrugging. "I can't do anything about the walls. I had to borrow them, locally, to show you this. But the wine, the bottles, the chess set..."

"I don't see a chess set."

"No? Maybe it wasn't so complete a transfer as I'd intended. No matter. I know you've played the game, and played it well. I believe you were a champion of some sort."

"Seventh grade," Denise says. "That hardly counts."

"Regardless of when, you can learn. And you and Tristan here will have all the time in the world to learn."

"I don't know who you think you are or what you think you're doing," Denise says, "but I'm not about to be part of some imaginary zoo with *Tristan* for your enjoyment."

"Oh, it's not for enjoyment," Lucy says. "Not entirely. I'm something of a natural scientist. I needed a breeding pair."

Denise punches Lucy. There's no thought, no preamble, no wind-up. She'd been trained, so the punch comes from nowhere to strike the side of Lucy's jaw.

The jaw is sharp enough to cut Denise's front two knuckles.

The punch is strong enough to send Lucy reeling back into the concrete wall. Something in her skull cracks—maybe something small, maybe something big. Lucy inhales deeply, doesn't bother exhaling—breath is apparently an affectation—and glowers at the human woman who lives in the house upstairs.

"I guess you don't know everything about me," Denise says.

"I don't think you'd be a suitable mated pair at all," Lucy tells her, finally letting the breath out in a stale stream. She glances at Tristan, sitting frozen in time.

As he fades, he comes to life again, long enough to say, "I suppose this is another one that won't work out quite the way you intended." He even manages a wink at Denise before he's gone. The chair follows. Then the table. The wine bottles fade individually, and Denise realizes she doesn't have a lot of time before the entire makeshift basement will vanish.

She scrambles up the stairs, which are steep and narrow and no longer as supportive as they'd been. She pulls herself the last few steps by the back of her washing machine. Lucy's voice follows with a stream of profanities in a dozen made up languages.

When she looks back, the drywall is in place as it should be. No trip to the hardware store will be required. Denise knocks on the wall, which sounds hollow but only because the other side is her walk-in closet. There's no indication of movement, of drywall dust, of anything, not even an echo of the unreal woman's voice.

Denise goes to her own collection of wine—five bottles only, none of them expensive—and pours a generous glass. Tristan had seemed quite pleased that the plans of the woman called Lucy weren't going smoothly. Denise drinks a toast to the gentleman from another century, then rings her friend, Anne, whose knowledge of witchcraft and iconography and wards is deep. "I'm not sure what we need to do," Denise tells her. "Either a protection spell or a rescue."

"Have no fear," Anne tells her. "I'll be right over."

RISE

Ravens circle the castle.

It's an old castle. The people inside are as ancient as the stones, more so, refugees of another earth that preceded our own.

The castle hides in the mountains. It's not invisible, but it is hard to reach, and hard to see with satellites in part because the stones of the mountain. Half the castle, maybe more, is carved straight from the rock, including all of the dungeons.

Those dungeons go on forever in all direction, especially deeper, and hide a great many forgotten secrets. Treasures. Dragons. Traps. Enticements. From deep, the heart of something beats, something not seen by any eyes in ten thousand centuries.

It won't be seen today.

But its heartbeat reaches the ears of a prisoner long chained to a gray wall in a dank, forgotten hole. It gives him a breath of hope, an ounce of strength, a glimmer of a future.

When he moves—this former raven god—the birds outside circle more tightly and make agitated noises and eye the windows with malicious intent.

The raven god squeezes his hands into fists. This tightens the muscles in his arms and wrists, despite the atrophy, despite the dust. He inhales, and perhaps it's the first time in a thousand years.

He breaks free of the chains.

He climbs from his hole by digging handholds into the walls and pulling himself up one excruciating inch at a time. His skin cracks as he climbs. His bones tremble. His muscles split.

He sniffs the air. He tastes the floors for any sign of water that might have once rolled across them. He feels his wings spreading, his feathers sprouting, his teeth sharpening. It's a long time since the raven god has eaten.

Rising into the castle, he walks between shadows, folded out of view of even the most elemental of servants. He's not interested in merely a meal. He seeks vengeance.

In the court, he discovers what's become of the kings and princes, the queen and the fool, the musicians, the tasters, the seers, and the guards. They're pathetic and insubstantial whispers of what they once were, their flesh reduced to ash and held in place by momentum. He could blow one over with a puff and scatter them to the wind.

That kind of revenge will not make a satisfying meal.

He listens, instead, for other sounds. The heartbeat of the beast beneath echoes the rhythm of the princess's heart. The raven god doesn't remember the princess. She's younger than he is, though not by more than a hundred years. She's radiant like a spider's web, her thistle hair silvery gray, pale and colorless; but once upon a time it was vibrant, and she was vibrant, and the realm itself—now barren granite and decaying forests—had teemed with life.

A tear escapes the raven god's eye, despite that he cannot afford even a single drop of moisture. He catches it with a finger, touches it to the princess's lips.

And she drinks.

It's only a tear, a single drop, but an indication of more to come. She grabs his hand, sucks on his finger, draws blood from its tip, and refuses to release him. The raven god hasn't got strength enough to break free. He cries out, he struggles, he writhes in agony as the princess sates her thirst on every hint of moisture within him—every dribble of spit, every bead of sweat, every drop of blood, every trace of poison.

The princess desiccates the raven god. She leaves only his withered skin like a gossamer statue. She stalks out of her chambers. Color has returned to her hair, the black and other colors of ravens; to her eyes; and her fingernails and lips and more. She leaves a trail of soot and ash, this princess of dusty things and pallid dreams. In the throne room, she feeds from her family, her father the king, her brothers, the guards and tasters and seers and fool, and finally stares into the eyes of her mother.

Her mother.

Her mother moves with the speed of trees marching toward oceanic volcanoes, which is to say there's life in her eyes but they're merely aware. The princess doesn't drink from her mother, but scatters the fragments of her. Maybe in time she'll reform.

The princess calls to the ravens, draws them to her, and together they flee the collapsing castle, listening all the while to the echoes of deep heartbeats not yet ready to rise.

THE DAY THE SUN FIZZLED OUT AND LIGHTNING ROSE INTO THE SKY

Lightning in the corner of the sky is all we get. Everything else is dark since the sun fizzled out. Yeah, the scientists never saw that happening. You know why? Because the damned scientists never take magic seriously.

I mean, magic was the thing that got us through the dark ages. All those witches they put to death? People killed them at their own peril. Those were some powerful users of magic. I'm not talking Penn & Teller magic. We all know that's just for the stage. It's illusion. Yeah, that's a form of magic, but it's not the kind of thing that cuts paths through seas, raises armies of dry bones from the desert, or transforms base metals into steel. Yes, steel is far more useful than gold. A variety of steels are used to make knives, which can then be used for utility, for self-defense, and for killing. Outside the movies, no one dies because their skin is painted gold.

Yet here we are. Scientists are stumped because they can't accept magic. Magicians are stumped because they don't understand the mechanics behind this magnitude of spellcasting. And the sun? The sun stopped casting light and stopped casting heat with a sound not unlike popping the tab off an old can of cola.

I guess it's up to me to do something, but I'm not sure I can be bothered. I mean, the temperature's dropped nearly thirty degrees in the past hour, here and everywhere else, and I'm of half a mind to just snuggle under my covers and let the world stay dark. Humanity, as a whole, just ain't worth the effort. No one will thank me, no one will reward me, no one will replenish the supplies I'd use up in an attempt to revitalize the sun. I say attempt, because even with me, there's no guarantee it'll work.

You want proof of that? Look at the news. The looting. The killing. The ridiculous speeches of politicians claiming to have solutions, claiming no solutions are necessary, claiming this is the work of a foreign agent. They're all idiots.

But then there's the lightning. In the corner of the sky. Being all peculiar. Shooting upwards. There are no clouds, no storms, no movement of wind, nothing to explain the lightning. Sure, it's the edge of the world. I live on the beach. I look down on the sand from my penthouse, bought and kept by the use of arcane magical formulas and the stock market. I look out at the ocean rolling in, waves of whitecaps, from my balcony with a glass of red wine, and I curse.

I curse a streak of red, blue, and green.

Reluctantly, I drag a one-man airship into the sky from a parallel place. The man inside is surprised, but I offer him wine and explain the situation. I point at the sun. He has an innate understanding. I give him a glass of wine, then pilot the ship north, over the Atlantic shore, toward the lightning. My guest salutes me with his glass—good wine, too, why should I not be generous considering his amiability?—and wishes me well.

Mine's not the only penthouse on the strip, but I am surprised to find someone else utilizing the esoteric arts in such a way.

It's cold out there. I shiver. That's how cold it is. I never shiver, and I was there when Shackelford made his fateful journey. I was there when they opened the ice mines in Scandinavia, but I suppose that was too long ago for you to remember.

I pilot north, to another tower, a narrow building overlooking this particular end of the world, and tie the ship to the railing on the balcony. The couple inside the living room are surprised. They didn't know I was coming. They'd broken out the good tequila. Makes sense. If it's the end of the world, no reason not to finish off the top shelf. They ask who I am. They don't realize I can see their naked bodies and dripping sweat. They've forgotten the lights are still on inside, the electricity still flowing through the wiry veins of the city. I rarely see people get that drunk. "Don't mind me," I tell them. "I'm just here to save the world."

And I admit it, that's exactly what I'm here to do. Damn. No one's going to pay me.

"No, really?" the woman asks.

"Tell you what," I say. "Fifty thousand bucks says I can do it. If the world doesn't end by tomorrow, I'll come back for payment."

The man says, "And what if the world does end?"

"I'll sweeten the deal, then. Your fifty grand to my half million."

"Deal," they say simultaneously.

Outside, the lightning is shooting up the sides of this building, using lightning rods in exactly the way they were never intended. This building is the source, but it's coming from low, lower than the ground, down in some basement.

I exit their penthouse and use the elevator to descend as low as it will go. I con the machine into traveling all the way to the bottom despite not having the secret code to make the elevator work. I'm good at this sort of thing.

The elevator deposits me in the midst of a vast warren of catacombs and labyrinths. This isn't even supposed to be here. I conjure a kind of swallow and tell her what I need. She flies off in one direction, crosses back to try another, finally returns and leads me through the darkness.

Yes, it's a steel door. Probably used to be lead or even gold. I thank the sparrow and send her back to where she came from. I shift the locking mechanisms and open the door. Inside, the scene is rather explicit: a dungeon, a sex dungeon, a man in vinyl properly tied to an apparatus I hesitate to describe, a woman suspended from the ceiling wearing only the ropes that bind her and a series of scars. There are bottles in weird shapes, beakers of bubbling liquids, old leather books, a scattering of icons and iconography. The symbols being called upon are surprisingly clear and precise.

They're both dead already. Not a surprise. I walk toward the machine generating the electricity. The temperature has dropped another thirty degrees since I left my penthouse. The woman, dead and suspended, says, "You cannot interfere."

I glance at her. "You can't really stop me, all tied up like that."

She snarls.

The man, dead and restrained, says, "There will be consequences."

"I know. I'll earn fifty thousand dollars. Not much of a payday. Now, however, I see I'm being overpaid."

They rattle in their various suspensions. It doesn't stop me. I throw the switch. The electricity running through the ceiling, up the walls outside this building, and into the sky crackle as it rails against being shut off.

The couple breaks the ties that bind them simultaneously. They amble toward me. I never understand why a corpse can't be properly driven. They're rancid. The stench is the closest they'll come to killing me. With a touch to the forehead, I disintegrate the atomic structure that holds her together. It looks like she's melting, in flakes rather than liquids, but she doesn't last long because the individual atoms she's decomposing into are microscopic.

See, I may know my magic, but I also know my science. I'm well-rounded.

The man in his vinyl pauses. He says, "I'm just passing through. I didn't make them use the book. I didn't even lead them to it."

"I know." I touch his cheek tenderly where a welt had started to go purple before he died. The molecules of his body slow as their temperature drops. It seems appropriate. He's not physically frozen in ice or anything like that, but I've slowed his macro and micro movements to the point of equivalency.

Then, because I was really enjoying that wine and the starry daytime sky, I punch him. He shatters entirely. Unlike the woman, there are remnants. The possessor remains trapped inside. It may never be freed, but I'm careful so I gather the fragments and slide them into a dimension without time.

The elevator returns me to the penthouse couple. They're shivering now, aware of their nakedness, and aware of what I'd done.

"I don't know how you managed that," the woman says.

"You have your areas of expertise," I tell her. "I have mine." I pilot the airship back to my penthouse. My guest and I finish off the wine as the sun starts to reignite.

"Much longer, and the world would never have recovered," the pilot says.

I shrug. "I've survived worse."

DARKER

It's getting darker out.

Every morning, the sun rises and throws a bit of sunshine around, then it hides behind clouds that keep getting thicker. I try to drink up the cloud stuff with a Crazy Straw, but even with all its crazy, it absolutely refused.

I go to the preacher man. He sits in his big empty church basking in light that falls through those beautifully stained windows. He believes it's the light of his god, and maybe it is. There's not enough sunlight to explain it, not all day like that, not all of it falling in the center of the church like a spotlight. He stands in that circle of light in front of the altar but refuses to leave. "There's only one path," he says.

He's mistaken.

But I'm not surprised.

I go to the line cook at the cafeteria down on Elm. He's cutting onions and wiping tears from his eyes and says there's a reason for his tears. I understand him, I do, but I don't believe him. It's a lie. He's a damn liar. I tell him, "There's only one path."

He doesn't believe me and says I'm the one mistaken. I tell him about the preacher man. He looks at me aslant and tells me to get my head checked.

I go to the tattoo artist. She's working on a rose on someone's shoulder. She probably shouldn't allow me in the back room like that, but she once said she'd never refuse me anything, and sometimes I like to believe her. The rose is pretty. The woman receiving the ink looks at me and smiles and says, "We should get a drink tonight."

"We should," I tell her. But I don't tell her it's already night, it's always night now, the sun is getting less and less intense so we have to find our intensity elsewhere. I'm not sure a glass of gin is the answer, no matter what it's mixed with, but it's at least proof of a second path.

The artist winks at me and says, "She's mine tonight. Don't even think about it."

I don't. Honest. I'm worried about the sun. Or is it the clouds? The sun's a big old star and probably isn't going to change drastically at any one time, not until long after I'm dead and buried and dissolved back into the earth and all my atoms have been fused into plants to be consumed by little critters hunted by predators.

Cycle of life stuff. The sun ain't at the end of its cycle yet, is it?

No.

Can't be.

But it gets darker every day. On the highways, all the cars have their running lights on throughout the day, or their headlights, or their high beams, and sometimes flashing lights because there's an emergency of one sort or another. I go to the ambulance driver who used to be a mechanic and say, "It's getting darker."

"Damn right, it is," he says.

He gets it.

"What do we do?" I ask.

"Damned if I know," he says.

I go to the florist. I say, "What's a good flower for sunset?"

She smiles at me. "Something red, perhaps."

But there are a lot of red flowers. Roses. Carnations. Asters and chrysanthemums and poinsettias. They all mean different things, and maybe different things to different people. I never understood the language of flowers. There's love, and there's love, and there's a third type of love, and I've never understood all of that, either.

So I pay for a purple orchid.

I take the orchid in its little pot home, but I don't put it in the windowsill because I know orchids can't have too much direct sunlight. Not that there's all that much left to be had. It's another day, a darker day than yesterday, and I know winter's coming but that can't be all it is.

I go to the eye doctor. I ask, "Is it just my vision?"

The doctor looks into my eyes with a tiny light and a scowl. She says, "No, it's not just your vision."

"So it really is getting darker."

"Yes it is."

"Thanks, Doc, you've been a tremendous help."

"You still have to pay," she reminds me.

I shrug and give her a credit card. If there's a later to be had, I'll pay for it then.

I go to the magus. He's just a poet who conjures images straight into your head with the power of his words. He's also insane. I tell him, "The doctor says I'm right."

"The doctor is a fool," he tells me.

"Why didn't you tell me?"

"I did. You haven't been listening."

He may be right.

Another day, I move the orchid onto the windowsill because there's not enough sunlight anymore. It's still purple and still happy, but it doesn't need water so I don't drown it. I killed my last orchid and I didn't even mean to. I still feel bad about that, but I've never confided that particular failing to anyone before.

You can call me an orchid killer. It's okay. We've all got something in our past we'd change if we could.

I go to the bartender. She models by day, but the days are getting shorter so I fear her career is near an end. I tell her this. She doesn't really talk to me, but she gives me something strong. There's the woman with the rose tattoo, and I realize there's something that can be done, something to save the world and all the people in it—most the people, anyway, just maybe not me.

Fueled with bourbon and a new understanding, I go back to the artist and tell her, "I need a sun."

"Any particular sun?"

"I've always liked vintage suns, the way they smile because they know an important secret but will never tell you."

"Any particular location?"

She puts the sun on my back between the shoulder blades. She works through the night. The needles hurt as they infuse my skin with crimson and gold. She tells me stories all the while about sun gods and sun goddesses and sun worshippers and beaches and oily coconut suntan lotion.

It's a magnificent rendering. I kiss the artist and thank her and give her my credit card. I tell her I have something to do and I hope to see her again but I don't know. She understands. She sheds a single tear, but it's the most amazing and awesome tear ever shed, like a tempest in a single drop of salt.

I go to the preacher man. There's no difference anymore between day and night. The moon revolves freely around the earth but never gave us sufficient light.

"That's a good sign, though," the preacher man tells me. "The moon reflects the sun. The sun's still got light to give."

So do the stained glass windows. I tell him, "Your work here is done." I remove my shirt to display the sun tattooed on my back. "It's my turn."

The Museum of Curiosities

He relinquishes the circle of light as I step into the center of it. He lays himself down to sleep—the long, final sleep—and I extend my arms and raise my head and let the light burn through every line and curve of the sun on my back.

Outside, the clouds dissipate.

And I become the preacher man.

PIE CONTEST

A queen rose from the snow. You probably know a story like that.

You may even believe the queen was evil or wicked or ill-tempered; and perhaps there was such a queen in some other land. But in the land of December, the snowy queen was in fact anything but icy.

She sent out hunters for a contest. "Bring me," she said, knowing full well what the tales might think she'd ask for, "the best pie."

Yes, pie. The snowy queen loved pie. Blueberry pie, sweet potato pie, pecan, even chocolate pudding pie.

The hunters travelled far and long to bring back the best pie makers they could find. They found a man from Paris, a grandmother from Virginia, a child prodigy from Kiev.

In all, a thousand pie makers gathered in the land of December for the contest.

In the first stages of the contest, pie makers were divided by their specialty and competed to represent their particular pie. So many chefs made apple and cherry pies, those contests had to be divided into multiple phases, complete with semi-final rounds.

Grasshopper pie had only a few hopefuls, while lemon meringue caused the greatest controversy when one of the bakers fell over dead before pulling her pie from the oven. They concluded it was natural causes, but no one was happy that her pie had been left in the oven to burn.

But make no mistake: there were murders and numerous attempts at sabotage. Most, however, were not believed to have a negative impact on the overall contest. Further, the snowy queen made a point of attending all the necessary funerals.

In the end, fifty pies were prepared for the snowy queen to taste herself. Hers would be the final judgement.

And judgement came swiftly. On the second day of the tasting, the snowy queen declared the shepherd's pie of an Australian woman to be the most outstanding of all the meat pies, which of course disappointed the Britannic contingency.

She chose a peach cobbler over the rhubarb pie, which upset some based on technicalities. A day later, she declared the grape pie to be the most surprising.

The snowy queen also took a second helping of butter pie, which went a long way to appeasing the Britannic contingent.

She also liked the flan and the empanada, which left some people confused. For a while, it looked like the Mississippi mud pie was going to be her favorite—prepared by a man from Gulfport.

Instead, the snowy queen selected a New York man's key lime pie. She said she found it refreshing.

She also said another day, she might easily select something else. Therefore, in the land of December, pie contests are now an annual event.

BOOKIN'S WEB

In the bookshelf, between two thick old books meant for children a hundred years ago, where the musty scent is inescapable and the words faded with age and use, there lives a bookin. Maybe you haven't heard of bookins. They're not as famous as elves—none has ever fought in a war against dragons—and not one has ever sat upon a throne and ruled as king or emperor. But they're old as any empire of men, and they're magical as any fairy you're likely to meet.

And they're small.

On this particular bookshelf, the bookin lives in an apartment he himself carved into the spine and back of a book so rare no one alive remembers its title. Of course, he's left the story untouched; he's far more interested in the words, the phrases, and the hero's journey than the value attached to the physical substance by merchants and death dealers.

On the day later known as the Great Horror, nothing noteworthy happened, and the bookin wasn't even aware. It isn't until later, when the man's heirs start rifling through his belongings and divvying up the silver and the art, that the bookin becomes aware of the Great Horror.

Other books have already been packed, sealed, and sent away in heavy boxes to libraries and museums. But the bookin has made a home, and he's been comfortable roaming the streets—no, the *worlds*—of his neighborhood. *Paris in the Twentieth Century. In a Glass Darkly. Lost Horizon.*

The bookin simply cannot allow his neighborhood to be sold part and piecemeal. For his favorite restaurants and parks to end up on obscure bookstore shelves in places like Omaha and Karlovy Vary.

On that first day, the giants—compared to the bookin, whose kind were known to ride dragonflies as though they'd been born in Pern— didn't reach his neighborhood, but he can see the damage they've done. Half the constellations in his night sky have been rearranged and no longer resemble The Emerald City, the Shire, or Neverland. Instead, there are new, empty places, like black holes, except they are formed of rich, thick wood shelves, leftover busts of dead composers, one skull that might be human, and cobwebs.

That gives the bookin an idea. He sets a green light out on his porch, and in the middle of the night receives a visitor.

The spider is black as night except for a red hourglass on her abdomen.

"These are indeed tumultuous times," she agrees, after hearing his story and proposal. "Of course I'll do it. You have been most kind to me, and to my mother before me, and her mother. You are long-lived, bookin, and always have the most amazing stories."

"We'll have another after tomorrow, I am sure," the bookin says.

In the morning, the giants arrive with moving equipment and boxes and charts and paperwork, but in the library they discover an erratic web, as though cast by an inebriated spider, which forms letters. Together, the letters form words, a number of words, and those words form a phrase: *leave the books.*

The heirs take pictures of the web, lighting it in just the right way, unaware that they're also photographing the front façade of the bookin's home. They post it on social media, and pass the story to some clickbait site, and they manage to spin a bit of money out of the incident.

"It looks photoshopped," the youngest of the heirs complains.

"Shut up and take your check," the others tell her.

When the movers are done, the catalogs all taken, and after three other messages courtesy of the widow, the library, the bookin, and his home remain in the house.

The house, unfortunately, has a tragic tale of its own to tell, but that's for another day.

MARIGOLD AND THE BRICKLAYER

She slipped into the human outfit. It didn't fit properly, a bit tight in certain places, the hips, the lips, but she'd often heard humans complain about not fitting into their own skin, so she imagined it was normal. She took a breath of orchid and a breath of butterfly wings to lighten her step, and ate a chocolate because, well, chocolate. Then she set out of the house on her grand adventure.

The house let her out onto a city street. She had imagined woodlands, maybe rivers, maybe even oceans. This was not what she expected, but she went with it. Humans often found themselves in places they didn't want to be, so this was probably a good way to understand the full experience.

She went into an office building. It was a thousand stories high and housed half a million people, by her estimate. She'd never been any good with numbers beyond the twelve needed for the clock, and those were strange enough already, the one also meaning five, the five also meaning twenty-five.

She met a man behind a big desk and said she was there for an appointment. "With whom?" the man asked, his voice clipped and proper in a way that meant he could only and ever be serious, serious all the time, serious like everything mattered and the weight of the world would crush everyone else if he so much as shrugged his shoulders in the midst of a laugh.

"I'm not quite sure," she admitted. "What is it you do here?" She realized her voice didn't sound like his voice. It was lighter, higher, quicker, more musical, with an undertone of little glass bells the man simply couldn't comprehend. He stared at her—no, he glared—he tried to wither her with his eyes.

Eventually, even the ever and always serious man behind the desk had to admit she wasn't going to back down. "Fine," he said, shoving a clipboard and pen at her. "Sign in with your name and the time, and sit over there." He indicated a series of stiff cushioned lounges that had never been intended for lounging.

She signed her name, or something like it, a series of lines and squiggles he probably couldn't read anyway. The big imposing clock in the grand imposing wall behind him told her the time—those were numbers she knew—so she was able to get that part right, at least.

Then she sat.

Around her, there were men in suits, and women in suits, all carrying briefcases and checking their fancy wristwatches. One clutched his fingers in a fist. One wiped her brow repeatedly, despite that there was no indication the waterworks inside her had been malfunctioning. The air didn't move well inside this room, despite those big doors opening and closing all the time with little electronic swooshes.

Two or three people were called before her. "Ms. Marigold?" the man eventually said. It was the blandest, driest, dullest way anyone had ever said her name in all her life, which had been long and mostly lovely.

"That's me," she said, glad to pop up from that seat.

"Mr. Bricklayer will see you now."

She didn't catch the real name of her host because she misheard it as Bricklayer intentionally, and once that was there, it stuck. She went to the elevator, as instructed, and ascended to the thirtieth floor. When the doors opened, she entered a hallway occupied only by one tall tree made of plastic and poorly painted.

She followed the corridor to the end, where a secretary—it said so on a nameplate at the front of her desk—suggested she wait a little longer. So Marigold waited, this time able to look out over the vast countryside and all the city buildings that rose this high—there were a lot—and also the clouds in such a way she never got a chance to see them from the ground. They were beautiful, but she was separated from them, and the air tasted stale and gross.

"Mr. Bricklayer will see you now," the secretary announced, though not before Marigold caught sight of a couple of cloud farmers and a beautiful cloud lady in the midst of knitting swords together.

"Thank you," she said, then entered the indicated room.

One wall was all window, but it didn't seem willing to open. Mr. Bricklayer wore a fancy suit that probably cost him several fortunes, had maybe been made by hand, and was certainly cut to fit his body exclusively. The man offered to shake hands, but Marigold went instead to the window. "It's a lovely room you have here."

"Thank you," he told her. "I earned it."

He sounded as serious as the man downstairs, if less stoic. Maybe she'd named the wrong man Bricklayer. He didn't have the build for it, the chest or the hands, and his eyes had not yet seen a day of suffering.

"Oh, you've earned a great many things in your life, Mr. Bricklayer," she said. "Of that, I'm sure."

"Did you call me Bricklayer?" He seemed surprised, maybe a little amused, but also indignant. "My name is Mr. Bricklayer."

"I'll be honest with you," Marigold said. "I don't know what you just said. I only heard Bricklayer, and that's all I'll ever be able to hear, I'm afraid."

He came to the window, stood beside her, arms clasped behind him like some famous general posing for a statue. He didn't look at her, but he couldn't see the cloud lady, either, or her beautiful bouquet of white knives. "You're not here for the job interview, are you?"

She shook her head. "I'm not really good at interviews," she said, "and I rather like my occupation."

"We can pay you well here at Bricklayers International."

"I appreciate that," she said, "but you said Bricklayers, and you didn't mean it at all. You're playing with me, Mr. Bricklayer, and you don't even know why."

"I guess not."

"It's because I'm naturally playful, Mr. Bricklayer." He didn't seem to have a response to that, so she continued. "I'm going to go back home soon, Mr. Bricklayer. It's too claustrophobic in here for me, and I don't think this skinsuit fits me properly. It's all snug in the wrong places, loose in others, and it's beginning to stink, though not like yours. I guess you never take them off at night, do you? You never launder your skinsuits, or replace them, or anything?"

"Actually," he said, "we are constantly replacing our skinsuits." He bristled at the word, but he'd been drawn into this conversation regardless of his wants and desires. "Every seven years, I'm told, we replace every cell in our bodies."

"Every cell, is that so?" Marigold asked.

"It is."

"That's good to hear," Marigold said. "I was afraid if I removed your skinsuit, you wouldn't recover."

He wasn't even taken aback by that.

Marigold left with his skinsuit tucked into an briefcase that usually carried a laptop computer. She stopped at the secretary's desk. "I believe Mr. Bricklayer would prefer to cancel the rest of his appointments for the day."

"Your lipstick looks redder than earlier," the secretary said. "That's a lovely shade."

"Thank you," Marigold said, "but I don't wear lipstick."

The elevator brought her back downstairs, and the big glass doors let her out into the city. She wandered among the stone and metal skyscrapers for a while before finding a park. It was small, but green, and she could breathe better here than she'd been able to inside that stuffy building. She purchased a red popsicle from a man at a cart, then sat on a bench to enjoy the feel of the sun on her flesh. After finishing the popsicle, she unlatched the briefcase.

She unfolded Mr. Bricklayer's skinsuit carefully, unconcerned with witnesses who, essentially, seemed equally unconcerned with her. She laid him out on the grass, used a needle and thread to stitch the tear she'd made at the nape of his neck, and stood back to let him come fully into himself again. He took a deep breath, opening his lungs to full capacity, and stretched his arms, luxuriating in the bath of sunlight.

"Thank you, Mr. Bricklayer," she said. "I appreciate your willingness to consider our offer."

"I don't know that you made an offer," he said. "I don't know that you gave me a choice, but here I am."

"Here you are," she agreed. "Now, would you like to escort me back to my door, or should I leave you here to think?"

"I'd love to walk with you."

"Of course you would," she said. There had never really been any doubt. They walked in a comfortable silence until they reached her door. It was only about fifteen minutes, but the steps felt heavier to Marigold because they felt lighter for Mr. Bricklayer.

"I suppose that's it," Mr. Bricklayer said. "Now I return to the mundane."

She smiled at him, booped his nose like she might a small kitten, and said, "I would suppose no such thing." Then she went into the house, shutting and locking the door behind her, leaving Mr. Bricklayer alone in a city with fresh knowledge of things unreal and uncertain, and a new outlook. Inside, she slipped out of the skinsuit, and put it in the hamper so it could be properly laundered for the next adventure.

A LOVE STORY FROM THREE POINTS OF VIEW

Jack strode into the bar. A man on a mission. He went straight to the bartender and asked for his drink, then turned to survey the scene.

There they were, in the corner, as though nothing had happened. They hadn't seen him yet. Of course not. They were too absorbed in each other. The whole rest of the world didn't need to exist, forget about one lonely little man from Long Island.

The bartender gave him his drink. He finished it in one gulp. It tasted—well, it tasted sour, like revenge, like the culmination of a thousand and one nights of torture.

Jack had suffered enough.

He asked for another drink. The bartender grunted, but she brought him what he wanted. This time, he carried it over to the table.

Jill saw him first. The surprise on her face was delicious.

"Well," he said, setting his drink slowly on the table between them. "Fancy meeting you here."

Jill grabbed his arm and leaned toward him, lowering her voice as if the three of them were co-conspirators. "You're supposed to be dead."

"Yeah, well, life has a way." Jack smiled for them. He smiled big. He would've show them the scar from the bullets if that would've made a difference.

Jill lowered her voice more. "You can't be here."

"It's too late for that," Jack told her. "The doctors did a hell of a job, don't you think?"

Her companion—Jack knew his name but didn't care—stood suddenly and said, "I think you ought to go now."

But that's not what happened.

Paul brought two glasses of wine to the table, sat opposite Jill, looked into those intoxicating eyes, and almost couldn't say anything.

She saved him, as always. She picked up her glass and smiled and clinked. "To another wonderful week."

"I still can't believe it," Paul admitted. The wine was sweet and went straight to his head. It made her even more beautiful, her voice richer, her eyes deeper. "Every time I look in your..."

She touched his hand to stop him. "So you've said."

She sounded like she appreciated the words, but she was gently hinting he'd become repetitious, and even Paul knew repetition led to boredom and boredom led to slow death.

A man slammed a whiskey glass on the table between them. He stunk of gutters and Dumpsters and horse stables. He stunk of bourbon. "Well," the stranger said too loudly. "Fancy meeting you here."

Before Paul could even think of what to do, Jill grabbed the interloper's arm and whispered, as if to a lover, as if to Paul instead, "You're supposed to be dead."

Paul knew her work. He knew what she did, what she was trying to do, and it didn't take long to realize this man was the previous victim of Jill's eyes. He'd fallen in, gotten boring, and paid the price. That explained the stench.

"Yeah, well, life has a way." The smirk, more than anything else, caused Paul to tighten his fists.

"You can't be here," she said. She was speaking too fast, as though she'd lost control of the situation.

"It's too late for that. The doctors did a hell of a job, don't you think?"

That was when Paul drew in a breath, pushed back his seat as he rose, and said, "I think you ought to go now."

The stranger looked at him. Jill looked at him—her expression now all business calculations. The romance was gone, possible gone forever.

The stranger opened his mouth to say something, and Paul punched him.

Kristen poured the bourbon neat and watched the shell of a man throw it back like water. Did he even taste it? She doubted it. Would it waste him? She doubted that, too. He was already gone. When he asked for another, she eyed him suspiciously and poured it. He strode over to the table with the doctor and her latest prey, and that's when the bartender recognized the man and his swagger. Quick math said it had been seventeen days.

His stench lingered. She'd have to air out the whole place again. She busied herself with wiping out a clean glass, watching without looking like she was watching, waiting for her cue to enter the dance.

It came when the new prey threw a punch. It was a sloppy punch, wide, signaled from miles away, obvious and blatant and unbalanced. It surprised the dead guy, but didn't knock him over. Kristen pulled a machete from underneath, slid across the bar, and landed in a crouch between the potential fisticuffs, essentially stopping the fight before it could start. Both men, pseudo-men, whatever you wanted to call them now—both of them stared at her, but all her attention was on the good doctor and the glass of Malbec she still clutched in one hand.

"I've been watching you."

The doctor smiled so prettily. Other patrons gave them a wide berth. The dead man clenched his teeth. The doomed man emitted only half a whimper. Pathetic.

Another woman might've given way to those eyes. To that smile. To the reek of pheromones pouring off the doctor. But no one cared about the bartender in their stories of love trysts and reanimations gone awry. Over time, a person could develop a tolerance to anything.

Even still, Kristen's heart raced and her arousal intensified, so she buried the machete in the good doctor's throat. The blood was messy. The woman fell and clutched at the wound and convulsed for a while. The pheromones continued to work.

The dead man stared. Kristen couldn't handle the stench or that level of decomposition. It took three swings of the machete to free his head from his neck. Then she turned to the doomed man, frozen in place with his ineffectual fists still closed. Throwing the machete to the ground, she told him, "You're never gonna get another chance." Then she kissed him.

the museum of curiosities

A TRICKLE OF SIMPLE NOTES

He sits at the piano, trailing his fingers over the keys, picking out not a tune so much as a series of notes that somehow indicates his emotional state. They're high-pitched lies, as he plays along the far right edge of the keyboard. The notes are like a mask, a disguise, so the other phantoms hiding in the dark crevices of shadows can maintain their anonymity. No one needs to talk if there's music. Maybe it's not music, but it's sound, and for the moment that's got to be enough. It's a dark bar, but it should be darker, and it really should be quieter, but he can't abide the silence. His ears fill the void with a buzz, something like a buzz, a kind of constant scream just beyond the capacity of anyone else to hear. He doesn't like being unique.

Outside, up and down street, all the lights have been going dark, and even above the tinkling notes everyone hears the advance of the soldiers. Laughing. Shooting. Killing. Breaking windows and bones as they progress.

They're hidden in the bar, but not if the soldiers hear even a single note from the piano. Someone gently pulls him away. Another person closes the fallboard so he won't be tempted back to the keys. It's a genuinely nice gesture. And smart. It might save their lives.

They're all refugees in this room. They've each been running a long time, in and out of danger when necessary. Thirty men and women, give or take, and only enough whiskey to dull the very edges of what they're feeling. Oppressed. Exposed. Frightened. Even heroes can experience fear.

The soldiers are coming closer. Their boots echo loudly on the cracked and broken pavement. Their guns, when not being fired, click metallic teeth. Their hearts beat with the frantic rhythm of a thirty piece percussion troupe. They breathe so loudly between bouts of laughter, it's a wind tunnel in his ears—a maelstrom that could be calmed by random piano notes but are amplified by the silence. He looks about the room, willing his eyes not to snap so audibly as he glances between one co-conspirator and the next.

The soldiers are still far away, but even the sweat rolling down the napes of their necks sounds like a river rushing toward oblivion. He knows he's going to break. He knows it, and he can't help it, and even biting down on his forearm hard enough to draw blood isn't enough to distract him from the cacophony of inevitability.

So before he can break, before he can bring death to thirty people he might, under other circumstances, have called friends—or even better, never known—he flees.

No one tries to stop him, and he doesn't blame them.

He runs out the back, into an alley behind the bar and parallel to the street. His feet hit the ground like he's pounding on a timpani. They must hear him already, so he takes a full breath, as deep as he's able, and he screams. He screams to drown out the noise. He screams to kill his fears. He screams to draw the attention of thirty enemy soldiers rampaging like wild beasts on the streets of his city.

His pistol has three bullets. He lets all three fly with new screams, new cries, though a trickle of simple notes might have saved him.

The soldiers gun him down. But their joy has been broken, they have taken wounded of their own, and his co-conspirators will use this brief diversion to avenge him.

MY FINAL OFFER

Eager, they were, and insatiable. They crawled through the vents, broke through the windows, jammed themselves into the doors. They were on the roofs, fighting to get in, and finding their way to the basements.

So we ran to the subbasements and hidden cellars, where we would have maybe an extra ten or twenty minutes to do something meaningful before they reached us.

Ammo was low.

We might've been the last living souls on the planet.

And we, alone, were never going to be enough.

Katie did the stuff with the salt. Joey lit all the candles. He might never have believed, but when you've reached your final half hour and the countdown it running, you might as well give it one last go. I read from the book. Because I was the only one who could translate it. Because it was my book. Because I was old as the gates of Hell.

(Not the original gates. No one is that old.)

Within our circle, I recited the words. The earth shook. Outside, above our heads, and certainly unseen, clouds gathered. A little maelstrom. A tiny storm. A spray of lightning. The thunder rocked the walls even this deep.

After almost ten minutes, a fissure opened in the floor and a demonic thing that defied description rose from it. The beast exhaled sulfur. Its skin was a patchwork of burnt flesh, soot, and ash. Its eyes were—well, I'm glad we were within the protective circle.

The beast started by demanding to know who we were, how we could be so impudent, why we would disturb its slumber knowing that it would be forced to devour us with excruciating slowness and deliver our souls to eternal damnation.

Then it realized two things. First, it was outside the circle, not within it. Second, it slowed down in its litany of curses and oaths to look me in the eye. Yeah, that shut it up. It took in a deep inhalation and said, "*You.*"

It was as much accusation as surprise. I think Joey was awfully surprised by this note of recognition. And I could see it in Katie's eyes: she suddenly found herself wondering if she was on the right side of the salt.

I gave the demonic thing my best crooked smile. "Hello, again."

"I will floss my teeth with your veins," the creature told me, but it couldn't get any closer than the circle of salt would allow. I know my spells, I know my wards, and I know my limits. Most hellborne cannot say such things.

"That sounds pleasant," I said. "But, we are in mixed company." I nodded toward Katie and Joey cowering at the far side of this too-small circle. "Anyhow," I said, "you're too late. I'm not here to bind you, command you, control you, or even manipulate you. The world is ended. The zombie horde is on our heels. We would feel their breath on the back of our necks if their lungs had any capacity left."

The beast's eyes narrowed. It took a deep breath, sniffing at the air—in a way, getting the lay of the land.

"I haven't had time for calculations," I told the beast. "My friends here—I don't believe they're capable of it."

The beast lowered its voice to an agitated rumble. "What do you want?"

"Only one little thing," I said. "In the meantime, you're free to gorge yourself. There's a world full of—I believe almost eight billion shambling things, all trying to make their way here because we smell so damn alive, and they will tear each other apart to be the corpse that gets a seat at the last feast."

"You're giving them to me?"

"Confusing times, I know," I told the beast. "But yes. All of them: yours. One simple thing, that's all I ask."

The beast did not like the way I said that. Probably because of our prior experiences. That was okay. I knew it would take this deal. "Leave these two alone to repopulate the earth," I said, "and leave me alone to protect them and theirs for the next—say five centuries?"

"That's not enough time," the beast said.

"And anyone else out there," I added, "who still happens to be *alive*. Give them a fighting chance."

The beast narrowed its eyes and turned them on Joey and Katie, the last two human morsels I was aware of. "Why?" it asked. "They look delicious."

"Oh, I'm sure they are," I said.

"I am *not*," Katie said, slapping my arm. "I'd make a terrible meal. You don't want me."

"You don't want them," I said, ignoring her. "Or the rest of your eternity will be filled with nothing. No new lives to take or torture. No playthings for your amusement. No new meat."

"I like meat."

"There's meat, right now, outside that door," I said. "All of it, a whole earth full of it. Yours. Just keep them away from us."

The beast grinned. Oh, it was a wicked grin. There were so many weaknesses and flaws in the deal I was proposing. The beast was aware of some of them. Others would, in fact, bind it to us for a while, and it would not like that. But it would obey the intent. It knew the consequences of ignoring my final offer.

While it considered, I listened to the noises from the hall. This last, deepest, most secret and hidden basement, was on the verge of being overrun. There might only be a few hundred thousand zombies out there right now, but there would be more tomorrow, and more again after that.

The beast said, "I accept."

I extended my hand and crossed the line of the salt. "Consider us agreed, then."

It took my hand with its calloused, scarred, blistered appendage, and we shook. We thereby shredded the protections afforded by the circle of salt.

The zombie horde reached us.

The beast fell upon the first to arrive with wild abandon. I ushered Joey and Katie to the corner furthest from the carnage. This was going to take a while. "We should be safe now."

"Safe?" Joey asked. "You made a deal with the devil."

"A devil," I said, "not *the*. And yes, yes I did, and now you're safe, and your children, and their children, for a long time."

Katie grabbed my arm and looked into my eyes and, indicating Joey with a nod, whispered, "But I don't even *like* him."

Behind us, the beast wasn't beginning to tire, but it would. It relished the start of this, but in the end would rue the unceasing butchery. I said, "You should have thought of that before. Now you're the last two, so it's either the two of you or no one and nothing at all."

"What about you?"

I shook my head and smiled. "I've got to keep an eye on my brother here," I said, indicating the beast with a nod, "or things will go horrible awry."

the museum of curiosities

ARCANUM

The light of the moon made a path through the wrought iron arch and into the garden. It swayed and shimmered in the way such a path should not have. It ducked behind the poisonous nightshade and past the sharp thorns of the roses. It slid around the periphery of statues of monsters and goddesses, then led directly to a small chunk of granite at the center of the garden.

Stephanie was surprised she'd never noticed it before. The stone wasn't more than twice the size of her fist, which was small, but had a word etched into it.

She had to strike a match to bring enough light to read it.

It was a name and a date: *Lucy.* Today's date, 1967.

That was before Stephanie was born. A long time before she was born. She wasn't even sure her parents had been alive yet.

She touched the stone and said, "I'm sorry." It was an expression of sympathy. She wasn't sure why. She didn't know if Lucy had suffered, or if she'd lived 102 years before she'd died, or if she'd been kind or wicked.

Stephanie only knew the name. Standing to look at the garden around her, she realized the whole thing had been a memorial. Quite suddenly, she knew why she was apologizing. "We forgot you," she said, though it wasn't necessarily fair to say she'd forgotten something she'd never known. But someone had arranged all of this, and someone had failed Lucy.

"You're supposed to be remembered," Stephanie said, stroking a spray of white and pink snapdragons. "This is supposed to keep the memory of you alive."

One day, Stephanie knew, she would die. Another day after that, everyone who ever had known her would also die, and the memory of her would vanish from the earth.

Just like the memory of Lucy.

So she did some research. Stephanie went to the library. She pestered Mrs. Merriweather at the library for days, then weeks, looking into everyone who had lived in her house before. Because it was a big house with a fancy reputation and a good deal of local lore, including stories of ghosts, aliens, murder, and kidnappings, it proved difficult to parse out the truth.

The most sensational of the stories, which seemed to have no basis in reality, were repeated every year in the local papers like a Halloween tradition. The most disturbing appeared in a local historian's collection of ghost stories; though it was rarely referenced in other places, there was some question as to whether the historian, now deceased, had fashioned the story from truths or from scratch.

"All stories have some truth," Mrs. Merriweather told Stephanie. "That doesn't mean the truth lies in that house."

Every night, Stephanie visited the garden, knelt beside the granite, and told the spirit, who seemed at rest, "I'm working out who you are."

But stories had a way of twisting and distorting with time. Original sources disappeared, or gave only the barest facts. So Stephanie found out Lucy was, in fact, Lucille Harrington, and she'd been six when she'd died, most likely from poisoning. Was it murder? An accident? Had she swallowed something in the garden?

That was impossible. The garden was a memorial to her. It couldn't have fed her deadly nightshade if they hadn't been planted yet.

Stephanie could find no pictures to confirm there was never a garden before 1967. And Mrs. Merriweather, old as she was, hadn't even lived here then. She was from New Jersey, of all places.

Finally, Stephanie had to admit she was stumped. She had researched as much as she could. She had gone deep. She knew the names of Lucy's family, and when the house had been built, and that it was originally called *Arcanum*; the meaning and intention was lost to her. She hired a local artist who worked in iron to set the name into wrought iron.

She visited Lucy's grave at twilight and hung the new sign from the iron arch that led into the garden. She knelt at the granite, touched it, and maybe she even teared up a little as she said, "I hope you're resting well, *Lucille*."

Twilight always had a funny way of interacting with the earth. It sometimes hyper-saturated colors, and often stretched to steal an extra second or two, a whole minute when it was able. Most people would have said the twilight separated night and day, but the truth was the reverse: night and day kept dusk and dawn apart.

For a brief moment, as Stephanie passed under the arch and out of the garden, the super thick yellows and greens of twilight tightened their grasp on the earth. The moment strained. The dusk clung to the iron letters of *Arcanum*, and something under the earth stirred.

Something under the stone.

Something dead more than fifty years. Something that should be nothing but dust and bone.

Lucy broke through the soil. She upset the stone and upset the snapdragons. She reached into a stray beam of moonlight cutting through the long twilight. She was a girl when she'd died, but that was long ago; she wasn't a child anymore. She stared beyond the gate as Stephanie retreated to what had once been Lucy's house. The emotional turmoil inside her was like a maelstrom, a thunderstorm, a cyclone.

And though Stephanie lived in her house now and slept in her room and walked through the garden as though it belonged to her; and though Lucy's anger would have been completely justified, a lone tear escaped her eye and rolled wetly down her cheek. That intruder had tried to do right by her, even if she hadn't learned anything. And it was nice to have the name back. *Arcanum*. It gave Lucy life.

She took a breath. She inhaled the depths of twilight. She ingested the extended dusk and told it, without words, *not yet*.

One day, Stephanie would leave the house. She would die, or sell it, or something worse. Someone else would arrive. Someone else would paint the walls and polish the banisters and dust the shelves and cook on the stove. And if someone else ever took down the name again, if they removed the sign Stephanie had planted, Lucy would rise again. She would bring the long twilight and reunite the dusk and the dawn in a fiery cacophony.

The Thief on the Run

This isn't a story about what he stole. It's in his bag now, and it doesn't really matter so much as the fact that a number of people want to retrieve it. The prince put a price on its retrieval and made it clear that he didn't care if the thief lived or died. It doesn't even matter that the thief only took what was rightfully his, and that a court of law, if such a thing even existed in this place, would have found it difficult to convict him.

This isn't a story about the object of the theft, its convoluted history, even its magical properties, assuming the legends about it have any truth. It's about the thief running through a city where every citizen knows his face and his name, and not a single one isn't enticed by the offered bounty.

It's not about the underground, the shadowy world of assassins and cutthroats and conmen to which the thief does not truly belong. He runs through their world, turning at the darkest corners, gasping for breath in the briefest doorways and alcoves. Some watch him, and some will turn him in, and some will do so not for the bounty but to remove the one hovering over their own heads.

No, this is a story about where the thief hides. Because in the end, there's only so much running a person can do before they lose their breath, before their muscles burn and fail, before they're simply unable to run anymore. So the thief, knowing this will happen soon, shimmies up the side of a sturdy-looking hovel and slips in through a window.

It's the middle of the day. The thief doesn't know if witnesses watch him from the outside, across the street or down the road, other rooftops, cafes—though not cafes in this part of town He knows only of one witness: the woman inside the room.

He had expected the place to be empty. It looks empty. It has the air of neglect. Abandonment. Yet there's a bed in the room, with silk sheets, and a woman sitting on it watching with tears in her eyes as he crawls into her room.

The bed looks extraordinarily comfortable and completely out of place in a hovel such as this. Maybe it belongs in a palace, maybe a small palace, or at least the estate of some middling lord who hasn't really got any money anymore but maintains all the prestige of his position.

"Who are you?" he asks.

She shakes a head of long blonde hair. She's beautiful in the way of princesses and goddesses, without any dirt on her face or under her fingernails, which are in fact perfectly manicured and the color of blood. "This isn't a story about me," she tells him.

He knows it's true, but insists. "I need to know what to call you."

She smiles for him. It's a sad smile. Her eyes are red from crying. "Call me Death, then, why not?"

The thief steps away from the window. He's torn. He didn't intend to intrude upon a woman in her bed, no matter who or where, but he also runs for his freedom and his life, and the burden in his bag is heavy. He sets it down at his feet and says, "You don't look like Death."

"Oh? And what would you know of it?"

What indeed? The thief, once upon a time, had a run-in with Death, but that Death was an elderly man with bony fingers and a crooked smile and nasty body odor. Also, he cheated at cards. His hair was oily, stringy, thin, and the kind of gray that makes one think of sackcloth and ash. And he'd spoken with a foreign accent, though not an identifiable one, as though he'd invented his own.

"I met Death, once upon a time."

"I remember," she says, but she doesn't elaborate.

"Tell me," he says, because he's soft-hearted and hates to see anyone in distress, "why do you cry?"

"I've told you. I'm Death, and I'm waiting for my next victim."

"Waiting? Does Death not seek out victims?"

"Oh, they come willingly enough."

Outside, the constabulary reach the street noisily. They're shouting, jostling the general riffraff, rounding up all the usual suspects, that sort of thing, in search of the thief.

"I don't believe you're Death," he tells her.

"You don't have to believe."

"But I do believe you're sad."

"You would be, too, if every man, woman, and child you ever met perished before your eyes."

"Have you lost someone?"

She shakes her head. "*Something.*"

"What's that?"

"Would you tell me what you hide in your bag?"

It rests at his feet. Quiet. Silent. A reminder of another life, another time, a better place. He's half tempted to show her, but he's afraid removing it from the bag will bring enough attention that the men chasing him will be drawn to it like a sailor to rum. He touches the bag with his foot, not a kick, just a little nudge, and says, "What if I told you I carried Death with me?"

"Anyone's death in particular?" she asks.

"Not yours, I hope."

She smiles. "That's sweet of you, but I'll never be given that chance."

Outside, there were witnesses, and they're now pointing toward the building he'd entered. He steps away from the window, lest they see him. "Would you allow me to hide?" he asks.

"Are you a murderer?" she asks quite enthusiastically.

"They call me a thief."

"Then hide, yes, under the bed but up in the bedframe. Only the sheets are mine, you see. The mattress was already here, though I must admit, a pea would make it more comfortable."

He crawls underneath, dragging his bag with him, and pulls himself up into the mattress directly beneath her. Briefly, it seems impolite, or at least ungentlemanly, but she says, "Be still, and be quiet, and be good down there, or I'll reveal you inadvertently and all will be lost."

That's when the knock comes to her door. Raised above the floor, the thief cannot see how many deputies there are, but it sounds like more than enough.

"There's a wretch," one of them tells her. "A scoundrel. A rogue."

"Loose in the city?" she asks, feigning surprise and concern and genuine fear. "Well, I do hope you catch him, and hang him by his ankles, and whip him until he's dead. I do not like to hear of scoundrels and rogues terrorizing this city I call home. Forget the meaning of the word mercy, when you catch him, and I pray that you do in good haste."

The deputies, who had believed he'd be in this room, seem unsure how to respond. "Thank you, ma'am," one of them says. "But can we look around anyway?"

"I'm in my bedclothes," she tells him.

"It's part of the job, ma'am."

They look. They open her closet, but it's empty; and they peek under the bed, but the thief is suspended within the frame of the mattress itself and beyond reach of their eyes. "Thank you, ma'am," the deputy says again. "We're sorry to have wasted your time."

"Stop ogling me, please," she says, "and go catch the wretch."

A moment later, the door closes. When the thief doesn't immediately relax, she bounces once on the worn mattress, touching him with parts of her about which he shouldn't have knowledge. But he likes her, he can tell this already. He wonders if this is the story of his true love, of meeting her while acting the role of the thief on the run.

"You can come out now," she tells him.

He drops back to the floor, rolls out, looks up to see her staring down at him. The whites of her eyes are still red, and a fresh tear drops from her cheek directly into his right eye. It burns. He blinks, then smiles. He pulls himself completely out. "You were wonderful."

"And I didn't know you were a scoundrel *and* a rogue. That's a lot for a single man to be."

They smile at each other, inches apart, she still on the bed and he next to it.

"This is the part," she adds, "that I don't think I'll like."

'What do you mean?"

"Kiss me, you wretch."

He doesn't have to be told twice. He kisses her. And in the process, he loses his breath. He collapses coldly onto the floor. He stares at her for a moment, unable to look away, unable to breathe.

"You may have won at cards," she tells him with a sigh, "but your reprieve has ended." She smiles. It's a sad smile. A heartbroken smile. Truly, a lamentation without voice. She steps off the bed, and with her foot nudges the bag with the stolen object inside. It doesn't matter what it is. It was never truly important to her. She bends low so as to whisper in the thief's ear before he finally surrenders his ghost to her. "It was *you* who cheated at the card table."

The Envelope

I moved in on a Sunday. The short term apartment included a bed and couch and television, all of which I expected. The envelope on the pillow, however, was a surprise. My name—my full name, not just my first, which could've meant it had been for anyone—my name had been written in bold red letters. No one was supposed to know where I was. I needed alone time, a hole to hide in, and I'd booked this room under an obvious alias. My real name, all in red, those big letters filling the front of the envelope, told me—screamed at me—that I'd failed in my hiding.

I opened the envelope with my finger, slid the single sheet of paper out, and stared too long at the handwriting. Small. Tight. Neat. Utterly recognizable. Jill had written this letter. I'd come here, in part, to hide from my memories of Jill. Her hair dancing in the wind. Her laughing at my silly little jokes. Her pale blue eyes and the way they caused my heart to skip a beat every time they caught me unaware. Her, curled up on the couch asleep, chest rising and falling in a gentle rhythm.

I looked at the letter for a long time without reading it. You can't read when there's something—okay, I'll admit it, tears—in your eyes. Finally, sometime around 3am, when the loneliest light of the moon fell through the single window with a view, I read the words.

The first line was, "I will never forget you." Somehow, that made it worse. I threw open the window as wide as it could go to let in all the winter air. I went to open a bottle of bourbon and realized I'd already done it, so I poured another. I read the second line and the third, specific memories, things she knew I'd forgotten. The last line said, "I will never be far away."

That sounded great. I didn't want her far away. I found a pen and wrote. "Jill, I wish I didn't have to forget you. But it hurts." I fell asleep, passed out, blacked out, something.

It was still dark when I opened my eyes. I didn't remember closing the window or turning the lamp off. I switched on the light, looked again at the letter, and read her response: "I will always be with you, and I can wait until you're ready."

I cried some more. I suck at hiding. I went to the bathroom to rinse my face with cold water. Briefly, looking at my reflection, my brown eyes went pale and blue.

THE VIOLINIST VERSUS THE HURRICANE

A cat 5 hurricane looms off the coast of Florida. It's slow moving, but its winds are fierce. The damage it's already done in the Caribbean was catastrophic. Islands are gone, according to some initial reports.

Violet, the violinist, lives in a small community south of Daytona. She's basically at ground zero for the oncoming storm. Though they've evacuated much of the coast, there's always people who decide to stay.

Hurricanes are basically unfettered violence. With wind gusts approaching 200mph, this one's going to rip buildings out of the ground by their roots. The storm surge is already at record heights and only promises to get worse. There's a chance—a worst-case scenario—that the waves pushed by this storm will wash completely over the peninsula and reach the Gulf on the other side.

There are a lot of frightened people.

Violet, the violinist, is not frightened.

Violet, the violinist, has studied with the Maestro. Though it seems like long ago, it might have been only yesterday. Time is subjective and malleable. A hurricane, however, is neither. A storm is a verifiable force of nature. Nothing can stop it from doing what it will.

Nothing, perhaps, except magic.

Violet, the violinist, did not study musical theory with the Maestro. She's forged herself into a weapon. Facing the hurricane—Lucia, they've named it—she thinks of this as a test. If she passes, if she survives, she can seek the revenge her studies were meant to give her. If she dies—it's not up to her to decide her own fate.

The winds are already vigorous. She's far enough back from the shore that she shouldn't be touched by the incoming waves, but the water licks her ankles. She can sense dolphins out there, and sharks and rays, all of which have fled or descended to escape Lucia's wrath.

Violet, the violinist, snuck the Stradivarius from a royal collection in a European palace. It wasn't their only, though of course it dominated headlines for at least a few days. Now, in Florida at least, there's no room for news outside of the storm.

If she'd been faster, she might have met Lucia on Martinique, and maybe then she might have saved thousands of lives. The weight of those souls will either support her now or destroy her. If even one note is half a step off from where it must be, all her work will be for naught.

The rain reaches the shore.

It tickles her skin. The drops are colder than she'd expected. They're like needles on her face, at first, and soon like bullets. Violet, the violinist, lifts the stolen and priceless instrument to her chin, and raises her bow like a wand. She gives the storm and the near-silence a breath.

She can't really see the storm. Lucia is the horizon. Lucia brings darkness to the noon.

She begins to play.

She plays for joy and for heartbreak. She plays for love and loss and life and death. She prays for salvation. She wrings from that instrument notes that haven't been heard for most of four hundred years. The song resonates with souls and with flesh. The sound waves vibrate through the air; and Lucia drinks them in, all of them, every wave and every note and every ounce of passion, hope, and fear.

Violet, the violinist, plays for her most demanding audience. It's not like the opera house in Sydney. It's not like the Musikverein in Vienna. It's not Carnegie Hall or even the metro in Paris. It's a storm, an insatiable fury, a kind of goddess if such a thing can be real. She doesn't pretend to know. She swirls thought and intention into the music, a song written centuries ago and played only two times before. The wind whips her hair and dress around her, and tries to claim the violin.

Violet, the violinist, steps defiantly toward the ocean, toward the storm, toward death itself. She cannot see Lucia's face or figure, but knows she's got the storm enraptured and ensnared.

Violet, the violinist, plays with fury to match the hurricane. She plays with intention and unbridled talent. She plays with energies siphoned through the sand beneath her feet from the iron core of the earth.

The song goes for an hour or a day, and the storm, placated, turns.

The song goes for a month or a year, and the storm, comforted, calms.

The song goes forever, the notes straining against the fabric of physicality, and the storm, awed, comes apart.

Violet, the violinist, drops to her knees but plays until the final strand of bow hair splits. Briefly, that last note vibrates off key. Its echo reaches back to unravel all she's done. The storm draws in a breath. Violet closes her eyes and allows a tear to slide down her cheek. It moves silently, somehow missed by all the rainwater pelting her. It drops into the tide, mixing its salt with the Atlantic's.

Violet collapses. She'll never opens her eyes again. It cost too much to play the song. But Lucia, in the end, is satisfied, and lets out that breath; she recedes and retreats and dissipates.

Meteorologists will not be able to explain it.

Crabs will drag Violet's corpse into the sea. The tide will take her away.

A child will find the Stradivarius and collect a great reward and be flown to Madrid as a hero.

The Maestro will record what's happened today in his book.

And Violet, the violinist, will be placed amongst the stars, even if no one knows the stories of her: the myths, the legends, or the truth.

The Museum of Curiosities

HIDDEN FUTURES

He pulls a card.

The nature of the card is unimportant. It's his belief in the card that matters. The artist, even if famous, has no impact on what it means or how it's interpreted. He pulls a card, looks at it briefly, frowns, and sets it on the table facedown.

It's a matter of nuance and understanding. He doesn't need a card to tell him the future. Everyone has the same: some good times, some rough times, some terrible mistakes and terrific joys, until it all comes to an end.

The patron smiles, and looks at the card, the back of the card, obviously wondering what future it hints at.

"You have to understand," he tells her, "this is a unique set of cards. They're indefinite."

"I don't know what that means," she says. "I thought all cards were read in relation to the cards around them, the future and the past and the present coalescing to form the kind of celestial guidance I came here seeking."

"Some cards," he tells her, "I've never seen before."

It's a windy night outside. Those howls creep around the fortuneteller's trailer in a strange orchestral cacophony. The rain holds off, but it won't for long. Not all prognostications require cards or tea leaves or palms.

"I find that hard to believe."

"So do I."

She reaches for the card, but he catches her hand by the wrist. He squeezes too hard, forcing her to stop before something happens. But futures aren't avoidable. The Greek myths proved that. Look at Oedipus. Look at the Gift of the Magi. At Irony.

He doesn't want to look at more things, so he meets the patron's eyes. They stare at each other, two powerful people, two wonderfully strong and mysterious people: the fortuneteller who plays with fate; the stranger who delivers fate at the edge of night.

She breaks their visual connection to look at her wrist. Her flesh around his fingers whitens. She frowns. She says, "I only wanted to know if I'd get away with it."

She doesn't tell him what it is. She doesn't have to. Even as a dealer in fate, he pays attention to the news. He knows about the theft and the murder. He sees the blood under her fingernails. She had cleaned up pretty well but not perfectly.

He lies. "You will."

Her expression shifts to a smile. "I will?"

"Twenty-eight thousand dollars," he tells her, "hardly seems enough to cover a life."

She tilts her head, looking into her own recent past. Such glee in her expression. "More than his was worth," she says. "Anyhow, I also got this." She raises her other hand to show the ring on her finger, a row of sparkling diamonds set in platinum. It's an engagement ring. She wriggles her fingers playfully.

"They've omitted that from the news," he says.

Her smile falters, though she maintains the facsimile of it. "They can't track me by this. It's special."

"How so?"

She lifts her hand to bring the diamonds closer to his face. He releases her other hand to take this one, turn it slightly left and right to better catch all the facets of those jewels. Inside them, like inside a crystal ball, he sees faces, agonies, suffering—the souls they've collected over uncountable years. Briefly, he catches his own reflection.

"You seemed nice," she says, slashing with a knife.

The blade slides effortlessly across his throat, cutting the windpipe, the arteries, the veins. It's deep and cold and precise. She displays none of the mania hinted at by the news reports.

The ring, briefly, heats up her finger as another soul is swallowed. It's getting crowded in there, even for such insubstantial things as souls. They're stretched too thin, stuffed too haphazardly, bound too tightly.

She doesn't understand how or why the ring works and she doesn't care. She giggles. The card, facedown, is sprayed with blood, but she turns it over to reveal her path—it's blank. "Well, damn," she says. "He caught his own future instead of mine."

She pulls the next card. The Hanged Man. She doesn't like it. If that's her fate, it's not a good one. She slashes the card, too. The ring swallows the soul of the whole deck. It makes her dizzy with power. Briefly, she thinks maybe things will work out. She's got the money in a bag in the trunk of the stolen Mustang. She's got an assortment of knives. She's got a few guns. Ammo. Poisons. A chainsaw. It's surprising how much can fit in the trunk of a car like that.

But she leaves the fortuneteller's trailer and, instead of finding the lonely Mustang in the dirt parking lot, she faces a dozen police cars, flashing lights, officers with guns drawn, and a hovering helicopter with a searchlight picking her out on the makeshift porch.

She lets the knife drop, raises her hands, puts them behind her head. She knows what will happen. She won't die here in the dark. They'll make her hang.

THE MUSEUM OF CURIOSITIES

STRAY LITTLE DEMONS

He bleeds. The wound is fresh and deep and terminal. After a mere thirty-three years, this is the end of him.

It came quicker than he'd expected.

The people in this city don't even see him. They walk around him and give him lots of room. They make disapproving noises and faces as though they'd just caught some horribly distasteful odor and need to get away as quickly as possible.

He doesn't say anything.

No one dares meet his eyes.

He growls. It's low, feral, animalistic. He likes tigers. They're powerful and remain respectful. Grace under the pressure of superiority. He considers options: a rain of hellfire, a plague of locusts.

They step around the pooling blood. He doesn't reach out to anyone, doesn't beg or even ask for help of any sort, though he holds his gut around the knife still stuck there.

The chill is slow in spreading.

He retreats into the corner of an alcove, an unopened door that maybe cannot open anymore, a slab raised an inch above the sidewalk and possibly protected from rain. He catches a hint of that stench.

It's okay, he tells herself. This is what he knew would happen.

A woman, just the one woman, a woman not of any means and not alone in her head, pauses as she walks by. Her voices tell her to move on, to get away, this is a bad situation and will only get worse. Perhaps she feels she has nothing left to lose. She stops, appraises him, meets his eyes, and casts an immediate and purely objective judgement: "You're dying."

He nods. Once. It's really all he has strength for.

She approaches. She kneels to look at the knife. The hilt is long and bloody but of fine materials. The blade itself is longer, a heavy steel, and did a lot of damage on the way in.

She shakes her head. She sits next to him, propping herself against the old door, and pulls her knees toward her chest. "Do you want to tell me your name?"

He shakes his head.

"Do you want to confess anything?"

He can't help it. He laughs. It hurts to do so.

"Sorry," she says. "I didn't mean that in a bad way." She holds out her hand and waits a moment. When he doesn't reach back, she takes his anyway. "I'm afraid you haven't got long."

"Not long at all," one of her voices says.

He shouldn't hear that.

She squeezes his hand. "I won't let you die alone."

"That's kind of you," he says.

She smiles. It's a sad smile, a scarred smile, a smile that comes from deep inside but has to be pushed out past all the nasty things she's seen and done and felt.

"What's your name?" he asks. Words come out slowly. He's not sure they're the right language. The city begins receding from his vision.

"It doesn't matter," she tells him. "You call me whatever you need to."

He gives her hand a squeeze. She's normal—well, she's mortal. The voices in her head have quieted, resigned to her course of action. He says, "I was looking for a sign of something."

"Anything in particular?"

He shakes his head. The movement is languid and peaceful and warm. "No," he says. "But I've found it."

The strength seeps from his hand. His eyes glaze over. He exhales one last time and forgets to inhale. It's over.

He steps away from his body. His corpse. His mortal remains. It's funny, sometimes, the way that works. He looks around at a city full of anger and hatred, but can only see this nameless woman—he knows her name, all the names she's ever used and the one her mother gave her, which even she never knew—and it makes him smile. He sees the voices, the embodiment of her voices, perched on her shoulders, hanging from her earlobes, clinging to her torso. Little demons. He can't take those away from her; she needs them as much as they need her.

Still, there's one that's particularly bad, startlingly mischievous, gloriously wicked. He reaches toward it with his incorporeal hand. It cowers, but then surrenders. It strokes his fingers with its forked tail. He whispers, "Keep your words and deviations for one who deserves them."

The little demon nods. He rubs its tail, then its head. The thing purrs like a kitten.

Then he slips a wad of cash—it hadn't existed a moment ago, but his head is clear now so it's the right form for this time and place—into the woman's pocket. She almost notices the brush of his ethereal skin;

she smiles, and she stands, and she accosts the first person to try to walk past his corpse.

"He's dead," she tells the passerby, "so you'd better call someone."

Someone—the proper authorities to deal with such matters as nameless murder victims—is called, and he chooses not to smite this callous city. Instead, maybe, he'll wander its streets and silence a few more of its stray little demons.

BREAKFAST WITH
MY DOPPELGANGER

I met my doppelganger at the edge of a perilous drop in the Rocky Mountains. He looked like me, and he looked at me; and he bared his teeth like a wild animal. "Maybe we can talk about this," I suggested, but he wasn't having any of that.

We wrestled under an intense sun in the forty degree weather. The light was bright, the cold impossible, and we were perfectly matched against each other.

He was vicious, of course. You expect such things. We all know the stories. The doubles come to replace you. Take over your life. They come through mirrors, out of shadows, or sometimes via unknown otherworldly paths. I wasn't about to guess, not then, not with our hands around each other's throats.

Below the ledge, treetops waited like spikes at the bottom of a trap door. The blue of the sky seemed unnaturally chalky. We weren't at the very top of the world, but we were quite high. Our collective breath was insubstantial. Our muscles ached, as did our hearts. Yet we fought until orange stretched across the western horizon. We were down to our knees, each gasping for breath. A thunder rolled over us from the north.

"This is stupid," one of us said, and the other agreed.

The doppelganger said, "I don't even hate you."

"Then why?"

"Destiny," the doppelganger said. "Our roles were written long before we were thrust into this world."

We stopped fighting. We sat at the edge leaning back and trying to fill our lungs. "You can never defeat me."

"There's usually a weapon of some sort available," the doppelganger said. "That's how we were trained."

"Trained?"

"Did you think this was accidental? There's a council running things that makes all these decisions."

"I wonder," and I wondered aloud, "if we can put a stop to it."

So there, at the edge of the Rocky Mountains, under an indigo sky, witnessed by a large yellow moon low in the east, we shook hands and agreed to make a plan.

Night so high above sea level quickly grew cold. We slept uneasily in my car. The doppelganger hadn't arrived with his own, as he'd expected to pick the keys from my corpse. We weren't quite ready to trust each other.

The next morning, we drove down the side of the mountain and got a diner breakfast. We ordered the same plates. The server thought we were twins and even winked at us, thinking whatever.

Over twin French toast and sausages, we devised the plan.

The doppelganger shifted the door so when we left the diner, we entered directly into the chambers of the council. There they were: seven ethereal beings, barely substantial, barely anything. We were armed now with sharp knives from the diner. The celestial things had no defense for the sort of physical attack we launched. They went down like clouds dispersed: a flurry of water vapor, no blood, no resistance.

"Now what?" one of us asked.

The doors—the actual doors to the council's chambers—opened. A page entered to announce the next arrival: an elderly man from the far east. No, the doppelganger of such a man. "I am ready for my mission," he said, and though he spoke another language we were able to understand.

"You have a new mission," the doppelganger said.

"Find your double and share his burdens."

The doppelganger looked confused.

"Share his joys, too," the doppelganger said.

"That is not the mission I expected."

"Go," I said. "Follow our instructions."

The celestial page didn't seem to notice we weren't the council, and neither did the new doppelganger. We watched via a giant viewscreen as the doppelganger reached through a mirror to choke the life out of his double. We were disappointed. The doppelganger then lived out the rest of the old man's natural life, which turned out to be an additional twenty years. Maybe he led a good life, but it had begun with murder.

The next doppelganger was announced and requested her mission. We told her much of the same, but specified that she should not murder the woman she was sent to replace. She seemed truly disappointed. The viewscreen showed how after she arrived, the two of them walked through the woods, and the doppelganger suggested they try these psychedelic mushrooms that were, in fact, poisonous. They picked their own mushrooms, and consumed them, and died together in the woods so as not to be found until after an almost three week search.

"This," the doppelganger said, "is not going as planned."

I considered. I thought the mushroom trick still qualified as murder. I'm no expert in legal details. But I agreed with my doppelganger. Nothing had gone according to plan.

So I stabbed my double with both knives from the diner. "A weapon," I said, "will always present itself."

"Why?" asked the doppelganger.

"Nature," I said. "Our roles were predetermined before we thrust ourselves into this world."

When the next doppelganger arrived, I sat on the celestial throne and said, "Go. Improvise." Then I returned through the door we had created, back to the diner at the very moment after we'd left, and ordered another plate of French toast and sausage. There had been nothing to eat in the council's chambers, and I was starving.

I thought that would've been the end of it, but later I found myself sitting with my feet in a calm lake reflecting the deeply saturated blue of the sky. My doppelganger—a new one, a replacement, a decoy—reached from out of the lake. Another rose from the surface to the left of me. Another from my right.

The clouds, impossibly low in the sky, practically mists about me, laughed. A council made of cloudstuff could never have been so easily put down. "Guilty," they each said, one after the other. "Guilty. Guilty. Guilty."

And the punishment? I only heard one speak it. "Death."

the museum of curiosities

BONE ISLAND

1.

Midnight behind him, Chris expected no problems. The alcohol might've helped, but he hadn't had too much, just enough to veil the world around him with a wonderful layer of haze.

When he stumbled out of the bar, he turned left instead of right and headed away from the docks, away from the cute little bed and breakfast and that woman at the front desk, and deeper into town.

He'd taken the ghost tour earlier, seeing all the darker and stranger sides of Key West: old houses where presidents used to stay and caretakers remained, dolls that refused to be photographed, and the bones the Spanish found when they first arrived. Thus the name: *Cayo Hueso*—Bone Island—bastardized into Key West.

Duval Street probably never closed, but Chris was done for the night. He'd abandoned those crowds. The top of the lighthouse, a block or two away, was visible; near the home where Ernest Hemingway used to live with his cats.

Chris was never much of a Hemingway fan, but he certainly liked the man's choice in bars.

If the lighthouse was on his right, then the cemetery must be only a few blocks to the left. The ghost tour had barely mentioned the cemetery, and gave no such stories. Why not? Wouldn't there be lots of ghosts there?

Chris didn't really believe in ghosts. He liked the stories, but knew they were mostly fiction. Didn't take a Harvard degree to realize that. Good thing; Chris didn't even know where Harvard was.

He was too restless to go to bed. Warm and happy, ready to do anything, he was sure he'd find something interesting.

So he checked his watch, saw midnight had passed without incident, and figured he'd make his way over toward the cemetery, see if he couldn't find a few ghosts of his own. He expected nothing more than chickens, which roamed Key West freely, maybe a few winos begging for drinking funds, maybe another thrill seeker.

The full moon gave him plenty of light. In the back of his mind, Chris knew full moons and cemeteries probably didn't mix well, but he trusted in clichés only a little more than the tour guide's stories.

He turned left at Angela Street.

2.

Trees canopied the road, darkening it, but Chris didn't mind. The sidewalk was mostly even, sandwiched between little buildings on one side and cars and mopeds on the street.

Most of the houses sat back from the road; ivy wound around their wooden fences. Out of range of the Duval Street shops and parties, the shadows set deeper and more darkly. There was little breeze, but without the sun's full intensity, the temperature was perfect, not much warmer than the Gulf of Mexico, where he'd been snorkeling.

Ah, the water had been incredible. Coral and fish—even barracuda staring at him like he might be delicious—and the shark. He'd never seen a shark up close like that, not without twelve inches of super-strength plastic separating them. It was a nurse shark, nothing to worry about according to the captain. "Just leave her alone, is all," the captain said. Chris did just that. He wasn't stupid. He'd heard stories. People think these creatures are docile and harmless, so they grab a tale or fin and lose an arm in the process. Chris had both his arms, thank you very much.

The scent of flowers, as he walked, shifted at every house, jasmine or frangipani, others his mom hadn't grown. Even in the night, purple flowers were purple, but maybe the reds became black and the whites somewhat luminescent. He didn't normally stop to sniff or pick flowers, but paused when he found a rose in midair. Its swollen bloom hung there, a dark shade of orange, at eye level, staring at him.

He could've walked around it, but it reminded him of the way the barracuda had watched him. Patient. Hungry. It hung from the top of a white fence. Another dozen blooms were intertwined within the slats, not nearly so interested in him.

"Do I look delicious to you, too?" he asked.

The rose bobbed slightly in the wind.

Chris reached into the back of his jeans and took out his pocketknife. It was small, one of those fake Swiss knives, with scissors and corkscrew and bottle opener, all sorts of important and utilitarian things. He pulled the rose down, snipped the stem about a foot long, and cursed when a thorn nicked his thumb.

The deflowered stalk popped up, out of his way, and Chris carried his orange rose like a trophy, like his own little piece of sunlight.

After only two steps, he realized he was being watched. He glanced left and right, up and down the street, but saw no one. He felt the same guilt kids had when they strolled out of the store with stolen chocolate bars.

For cutting a flower? Maybe, but it wasn't quite the same as taking a five finger discount; you only noticed that when the old clerk's hawk eyes drilled through the back of your head as you left.

The rose's fence guarded a bed and breakfast, two stories with tiny windows upstairs and a swing on the porch. There was enough light to see no one sat there, and no faces pressed against any of the windows.

The cars were empty, weren't they? Yes. Definitely.

He pulled the rose to his chest, as if hiding it, and squinted trough the darkness.

He took another step, and something moved on his right.

He glanced down, between two cars and into the gutter. Yellow eyes blinked back. It flicked its tail again, and then the cat turned and sauntered off, unaffected and unconcerned.

Across the street, the tabby paused, gave Chris one last disinterested look, and disappeared through fence slats.

"Ghost stories," he said, rolling his eyes. He wondered if this had been one of Hemingway's six-toed cats.

The street curved as he walked, bringing the cemetery into view. And also the woman.

3.

He only caught a glimpse before she slipped through the fence and into the cemetery. She wore shorts and a tee shirt, nothing you'd wear clubbing.

Chris didn't call to her, but ran to see her again before she was gone. He tried to move quietly, but his sneakers slapped the sidewalk and echoed.

He couldn't say why he'd run. Maybe the night had started to descend on him, seeping into his bones and accentuating his aloneness. He had a weakness for women, true, but no real gift with them, and he certainly didn't expect to strike up any conversation. For all he knew, she might be only 14, a little girl sneaking away from her parents for a tryst with her junior high school boyfriend.

Mostly, he was intrigued. He'd decided to continue that ghost tour on his own, and someone had beaten him to it. Of course, if she had been a he, Chris would probably not have run.

He reached the gate where she'd entered. At the edge of the cemetery, trees shaded the markers. All the graves were above-ground. A set of crypts were piled three high in solid sarcophagus condominiums directly ahead of him. Closer, broad areas were partitioned from the main group, like steerage and first class.

The fence was wrought iron, rusting in places, with barbed wire at the top to keep him from climbing. Two rails were slightly bowed out, wide enough apart for the woman but not for Chris. The gate was closed, its chains joined together by a Master lock, and had remained shut for so long, a crafty spider had weaved its webs across it.

He scanned the sea of stone, searching for any sign of the woman, unable to rationalize wanting to get a better look at her. He felt a connection with her, something unnatural and probably not shared. But they'd shared a thought, to frolic with the dead. Okay, maybe Chris meant to wander aimlessly and read some epitaphs, but the woman had seemed so carefree and casual—like she made this trip often.

He had to get over the gate.

A sign read, *Gates locked after sunset*, though this one looked like it was also locked before sunset.

Under the sign, some iron had rusted clear through. Not enough to break the bar away and slide past—he wasn't Superman—but it was exactly the right bar, and the rot had spread just enough, to pull the chain free.

After a brief check up and down the road, Chris grabbed a fistful of links and tugged. It braced against the rotted section, scraping away pieces of red metal. He gritted his teeth and put everything he had into it.

He saw movement in his peripheral vision; the woman stood at the far end of the long line of stacked tombs, hanging onto the side of the stone, watching him.

The chain broke through the rot. Chris lost his grip and fell to the sidewalk. The chain clanged loudly, the rose dropped, and a concrete chip tried to break his fall, digging painfully into his thigh. He slid sideways, scraping his palm and banging his knee—just enough pain to shake away most of the alcohol haze.

By the time he picked up his flower and got back on his feet, the woman was gone.

4.

The gate groaned as it moved. Chris pushed and pulled until rust flakes covered his hands, and finally opened it enough to slip through.

He didn't chase the woman. He had to walk carefully, as there seemed to be no actual paths in this corner. Every step was over soft grass or broken concrete. It surprised him, how many of the tombs at the very edge of the cemetery were broken. Many of the top slabs were cracked, and weeds grew through some of those crevices.

There wasn't much by way of broken bottles, used condoms, or discarded fast food wrappers, just bits of stone everywhere. This was an old part of the cemetery, except for the monstrous superstructure.

He almost climbed over one of the shorter tombs, but stopped himself in time. This wasn't clipping flowers or swiping candy. It was utterly disrespectful. And now, when so much marble glowed under the light of the full moon, he was exposed, easily seen by anyone and anything.

Any *thing*?

Too many ghost stories, Chris decided, too much beer, and one shot of Southern Comfort he should have left on the bar.

Some of the tombs were protected by short fences, not meant to deter anyone but to denote a territory.

The wind had died, revealing other sounds: distant singing—or was that chanting? The voices receded momentarily. At first, Chris thought they probably came from someone's loud television.

Rather quickly, Chris found himself out of sight of any of the roads, beyond view of the fence and gate—and safe from prying eyes.

Safe, but lost. He couldn't quite follow his way back; most of the graves he'd passed were so similar, the dark rendered them identical. Even the huge, marble house at the corner had been lost in the dark, hidden by monuments and statues.

He didn't know where the woman had gone. Maybe she wasn't real, his mind recalling the woman from bed and breakfast. She'd been small, too, with short black hair and brown eyes. She was Polynesian, maybe Japanese, with a touch of Puerto Rican or Cuban. Her skin was dark, tanned because she lived in Key West. On Bone Island.

Chris felt like he'd found the real Bone Island. Behind these marble walls, some skeletons were over a hundred years old. The original inhabitants, those bones found by the conquistadors, were perhaps beneath those.

Waiting to rise?

Chris continued, his way lit by the moon. He moved slowly, watching his step, finally reaching a wide gravel path that led deeper into the cemetery—and closer to the voices.

No need to go further and meet them. Ghosts weren't a problem — they weren't real—but people hanging out in cemeteries (like him)— something about that felt dangerous, like a person hiding in an alley behind a Dumpster.

He turned the other way.

Alongside the path, a man sat back on a gleaming slab of marble. He was darker than the shadows. Under the brim of his hat, he was perfectly concealed, even in the moonlight; nothing was visible except the red tip of his cigar and a glint of metal at his side.

He puffed deeply on the cigar; the end glowed more brightly, revealing the black pits of his eyes.

He moved his hand toward the metal that might have been a knife or gun.

Chris turned and ran.

5.

He should've known better.

Running in the moonlight, in a cemetery, wasn't a good idea. You go a few steps, turn, evade the stranger, and two things happen: you get more lost, and you find what you originally intended to avoid.

Chris had leapt over one tomb, rounded a corner, and crashed into a group of people sitting around a small fire.

The fire was inside a kettle.

Five men and women, dressed all in black, had covered their faces with grease paint. The smudges made geometric designs, arcs and triangles—even an eye on one woman's forehead.

He twisted, trying not to hit the firepot or trip over anyone, lost his balance, and landed on a flat slab of raised marble.

"Ghost!" one of the women said.

"Tie him!" a man said.

Someone grabbed his ankle. He jerked his leg away.

Chris managed to lurch forward as he got to his feet, and ran straight into the side of one of the mausoleums. Hit it so hard, his teeth rattled and white flashed before his eyes.

One of the five, trying to yell and whisper simultaneously, said, "Complete the spell!"

Someone grabbed Chris by the shoulders and pulled him backwards. The huge arms crushed him, making it hard to breathe. "No worries," the man whispered in his ear. "You're already dead."

He was stronger than Chris, bigger, impossible to resist, so Chris did the only thing he could: he jabbed the rose stem into the man's eye.

The grip loosened for just a moment, but that was all he needed.

Still clutching his rose, Chris rounded two corners and found the worst possible place to hide: inside the open door of a mausoleum.

6.

Crypts lined both sides of the stone house. The ceiling was just above his head. There were plaques, unreadable in the dark, and everything was made of cold, cold marble.

In the rear, there was a long, narrow stained glass window, but even the woman wouldn't be able to slip out through that.

Outside, two of the black-garbed chanters ran past the mausoleum.

Chris kept away from the door, moving about half way in. He stayed as still as possible and held his breath. He heard nothing. His pulse hurt in his throat, and a bead of sweat slid slowly down his cheek.

He was glad his sneakers hadn't made any slapping noises on the floor.

He was afraid to close his eyes, so he looked through the gap at the door. He tried not to think of where he was, but couldn't help feeling he'd violated someone by barging into their final resting place. He hated when his sleep was interrupted; why should death be any different?

Nothing moved outside.

He focused on the grass, the visible sliver of cemetery. He could almost read words on a stone across the path.

It was warmer out there. Maybe the breeze had returned; inside, Chris couldn't know. He might hear cars in the distance, or those roosters, or tour guides explaining the history of Bone Island. No one was sure if the skeletons had been part of a burial ground or the remnants of a battlefield. The island must have smelled stale then, frightening, not too different from the inside of a tomb with four decomposing corpses. The air was heavy in here, but too cold, like winter in New York. That bead of sweat made an icy line to his jaw.

Outside, he told himself. *Think outside. Forget where you are, and why, and focus on the damn grass.*

Chris still heard nothing. No more of the black-clad chanters passed. The man on the tomb hadn't necessarily followed him at all. What if that glint of metal had been merely a cell phone?

Middle of the night, with a full moon overhead, and he had thought exploring the cemetery might be a *good* idea?

Tentatively, he stepped toward the front of the crypt. His footfall echoed—but only inside, he hoped. Darkness had a habit of intensifying such sounds.

After a second step, he heard something else—like stone scraping stone, slow and gentle, but so very heavy. Behind him, a woman's soft voice asked, "Leaving so soon?"

7.

The doorway seemed suddenly tighter, too narrow for Chris, and too far away, so he clenched his fists, took a deep breath, and locked his gaze outside. This was real. He refused to argue with his senses. "It seemed like a good time."

"No," she said, her voice like a feather on his ear. "Stay a moment longer. Trust me."

Chris' throat was too dry to swallow. *Trust me* sounded like last words.

"If you can't trust me," she said, "talk with me. I get so lonely. Most people ignore my invitation."

"Invitation?"

"The door." It shuddered, or shimmered, or maybe a drop of sweat blurred Chris' vision. "I don't get many visitors."

"I can imagine."

"Can you?" she asked. She kept her voice at an even whisper, but those two words sounded harsher than any scream.

"It's a scary thing," he said, "walking into a tomb."

"You don't think I know?"

"I didn't say that."

"You're not very bright," she said.

"What?"

"I wasn't a jilted bride."

"I'm glad."

"But that doesn't mean a man didn't hurt me."

Chris hesitated, unsure of how to respond. *I'm sorry*, he thought, would be wrong. "I didn't hurt you."

"You've hurt somebody."

Chris thought he'd been on the receiving end more often than not. "Maybe," he said, "but I've also been hurt."

"We're not talking about you," she said.

"But..."

"Her name is Lily."

The abrupt change of subject caught Chris off guard. "What?"

"The woman," she said. "You followed her. I know you did, don't think I don't. Her name is Lily."

"Thanks."

"You won't hurt her." It was not a question, but an absolute, authoritative statement.

After a moment's silence, Chris asked, "Will she hurt me?"

She laughed, briefly. "Quiet."

One of the chanters walked past the mausoleum.

Her voice was softer now, icy on his left ear, and Chris felt her chilly hand on his chest as she leaned close to confide. "They think they know what they're doing."

"Do they?" he asked.

She ignored it. "Do you suppose, maybe, you'll think of me again later? Just think of me, that's all. You can do that, right?"

"Sure."

"Don't make a promise you can't keep."

"Sure," Chris said again. "I don't think I could forget."

"Good. May I kiss you?"

He hesitated, afraid of the consequences of any answer, afraid yet always willing to accept kisses.

Like a breeze, she pulled away. "I'm sorry," she said. "Go. Go on. I shouldn't have asked."

"No, don't," Chris said, suddenly too warm where she had touched him. "I mean, yes. Yes, please, I'd like that. A kiss." He turned to look into the farthest, darkest corner of the crypt. "Please."

Her lips were cold but soft, gentle, hinting at passion like the first kiss of future lovers, invisible on his mouth and gone too soon.

He was awed.

"Go," she said. "Good luck. Keep your promise."

Reluctantly, Chris walked to the doorway. It was easily wide enough for him now, wrought iron with stained glass, clean and well maintained. He paused, looked back, and asked, "What's your name?"

She smiled. He knew this, though he couldn't see it. "Jessica."

"Jessica," he repeated, and then lifted his orange rose. "For you."

"Thanks," she said, "but you need it more."

Nodding as if that made sense, Chris stepped out into the warmth of the cemetery.

8.

Behind him, silently, Jessica had closed her door. No further invitations tonight. Chris felt vulnerable, out in the open again. He saw no sign of the fence, but he could just pick a direction and walk. The cemetery wasn't *that* large.

A rooster called. "It's not dawn yet," Chris whispered.

It was supposed to be a short vacation. In two days, he'd be on the road again, driving up US 1 to Miami and his flight home. He'd enjoyed the trip, looked forward to doing it again, and had not flown straight into Key West specifically so he could drive the Seven Mile Bridge.

But two days seemed suddenly very distant, at least as far away as the end of the cemetery. There had to be an end, the iron fence, a place he could climb and risk the barbed wire. Another scratch or cut was preferable to whatever fate the chanters had intended.

He knew they were somewhere off to his right, so he thought he'd go left. But a sudden cackling erupted, a woman screeching more than laughing. Ahead of him, past a few thick trees and a line of sarcophagi, someone had been pounding on drums, *ba-da-boom, ba-da-boom, ba-da-doom.*

They were everywhere, he suddenly realized, singing around fires, dancing, maybe even slicing open sacrificial virgins with sacred daggers, trying to cast spells or curses or voodoo.

Jessica said they only *thought* they knew what they were doing. Didn't most horror films begin when someone played with ancient rites they couldn't control?

Behind him, past Jessica's mausoleum, sounded safest—quietest, at least.

As he started, retreating from everything else, he saw the woman again. Lily.

9.

He almost ran to her. She was looking right at him, standing in the shade of a tree so the moonlight didn't reach her face. When she finally turned and walked away, it was slow, a come-hither type of saunter.

Maybe twenty yards and a dozen graves separated them. She passed behind a marble obelisk and vanished. Briefly, Chris panicked. He couldn't lose her. She was the only sane thing he'd seen in here. He picked up speed, anxious now, nervous, and nearly tripped over a tangle of vines.

The cackle repeated, closer this time. The drums banged more furiously. A twig snapped under Chris' foot, sounding like bone. A sudden wind rustled leaves in the trees. He couldn't see Lily anymore, couldn't be certain she hadn't changed direction. Was she taunting him?

He should've just gone back to the bed and breakfast on Eaton Street. The woman in the front office would have coffee brewing by 8. Croissants. Cheese and apple slices. He didn't need to be staggering through the Bone Island cemetery.

But he simply had to meet Lily. The compulsion overrode common sense.

He didn't know why. Didn't care. Such compulsions were best answered, not questioned.

Chris reached the obelisk where she'd disappeared. No sign of her. Only the drums, whose volume hadn't diminished despite the extra distance.

And then a voice.

One of the chanters. Another answered, but the words were lost. They weren't tying Lily, were they? He couldn't allow that. He pulled his pocketknife out of his jeans. Wasn't much of a weapon, but the little blade was sharp. He unfolded it as he walked, following the voices.

"We almost lost her."

"We didn't."

"Quiet."

Chris paused, half way through a step, in case they'd heard him, but couldn't stop.

"Mix the rest of the ingredients. Hair. Bone chips. Blood."

Chris came alongside a tall chunk of granite. He peered around the edge, at the five people kneeling again around their burning kettle. One woman dropped the *ingredients* in as another recited them. Directly behind her, Lily lay atop a broken slab of marble, black ribbon wrapped around her wrists and ankles. Lit candles surrounded her. The makeshift altar included a lacy white material beneath her. She stared straight up into the sky.

Deliberately, the woman cut her palm with a gray knife. She held her hand over the flames and squeezed until several drops fell and sizzled.

She rose. The painted eye on her forehead glowed. The others remained on their knees. She announced, to whatever listened, "We have something for you."

With an incoherent cry, Chris jumped forward.

10.

The kettle erupted.

Flames burst like a geyser, rising high into the air and falling back in on themselves, widening, billowing black smoke.

"Yes!" one of the chanters said, a triumphant cheer accented by a shaking fist.

The flame split at the bottom, and one fiery leg stepped out of the kettle.

One of the men scampered backwards, suddenly afraid. The other's eyes widened, reflecting the firelight.

No one had even looked at Chris.

He'd stopped. The smoke and fire formed itself fully into the shape of a man, twice the normal height and breadth, and stood directly between Chris and Lily.

Lily looked now at the creature, but didn't struggle against the silk cuffs. Each wrist and ankle was tied to what appeared to be small bars of silver on the ground. They didn't look heavy.

In that moment, Chris' greatest fear wasn't the chanters; nor was it the fiery thing they'd summoned; rather, what if Lily didn't try to get up because she'd offered herself willingly?

The creature took a deep breath and spoke, its voice rumbling and gravelly. "The six of you call me."

"Six?" the standing woman asked, glancing at Chris. "No, five. Not that interloper." She pointed.

"Good," the creature said. Then it plucked her from the earth like a flower—with one hand that was more smoke than fire—and popped her, whole, into an impossibly wide mouth.

The others were on their feet instantly.

No one got far. The creature grabbed two before they took a step, and swallowed them without a sound. One of the men had gone a few feet, screaming as he ran. The smoky hand crushed his head, leaving only one final woman standing. She hadn't run, simply stared and shielded her eyes from the heat. "But we have a sacrifice," she said.

Through the smoke and flame, none of the creature's features were discernable. Maybe it had a nose, and eyes, but it was all very mutable. Still, it smiled at her, with a hint of patronization. Then it blasted her with a funnel of flame that enveloped her head and tossed her backwards.

She landed near the black man with the brimmed hat. He flicked open a chrome lighter and lit the end of his cigar, puffing three or four times before killing the flame with a soft clang. He leaned against one of the mausoleums, one leg bent so the foot rested against the side.

The whole thing had lasted maybe five seconds.

Chris froze as the creature turned its attention on him.

11.

Sweat covered Chris, partly from fear but mostly from the heat. He had expected Key West to be hot, but not like this.

The ghost tour had ended.

"They wanted to give me this woman," the creature said. "Have you got some other *ebo* for me?"

"*Ebo?*"

"Sacrifice," the cigar smoker said, stepping forward. "The *orisha* requests a sacrifice."

"I didn't call him," Chris said, not taking his eyes off the towering fire.

"Neither did I," the man said, "yet I give him my smoke." He took the cigar from his mouth and blew out a thick gray plume. He was an old man, wrinkled, darker than anyone Chris had ever seen, glistening in the firelight. "He won't wait long."

Chris looked up at the creature's fiery countenance—it was completely unreadable—and then at Lily on top of the grave. Did this thing seriously want Chris to choose between himself and the woman? That couldn't be right. He glanced at the old man, who had returned to his leaning and his cigar.

Chris clenched his fingers. If he said, *Take the woman, I don't know her,* the creature would devour him anyway. There was no way out of this. Maybe if he made the *right* choice, giving himself up so Lily could live, the creature would let them both live.

In his left fist, a thorn from the rose bit his palm.

Chris closed his eyes and raised his hand. "This," he said. "My *ebo.*"

The creature took the proffered flower. It did not burn. "Ah," he said, "like a sunburst. Very good."

Then he was gone. Fire and smoke retreated so swiftly into the kettle, and went out, the sudden vacuum pulled Chris forward. He kept the momentum, and knelt beside Lily.

She turned her eyes toward him but did not lift her hands.

He tried to move the silver bars, but they must've weighed a ton each. He tried to untie the knots in the silk, but it took too long. Finally, Chris cut the ribbons with his pocketknife, freeing her hands and then her feet.

Lily sat up, rubbing her wrists. She swung her legs off the side of the stone and held out her arms for Chris' help.

He pulled her to her feet.

She wrapped her arms around him and kissed him with cold lips.

"Thank you," she said. Then she dissolved into smoke.

"Impressive," the old man said, stepping up behind Chris. He had discarded his cigar. "Shall I walk you out?"

Chris said nothing. He had to force himself to resume breathing. Eventually, he nodded. With a hand on Chris' shoulder, the old man guided him through the graves.

The Long Journey There

Early in the season, he nevertheless turned at a bend in the woods and found himself under an iridescent golden canopy. Moss covered the foundations of the trees and much of the path, and that was glistening emeralds, but the brilliance of all the yellow was like a revelation. The colored leaves towered over him but seemed to bend down, heavy with the remnants of a recent thunderstorm. Though the trees obscured the sky, it was obvious the sun had finally broken through the clouds. The occasional red-leafed tree, much lower to the ground—a darker, more foreboding blood hue—stood like sentinels, soldiers, samurai in the forest. Birds sang in the distance, or nearby and hidden. The crash of a waterfall became more pronounced as he continued on his path. A kaleidoscope of butterflies—blue and black and orange and yellow like the leaves—fluttered around and through him, on all sides, over and under, some alighting briefly on his arms and hands. They floated haphazardly on the wind, which followed the same general path he found himself on.

Upon a time, it had been a well-traveled path, possibly connecting early settlements, used by merchants and bandits alike. But it had been a long time since human feet had shadowed the deer, the elk, the mountain lions that still regularly followed its course. There were no signs of people, no prints of sneakers or boots in the hardened mud, no discarded fast food wrappers or cigarettes or trash of any type. No mobile signal reached this far from civilization.

His name was forgotten, he had been walking so long. He paused when the scents of pine and wild apples and mushrooms were joined by honeysuckle and other flowers. Here, he first saw the creek flowing from the waterfall. Every step confirmed the stories, the legends, and the myths. He was close now, his journey near an end. But here, the path began to rise at a slight incline, and it curled back around itself, and through a series of switchbacks ascended what, in the grand scheme of things, was a fairly small mountain. The path grew treacherous. Steeper. Rocky. Unstable. A squirrel, chittering on the side of a tree growing from the mountain wall, paused to regard him. And other eyes spied him there, no doubt wondering about this lone human on a path humans never tread.

The ascent was long and hard but, at the end of the day, when the sun had hidden under an unseen horizon and starlight sprinkled the sky, he stopped in a hollow within the trunk of a lightning-struck tree, nothing left of it but a mighty foundation and charred wood, to rest for the night.

His rest did not go unchallenged. First, a bear stopped to sniff at him, but she ultimately grumbled and went on her way. Then a wolf prodded and snarled, a juvenile, but its alpha pushed the pack forward. When the sprites came, blue and black and orange and yellow like the butterflies, they danced naked on his thighs and raced up and down his hips and waist. They pulled at his hair, their tiny fistfuls grabbing only a dozen strands at a time. When one stumbled and fell and landed in his eye, he started, and the sprites scattered like wisps into the night with barely a chuckle like glass bells.

Finally, a progression of the dead passed by his sleeping hollow. The shades drifted silently along the path, their presence swallowing all other sounds, even those of the not-too-distant waterfall. Some held ghost lights aloft like lanterns. Some mourned. One or two danced, celebrating their recent departure, but most simply walked. The ghosts gave off their own faint light, like glowworms lost from the caves. He watched, and counted thirty-five before one of the phantoms stopped beside his hollow to look directly at him.

This one ghost was a woman, barely older than a girl. Her eyes were deep. Accusing. Unwavering. He closed his own so as not to look too long into them, for within them lay only madness and pain. He had plenty enough of both.

In the morning, birds sang and the wind shifted and the sounds of the waterfall grew loud. He rose from his temporary bed, rested but insufficiently so, brushed himself clean, quickly stretched muscles sore from weeks and months of ceaseless journey, and continued up the side of the mountain.

The path was more difficult this last day. He had to scramble over fallen rocks and navigate a ledge not wide enough for the butterflies, and for a time the sun's angle caused it to shine straight into his eyes. He nearly fell off the side of the path, which would surely have resulted in his being impaled by a pine. He nearly twisted his ankle and almost snapped his wrist and twice came dangerously close to cracking open his skull. By now, the colors were below him, all the trees this high skeletal and bare. If a branch did support leaves, they were brittle, brown, and desperate to drop their final flight.

A little higher, he reached the apex of the path. From here, it was sloped downward and in from the edge and not very far. Music accompanied him, wind chimes made by nature or preternatural creatures. The river ran beside him, this time headed toward the falls. From the opposite shore, a coyote watched curiously. A flock of small birds erupted from the treetops. And all at once, his long journey ended.

A natural ledge overlooked the waterfall. Only a slight spray was caught on the wind. Here, the ghosts had set up camp for the day. Where they basked in sunlight, which was plentiful now, they were thoroughly invisible.

Stones had been set into the rock wall long ago and recently by hands inhuman, ethereal, and transitory. He unhooked the pack from his back, set it down, and rested a while, a truer rest than he'd had overnight. Nothing and no one would disturb him here. Though he didn't mean to sleep, he did. And though he didn't mean to dream, how could he not? This was a place of dreams, of mists, of magic and mystery. Waking before dusk, he retrieved a stone from the bottom of his bag. Her name had already been etched into it. He found an appropriate place in the wall, even though he couldn't read most of the other cenotaphs, and inserted the stone. At first, he had trouble. The stone didn't want to stay. But he was helped—by the ghostly woman who had stared at him the night before. Her hands passed through his but were solid against the stone. He barely felt anything but frost. She occupied the same space as him, briefly, and in that moment he felt her breath. It was twilight; she'd have only this one moment to speak. She said, "The woman you mourn, she's long gone past these between places."

Then the stone clicked into place and for all the world would forever belong right where it was. He closed his eyes and told the ghost, "No. There will always be a part of her with me."

Then he began his long journey back.

BELOW

Swift, sharp footsteps in the hall. Those are some mighty fine shoes out there. Oxfords maybe. Very steady. Very straight forward. Growing louder every moment.

You watch the open door. The only other sound is the intermittent beeping of a call light from a faraway room. You haven't seen a nurse or orderly or doctor or even someone from social services. There hasn't been a visitor singing songs for you, despite that you hear the occasional strumming of guitars from down the hall. From another wing.

This wing is dark.

Plastic curtains hang over what must be your window. They block all the daylight. Or the moonlight, starlight, and streetlights. The lamp on your bedside table is about as bright as a single candle. What light reaches your door stretches a long way down that hall from elsewhere. It smells of plaster and loose electricity and flaking paint.

You would scream, but you can't find much by way of voice. You would press the call button. You see it, big bright and red, hanging just beside the bed. But you're strapped down. Leather bindings. You can no more reach that light than you can dance a tango.

The footsteps stop just outside your door.

Someone stands out there checking a chart, reviewing a file, taking a breath to prepare for whatever it is they've got to tell you.

It's okay, you want to say. Just give it to me straight.

Whoever is out there, the stray hall light reveals no shadow.

The room around you is as bare and functional as can be: a single dresser across from you, a dark television screen atop it, a chair beside your bed, safety bars on either side to prevent you from rolling one way or the other—despite the straps, apparently someone thought this was necessary—and an IV bag next to your bed.

The thing is, the IV isn't dripping. The line just hangs there. The needle dangles and catches all the light it can find and twinkles, winks, maybe even mocks you. You can see a bandage on your wrist where it must have been feeding you morphine or sedatives.

You can't remember why you're here.

You're hoping the person outside your door, the person whose shoes sound so damn expensive, will fill in all the gaps. They'll start with a greeting, and that's how you'll learn your name again. They'll glance at the chart they've just studied as if doing one final check to make sure they don't say the wrong thing, then pronounce something Latin—an illness, perhaps. Or was there an accident? They'll tell you. You feel no pain. You feel light as a feather. You feel immobile, not just because of the straps. But you can lift your fingers. You can wriggle your toes.

Enough time has passed that you begin to wonder if you imagined the sound of footsteps. But no, you hear someone inhale, and he comes round the side of the door from the darker end of the dark hall.

"Hello," he says, not including your name. All your best plans are dashed.

You try to speak, but it's difficult to raise your voice above a whisper. Pushing air through your vocal cords takes effort. It doesn't hurt, but it feels claustrophobic.

"Don't panic," the man says. He smiles. It's supposed to be reassuring. He's done this before, the smile suggests. He's dealt with hundreds of people just you like. He's old enough to have dealt with thousands. His hair's more salt than pepper, his eyes an unnaturally dusk-hewn brown with flecks of gold, his lips thin, his skin dry. "You have nothing to worry about." He's not looking at you, but at the table beside you, the one you've tried to avoid looking at, the one with four ceramic jars: falcon, jackal, baboon, and human. They've all been sealed. The table itself has been dried and cleaned.

"Those," the man who doesn't appear to be a doctor says, "are your organs. Not all of them. It's an ancient practice, I assure you, and well tested. We've saved your lungs, your liver, your stomach, and most of your intestines." He smiles again. The smile looks like a scratch on a record. It shouldn't be there. "We don't want your heart. We don't need your brain."

You want to ask questions. If you haven't got lungs, how can you breathe? But maybe that's why you can't ask your questions.

"Oh, you're panicking again," the man says, "though I just told you not to. Oh well, there's not much I can do. I just wanted to let you know the ceremony isn't over. There's still the wrapping. Don't worry. Our wrappers are very experienced at this sort of thing."

Four women arrive just as he says this. They're dressed as priestesses. Those aren't costumes, but actual clothes, some of which have seen better days. The gold is real. Their eyes are—well, *old* is the only way to describe them. Their bodies are young.

Each carries a roll of what you first think might be toilet paper, but it's gauze, thick and white. Their fingers are nimble, quick, even teasing as they begin to wrap you.

From down the hall, there's beeping from another call light. There's the strumming of an out-of-tune guitar. They wrap your center first: your stomach, your chest, your genitals. They wrap your legs together, not separately, so there'll be no chance of you walking anywhere. They undo the straps to move your arms into position over your chest. You haven't got strength to resist.

Once they've begun your arms, the man puts a small leather-bound book on your chest just above your hands. "A book of the dead," he tells you. "You'll need this to guide you. Whatever challenges you face below, this book has all the instructions. Whatever questions you have, this book has all the answers."

You want to ask how you're supposed to open the book.

They wrap your head last. One layer at a time over your eyes. You can mostly see through one layer. You can barely see through two. After a third, fourth, and fifth, you no longer see anything. You're not even sure if your eyes are open. They're not done wrapping. There are countless and endless layers of gauze. Then you feel what might be them pasting the gauze down with cold, wet brushes. It would all be very erotic under other circumstances.

The man's voice is muffled when he says, "We'll come back at midnight to bring you below."

You listen to his confident, expensive steps as he leaves. You don't hear the women leave, but you no longer feel their hands working. You want one of the nurses or orderlies or doctors or social workers to find you before they return. You don't want to go below.

It's a long, long time before midnight arrives. You don't hear them. You barely feel them. Numerous hands lift you effortlessly off the bed, deposit you on a stretcher of some sort, and roll you away. You hear the ceramic banging against each other as they gather your canopic jars. You remember your name, but it's probably too late for that. You remember your life, but it's too late for that, too. They left the brain intact. And the heart. That's why you're still alive. Your heart beats. Your brain thinks.

They bring you below, place you in what must be a sarcophagus, slide the heavy sounding lid into place, and shut out all the light.

This is what you'll know forevermore: the cold of the tomb, the darkness, the dampness.

Then you feel the scarabs crawling over you.

The Museum of Curiosities

FREEDOM AND SALVATION

The rain skiffs are out in force.

The storm started gray but is now black as pitch, as coal, as coal mines, and I'm afraid we won't make it out of here this time.

And we are close. So very close. I can practically smell the salt in the air.

Maybe I could smell it, if not for the downpour and the gale and the lightning making everything smell of fried ozone.

Thunder masks the sounds of the skiffs.

The pilots wear black helmets that gleam in the dancing electric night. Helmets like smoke and death and rot. I hate them. My brother piloted a skiff, or was shot down by one, or was kidnapped to work the mines. Truth is slippery. My mother's mind has always been broken.

We're huddled in darkness nearly protected from the storm by what used to be a Woolworths. There's an entire wall missing. One of the walls that remains stretches twenty meters over the highest floor. We shelter beneath that. The rain still gets at us. Wind is inescapable. And the rain skiffs get closer with every pass.

I don't know who they're looking for.

It might be me.

It might be all of us.

It's been a few weeks since I heard the engines of rain skiffs. They're meant for sneaking and stealth. They intend to come up on you while you're distracted and fire nets or tranqs or hot lead murder.

We're protected on two sides and from above. The skiffs will have a hard time getting to us here. But I don't pretend we're safe. I motion for quietness, for silence and stillness, for even the young ones to settle down for a few minutes.

Maybe they'll fly past.

Maybe the storm will recede.

Maybe something huge and powerful will rise from the ocean, like in the old stories, and put an end to this nightmare.

I see the lights of the rain skiffs. They move slow out there, scanning the wreckage and debris. Maybe it's just a routine search party. Maybe they're not even with the government. I can't know without seeing them. I can't see them without putting us all at risk.

But I can't protect us forever.

The skiffs are closer. I can see their lights through the windows. Through the cracks in the bricks. Through the night and the storm and the echoes of railway runners of previous generations.

A bolt of thunder shakes the wall behind us. A second bolt, and I have to accept it's not natural.

"Run!"

I don't know who lets loose the cry. Maybe it was me. It should have been me. We run, we scatter to the elements, and when the battering rams punch a hole in the wall to bring down bricks like a rain of red death, no one's caught in the avalanche.

"East," I say, too late because no one can hear me. East, because that's where the ocean waits. East, because that's where there's a boat full of refugees and an armed resistance and the tiniest sliver of hope.

East, because to the west are the mountains, to the north are the authorities, and to the south are the badlands.

East, because there's nothing else for us.

I dodge searchlights and lightning arcs and gunfire. I skip through the dark like it's a final obstacle course. At the end: freedom, and maybe salvation. If I get caught, it's a different, final kind of freedom — unless they decide to take me alive.

I won't let that happen.

I'll fight.

I'll fight, though I cannot fight. I'll struggle and resist and die with honor if I must.

The road is uneven and filled with fissures and crevices that descend straight to hell.

According to the old stories, once upon a time there were great roads that crisscrossed nations and led to places of work, worship, and play.

According to the old stories, anyway. I don't believe all the old stories.

And there it is, across the last great expanse of fractured asphalt and past the skeletal remnants of structures that once housed dozens or hundreds of people all in a single place: the beach, sand stretching forever to the right and left, and the endless black expanse of ocean.

There's no horizon.

There's darkness and oblivion but no ship, no transport, no resistance fighters.

Behind me, a dozen rain skiffs have picked up my trail. They're coming. There's no place to run but into the ocean.

So I race over sand, then wet sand, and into the surf.

The waves toss me back.

Three, five, seven spotlights pick me out in the water.

They shout something at me through a loudspeaker. The storm swallows the words.

It's okay. Let them shout. Let them scream and shoot. I won't let them have me.

The next wave is twice the size of the last. I dive in. There's nothing else to do.

The water's still only up to my waist.

And the next wave is bigger.

Bigger.

In the darkness, there's a shape, indecipherable and inexplicable, rising from the ocean. The water shoves me back.

The shape makes no sound. Or if it does, it's the sound of storms and thunder.

I've never seen rain skiff pilots turn their vessels around so quickly.

They scatter like we'd scattered.

They don't get far. The next wave swallows me entirely, and swallows the skiffs, pulverizes the architecture, and crosses the asphalt.

The next wave is bigger.

I cling to something, I don't know what, a flagpole maybe. The leviathan doesn't seem to notice me.

It advances on the shore.

It and others like it up and down the coast—I can only see the vague silhouettes of them but in every direction and further than I can see. I hope they've come to offer freedom and salvation.

For a brief moment, it shields me from the storm.

the museum of curiosities

THE TRAIN TO PRAGUE

A long cobblestone road leads toward the setting sun, to the city skyline that cuts out a stark silhouette against the reds and oranges. Shadows are long as Starling walks. She's not one of the pilgrims, even if she walks in the same direction. She carries a book in one hand and has nothing else but the dress she wears. Her feet are bare, her hair loose and free, her eyes sparkling with impossible depth. Some — many — have called her stunning or outstanding or unreal. Tonight, as dusk paints the city, as she enters the shop of the alchemist, she feels impossible. Like a white raven with blue eyes. Like a cat who likes to play the saxophone. Nothing can stop her now. Nothing can get in her way.

She steps straight to the counter, to the young man, a mere boy, sitting reading a well-worn paperback Romance. He doesn't close the book when he smiles at her in an automatic way. "Can I help you?"

Starling sets her book on the counter between them. She doesn't open it. She puts it down with all its weight of age and secrets, its mysteries unravelling at the seams. She says, "I need money, and you need this book."

The title is *Making of a Shadow*. The boy doesn't dare touch it. He swallows once. He dog ears a page in his book. The pages in her book are older but less worn. The ink is stronger, more vibrant. Starling's already getting impatient. She says, "Make with the cash."

The boy shakes his head. A bead of sweat forms on his forehead. It's not a desert city. There's no material need for it. He says, "I can't."

"You must." She's insistent, even desperate.

He doesn't touch the book. He uses his Romance to push it across the counter toward her. "There's no way," he says. "I can't invite that kind of trouble."

They're both desperate. It's obvious to her now. Starling says, "Then pay me now. I'll take the book with me when I leave."

The offer must be tempting. He closes the Romance and puts it down. He sucks in his lower lip. He scratches the stubble on his chin. "I haven't got that much cash," he says. No price has been discussed. "Maybe I can perform a service."

"I need a ticket for that train."

"To where?"

"Prague."

"Is that all you need?"

Sterling smiles. "I'd love a bottle of red wine."

The train to Prague is only about ten hours. Not impossible to afford unless you haven't got a dime in hand. She's a wandering mystic, young, pretty, and undoubtedly wild. She thinks he wants to go with her.

"I'll call the station," he says, picking up the phone. "I'll make the arrangements. What name should I give them?"

And that's all it takes. She feels a pang of love for the boy. She lowers her voice and leans closer to confide. "Tell them Starling," she whispers. "But, and this is only for you, my name is Kerolina."

He makes the call, recites the necessary numbers to the stationmaster, then requests a bottle of red and two glasses be waiting for them.

It's bold, and she loves him even more for it.

She retrieves the book, hugs it close to her, almost like a shield. He closes and locks the shop. They walk over cobblestones toward the setting sun and the darkening night. She knows the shadows chasing her will destroy his alchemical shop and everything in it just to make sure the book's not there. He must know something about it, too, unless with barely a sight and hardly a whiff of her cotton candy perfume, he's already enthralled to her.

"What's your name?" she asks after they reach the station.

But he shakes his head. "I'll tell you in Prague." Then he asks," What brings you there?"

She smiles and lies. "A clock."

It's a beautiful start to their relationship, no matter how it will end.

THE CLARINETIST

It doesn't matter whether they're a thrash metal bassist or a concert violinist, an operatic soprano or a hard core rapper. What matters is intent. Musicians make the music. Music makes magic.

The piper walking the streets of Hamelin, for instance, the flutists dazzling snakes into dance, even pedestrians whistling for taxis in New York City. Also: that cartoon mouse with the brooms.

And there's Bob.

You wouldn't think much of Bob. He's the epitome of low key. Sure, he's got a cool hat, and wears it at a jaunty angle—though to be honest, no one today knows what a jaunty angle is. The thing is, he wanders streets, alleys, parks, highways and interstates, and sometimes even the aisles of churches, with his clarinet in pocket specially designed for it on the inside of his long coat.

It's such a small thing, you wouldn't expect him to enrapture strangers. Yet men and women alike, if they hear a measure without seeing the man, go home to dream of beautiful, unimagined things.

He has a collection of phone numbers, illicit and unsolicited Polaroids, and ex-wives. Five ex-wives, to be precise, and each still tries to care for him somehow. Angelia sends money every month. Michelle makes his doctor appointments. The doctor never charges him.

On this particular night, he walks a well-traveled bridge. It's neither huge nor famous. As far as he knows, it's anonymous, just a regular bridge, but there's a woman on the wrong side of the railing looking down at the cold black river.

He withdraws the clarinet and does a quick little bit of improvisational jazz just loudly enough for her to hear.

She holds the railing with both hands. The wind plays with her hair as she leans over the water. But she's turned her head to instead watch the wandering musician. When he's close enough, she asks, "Can you make it all better?"

He pauses in the song long enough to say, "I'm sorry, no."

He continues the song, something that would make Jimmy Dorsey proud and Benny Goodman swoon. But it's short, and comes too soon to its natural conclusion.

"Then why do it at all?" she asks.

He shrugs. "I play because I play. Nothing more sinister than that."

"There was nothing sinister in what you just played," she tells him. "For a moment, I was in the clouds, in the sunlight again, surfing along the rainbows, in places I haven't seen since I was naïve."

"There's nothing wrong with that," Bob says. "Would you like another song?"

"Will you charge me?"

"I will."

"You can have all my money. I won't be needing it." She looks down to the surface of the river. It's an abyss, an endless obsidian drop into nothingness and oblivion.

Bob shakes his head. "I don't need your money."

"You'll want a final kiss, then, is that it?" Her guard is risen.

"No, that would be—ungentlemanly, and maybe unsporting," he says. "No, I only want you to listen. I want you to close your eyes as I play, I want you to hold tight to that rail, and I want you to not let go until I've finished."

"That's not much of a price."

He shrugs, and lifts the clarinet. "It's what I require." He takes a breath, but holds it until she nods her assent.

Then he plays.

This time, it's neither a simple nor complex piece of jazz, but something symphonic, and for a while it sounds almost as if an entire orchestra plays alongside him. When he closes his eyes, he sees the violinists, the cellists, the horns and trombones, even an array of timpani booming in support.

It's a transformative song, an epic journey and quest, in which heroes battle monsters for the hearts of gods and goddesses. It's a moving song, with slow, sad sections, but also with frantic swings of violence and vehemence. It's swift in places, and it's a good thing Bob closes his eyes as he plays or he might be swept away by what he doesn't see: the woman swaying, tears falling uncontrolled from kaleidoscopic eyes. Even as he plays, she leans back, over the edge of the railing; and before he finishes, she falls onto the bridge side. She twists her ankle and scratches her arm, but says nothing for fear of interrupting the song.

And when it ends, when Bob opens his eyes again and lowers the clarinet, she looks up to meet those eyes and says, "But, that can't possibly be the end, can it? It feels—unfinished."

"Oh, it's the end," Bob says, "of the first movement. There's more, but I won't be back until next week to play the second."

"How many movements will there be?" she asks.

"However many you require."

Briefly, she smiles, all her worries and troubles temporarily forgotten, and says, "I'll be here."

"Of course you will," Bob tells her. Then he winks, and slips the clarinet back into a pocket specially designed for it on the inside of his long coat. "I've put a spell on you."

The Gates of
Modern Bablyon

The old man at the back of the neighborhood built a fence surrounding his property. He had five acres back there, all to himself, filled mostly with woods. We used to take our bikes up and down those trails. We didn't know it was his property and we didn't care; we were barely teenagers.

He started building the fence by himself, a wood fence, hammering every plank into the earth. It wasn't pretty. When we asked, he said it was for our protection.

He told stories of ogres coming down from the mountains, of alien landing fields we had somehow not discovered, of snakes with three heads, rabid dogs with scorpion tails. Then he showed us a very official letter from some city department official directing him to build the fence or face fines, possible litigation, and potential jail time.

So we helped him build the fence. We had access to hammers, and we all wanted to drive nails into things, anyhow. We stole paint cans from our parents' garages, so the fence ended up becoming a series of ugly abstract murals. We all did something different on each section of fence. If we couldn't see through the wood, at least we wouldn't have to see wood, that was our thinking.

Jenny painted a giant cat's face looming over a horizon like sunrise. She was the artist among us. Eddy did flying saucers. Johnny made a tank; at least, we all believed it was supposed to be a tank, but we never asked. Sue did something with dancing rainbows and moonbeams. And I, stuck with too much red, attempted what was meant to be a dragon. No one asked me about that, either.

The old man was thankful for our help. The perimeter of five acres required a lot of fencing. He made us lemonade one day, chocolate chip cookies another. Eventually we came all the way back around to the start of his property. The driveway. The fence ended one car's width away from where it had begun.

"Will we make a gate now?" I asked.

"I thought you already had," the old man said.

So we raced around the edges of his property on our BMX bikes, around the crooked and uneven fence with its bizarre paintings, which we were mostly responsible for, until we found a gate painted on one. It looked to be huge, like to keep back monsters, with lions perched on towers on either side.

"That's got to be your work," I said to Jenny, but she claimed it wasn't. It wasn't any of ours. It was too good, really, so realistic, so sandy and hot. We felt we were there, at the gates of Babylon, waiting for the doors to open to let us in from the desert. We felt this way in the warm summer woods. On our bikes, we felt the desert wind and smelled the breads and wild fruits of the bazaar and—I can't say everyone wondered it, but I certainly wondered if we could get to the other side of that gate.

I returned alone at twilight. I knew something the other kids didn't know about the half-light, *die Dämmerung*, because my gram used to talk about such things when she was into her whiskeys.

I dropped my bike alongside a circus scene I'm not sure any of us painted and approached the gate with all due reverence. That was something else gram taught me. "Let me in," I said, "before the desert night consumes me."

They opened the gate and ushered me in. I had never tasted air so dry. Otherwise, it was like walking on the beach just at the edge of the high tide line. The sand was the same, except here there were prickly things and little orange bushes and horses and camels and elephants walking the streets. There was a juggler with colorful face paint like a clown, but so not like a clown I went another direction. I couldn't understand all the languages around me, though I caught hints of German and Irish and English, the things I'd been taught.

I found a woman with dark skin and red lips and a golden circlet around her head. She leaned close and exhaled all kinds of intoxicants, poisons, perfumes, and scents designed to bend my will to hers. She said something in a language I didn't understand, so I told her I didn't understand. "You're early," she said. "Come back in five years, if you dare."

Then she kissed me. I won't lie and say it was the first time I kissed a girl, but it was definitely the best. It was magic, that kiss, I swear it to this day. It threw me back through the gate, through the fence, all the way to the woods.

I tried to return through the gate but it was past twilight. I tried again every night that summer.

It's been five years.

The old man is gone. The fence has fallen into disrepair. Alongside the road, the new owners had sand-blasted the fence to clear all the murals. Jenny was in art school in New York now. Eddy had died, an accident; drugs were involved. Johnny's parents moved him to South Carolina, they say, and none of us ever heard from him again. Sue still lived in the neighborhood. I was back for the summer before my second year of college.

I got out my old BMX bike. It seemed small now, but it had been my everything once upon a time. I pedaled through the overgrown path along the side fence, recognizing the various vignettes we had sloppily painted on the old man's fence. Some, I didn't remember: the sugar skulls; the dune buggies; the prisms and pyramids. I put down the bike next to the circus scene and approached the gates of Babylon with all the reverence my gram had taught me. She was gone now, but I had a fifth of whiskey to toast her from the other side.

I said the same line as before: "Let me in before the desert night consumes me." They opened the gates and ushered me in. There was a stronger smell of incense this time, more vanilla and more spice, and a hint of citrus which confused me. I noticed the street urchins this time; last time, I had been one of them.

I found the woman with the dark skin and red lips and golden circlet around her head. She leaned close and exhaled all kinds of intoxicants, poisons, perfumes, and scents designed to bend my will to hers. She asked to share my drink. "For your gram," she said with a wink. We drank, and she said, "I knew you'd be back."

"You compelled me," I admitted.

She smiled. It was the most beautiful thing I'd ever seen. Then she kissed me, and it was more delicious than the first time. It was magic, that kiss, I swear it to this day. By the end of it, I had lost all my strength, all my youth, and most of my soul.

That's how I came to be here, on the streets of this modern Babylon nowhere near the desert, within a breeze's reach of the ocean, asking for just a few spare coins. Unless I find the right coin, the special coin, the one she wants, I won't be able to return to my old neighborhood and my BMX abandoned in the woods near a circus scene. I'm sure Jenny and Sue went looking for me, but they likely entered the wrong section of the fence thinking I'd be more attracted to the Ferris wheel and carousel. If nothing else, I need to go back to rescue my friends. I just need one magic coin, is all. Just the one. Please.

THE MUSEUM OF CURIOSITIES

THE DANCER

He sits, and she dances.

He sits and doesn't move, because to move is to fail, to move is to risk her wrath, to move is to die.

She dances, and it's slow, erotic, veils sliding around her, her curves and colors hidden and revealed and hidden again with every motion. She weaves in and out of the shadows, in and out of the music, in and out of his line of vision.

When she moves behind him, her silk brushes his lips, his face. When she moves around him, she touches his shoulder, his cheek, his soul.

He tries to remain still. He cannot. He's in love. He's enraptured. He's enthralled. And he's doomed, he knows it; he knows this more than anything else he's ever known. And he is a man who has known so many secrets.

She whispers when she dances. She bends and sways and tempts and teases. She leans close so he feels the warm breath of her words on his ear, but he comprehends none of the words, none of the meaning.

She sheds another veil. The red silk flutters, drifting languidly like an eel through water, until it lands on his knee. There's almost nothing now between his eyes and her skin, his hands and her flesh, his life and his death.

He wants to move. To reach out. To caress her cheek—more than her cheek—and find the sweetest words to whisper back to her.

But those teeth.

Not hers. The dancer's teeth are extraordinary under a brilliant and often seductive smile. But the teeth in the dark, and the eyes seeking out any movement, any sign of weakness or of strength, any indication of life—the teeth in the dark will shred his flesh, strip it straight to his bones.

He shudders at the thought. The teeth seem to shudder in response.

The dancer brings him back to her, drawing his gaze away from the darkness. Her eyes are like stars, kaleidoscopes, vivid abysses into which he would throw his heart and body and soul. In that moment, that brief connection, some of her words get through. "They'll devour me if I stop."

Just like that, his attention returns to the teeth. So much closer now. Can they hear her whispers?

He barely moves his lips. He says, "I love you."

A tear spills from the dancer's eye. It escapes the corner, trails down her cheek for a moment before the dance moves her away again, and the last of her veils, the last of her armor, the final thread of protection, slips free, glides through the shadows, lands in folded waves on his hand.

It's a weight like he's never imagined.

He moves. He rises abruptly from his seat, reaches for the dancer. She's drawn into the dark, fading back, and all he can do is stretch — his hand entangled by the veil — into darkness — and then: teeth.

Teeth like nightmares. Like spikes. Like stalactites. Like boulders crushing his bones as they strip away his flesh, his muscle, his sinew — his blood, his thoughts, and his life.

The teeth recede. Slowly, the dancer retrieves her veils, stepping again into the silk. The scent of him remains, briefly, and she savors it. She wipes her eyes. She says, "Not fair. This time, I think he really loved me."

From the darkness, an answer comes: "But you didn't love him."

She nods. She didn't. It's true. It's always true. She walks daintily through the darkness on spiked heels, retouches her mascara in a mirror of shadows, then finds the next victim sitting, sweating, young and supple and anxious and oh so scared, waiting for her to dance.

This is her punishment, not theirs.

SHADOWS DANCE

Shadows dance because there's music, and the music makers play only because they have so appreciative—and demanding—an audience.

Because even after the sun rises, shadows are thick and sharp and dangerous.

It's a stark sky, blanched white, scorched, harshly and unrelentingly hot. The bourbon flows, and the shadows laugh, and the musicians have been repeating themselves because their set was only supposed to be forty-five minutes.

Sometime around breakfast, the seer, having been informed of the emergency, arrives. He's dressed in fancy black lace and finery. His beard is precise, his fingernails pristine, his heart a thoroughbred about to place in the final leg.

The shadows simply laugh.

They dance around him.

They flip the pages in his conjuring book as he tries to read from them.

They blow out the matches in his hands before he can even light the candles.

"Will you just *leave?*" he asks, exasperated.

The shadows laugh and dance, and the musicians pick up the pace because they have to.

The seer snatches his conjuring book from the floor and runs. The shadows chase him down the street.

After a bit, the bassist stops playing. The drummer, momentarily confused, loses the rhythm. The guitarist finishes her solo, then stares out at the empty room. The singer says it first: "Have they all gone?"

The shadows chase the seer down the road, up a cross street, all the way to his apartment, where he has a vast variety of spices and incense and crystals. He has skulls made of resin and wax. He has rune stones and tarot cards and prayer beads that he clutches when he asks, "What do you want from me?"

The shadows dance. In his house, on his bed, across the surface of his scrying mirror. They dance in his windows and upside down on his ceiling.

The seer attempts a spell, attempts an exorcism, even attempts to serve them tea—and three of the shadows dance through the tea because they cannot drink it but they like the aroma.

The shadows make his séance table rock. They flicker his lights. They turn the dial on his radio until he's getting foreign voices speaking in foreign languages about secretive spy stuff he should absolutely not be hearing. They turn on his blender and his television and his washing machine.

The seer crosses himself and recites Jewish prayers and invokes Allah, the saints, the pagan gods, the angels.

An angel shows up at the front door and knocks. The angel radiates light and warmth and beauty. The angel snaps angelic fingers, snaps them in tune, and provides a rhythm so the shadows can dance.

Demigods and monsters play bone pipes and stringed instruments. The seer doesn't want to know what the strings are made with.

The seer screams and cries and ends up curled in a ball on his living room floor, eyes clenched tight, hands to his ears, shadows dancing over and around him and through him as if he's not even there.

Shadows dance.

That's the only point.

Shadows dance because they want to dance, because they want to be free, because they want to understand things beyond comprehension—mortal and immortal alike.

Shadows dance because everyone and everything dances.

The seer sees nothing. He sees money. He sees the basest insecurities inside people and preys on them. He never expected to see shadows dancing. He never expected to see angels or demigods or monsters. He's a fraud, the worst kind of fraud, taking advantage of tourists but also of people in desperate need and desperate straits.

The shadows don't care. They dance because shadows dance.

The angel maintains the rhythm, as back on the stage the musicians have called it a night and fled for safer ports.

The seer repents. The seer cries. The seer swears he'll change his ways. The shadows dance. Mephistopheles himself struts into the apartment, the dancing shadows making room and giving space. Mephistopheles leans down and says to the seer, "I am prepared to strike a bargain."

The seer cries, "Anything!"

Soon, the shadows dance in other places, in speakeasies and taverns, in dancehalls and stadiums, in basements and attics across the city, the country, the world.

The seer sees things he'll wish aren't real.

And Mephistopheles walks away wiping his hands as though shaking with the seer had left them stained and sticky. The seer might simply have joined the dance and saved himself...but it's too late now for that.

The Museum of Curiosities

MOUSE HUNT

She arms herself for the great mouse hunt.

She uses a toothpick as a sword. It seems appropriately sized. She might be much bigger than the mouse, but a full sized sword would simply be too much of an advantage. The toothpick is pointy at the end, and it's distinctly possible to only inflict a flesh wound.

She hunts by sound. The mouse is quiet as. Figures.

She hunts by smell, but she doesn't know what a mouse is supposed to smell like. She's never smelled one up close.

They look cute, except when they're running around inside the walls of her house and chewing holes in the upholstery. So she hunts by sight. The room may be big, but the mouse isn't climbing walls or crawling across the ceiling like a spider. That was last weekend's hunt. It had ended in something of a stalemate.

The runners along the floor show places where the mouse has been sneaking into and out of the living room. It doesn't need a lot of room. It's possible that this gives her a disadvantage. Maybe the mouse is small enough to stand perfectly still and avoid detection as if it was invisible.

The spider, however, had attempted just such a strategy, and it had failed.

She also sees where dust has gathered like tumbleweeds. Where paint has peeled naturally. Where there are stains she cannot readily identify, which disturbs her.

Some of those stains might be attributable to the mouse. It's playing with her.

So she hunts with a kind of determination she rarely employs. Against the spider, yes, of course, because those things are venomous and like to bite when you're sleeping. Against the mouse, now, because they skitter across the floor and frighten her cat.

Stupid cat, she thinks, looking at the cat perched on the edge of the couch. The cat looks back, obviously thinking *stupid human*. They have a healthy respect for each other, and maybe a perfect amount of mutual disdain.

"Who am I kidding?" she says. "You're my adorable little fluffball."

Of course I am, the cat must be thinking, because it purrs, albeit briefly, and flicks its tail.

Back to the matter at hand: the mouse. It's around here somewhere. She's heard its little paws when it ran, but right now it is silent. It will wait until something else makes a sound. It's a crafty little mouse.

"Come out, come out, and play," she says in a sing-song way. But the mouse does not come out, the spider tsk tsks from its perch in the corner of the ceiling, and the cat merely cleans itself.

Then the grandfather clock, big enough to dominate the living room, an inheritance from her grandfather, strikes the hour. One in the afternoon. One strike, that's all, but it's enough for the mouse to take off running down the side of the clock.

"Got you!" she says. "*En garde!*" She wields the toothpick like an expert. The mouse might've stopped, but the downward momentum on the side of the clock is rather irresistible. She allows for it to reach the floor, then says it again. "*En garde*, little mouse! Stand and fight!"

"No!" the mouse squeaks.

She thrusts with the toothpick and jabs the mouse in its flank. The mouse screeches.

"Point to the human," says the spider.

The mouse runs toward a hole in the floorboard. She parries, sending the mouse in the other direction. She feigns left. The mouse feigns right. They meet in the middle, and she accidentally kicks it halfway across the living room.

The mouse then runs for the front door. It's closed, locked, unmoving. The mouse hits the corner of the door and staggers backwards, dazed.

"Acceptable," she says, quickly unlocking the door and pulling it open. When the mouse doesn't immediately move, she jabs at it again. The mouse escapes the house and runs toward the fields outside where it will live a happier, healthier life anyhow.

She slams shut the door.

"Bravo!" says the spider.

The cat pauses in its cleaning and looks expectantly at her. Isn't now a good time for dinner, it wants to know.

She sleeps soundly that night, thinking she has vanquished the mouse invader and protected her home. But in the middle of the night, the mouse creeps under the front door and back into the house. The mouse trots toward one of the holes in the wall, tipping its hat to the cat, who watches it and yawns.

The mouse returns to its own bedroom in the walls, where it has been living for quite some time before the human decided to begin that horrible hunt.

But that's over now.

Next weekend, there'll be something else worth hunting.

the museum of curiosities

THE GHOST WHO HAUNTED ME

I told a ghost story once. It was good and also true, but the ghost didn't appreciate my ability to spin a tale. She followed me home, perused my library, read over my shoulder as I scribbled. Finally, I asked if she had a problem with me.

She was shocked. "Why would I have a problem with you?" she asked.

"I don't know, but ever since that night I told your story, the story of you, you've been haunting me."

She got this dejected look that made me feel I'd been overly harsh, then looked away and said, "But your story wasn't as true as you believe, and you conjured me out of nothing. If I haunt you, it's only because I'm bound to you who created me."

I considered what she said and the nature of my stories. Though I had trouble believing her, I said, "Then I release you. You are bound to me no longer. Go where you will."

She smiled and left and came back deep in the night. "Thank you," she said, waking me, "but if it's all the same to you, I'll stay."

The Museum of Curiosities

THE HOLE THAT APPEARED IN THE ROAD

A hole opened in the middle of the street one lonely night. It was not an oft-traveled road, so the hole might have been there a few days before Billy noticed it. His first thought was sinkhole, though he didn't know much about sinkholes. It was symmetrical enough to believe a supervillain had dug their way here from the other side of the earth.

He knew, in the back of his mind, that a straight line through the earth's center would lead to someplace at the bottom of an ocean, but no one required the villain to dig in a straight line all the way down until they were coming up. Who said they'd even gone through the very core of the earth? That was solid iron down there, and all that magma would probably take its toll on the paint job of their evil drilling machine.

Maybe aliens dug the hole. That made even less sense, because would they have to start by digging all the way through the atmosphere, leaving a vacuum without oxygen or nitrogen or any of the other gases trapped within the planet's gravitational clutches.

Billy edged close enough to the hole to look down. It was rather steep. He doubted he could climb that wall, and he was as good a climber as his cat, which was saying something. Straight up the side of the cat tower like a lightning bolt. But the walls of the hole were smooth, and it was too deep to see the bottom.

If he had a rope ladder, he could descend like that time he went into the dry well. It wasn't really as dry as people always claimed. It was damp, it was musty, and it smelled bad. If the bottom of the hole smelled as bad, surely he should've detected something of it at the top. But that's how deep it was.

It must've been fairies of some sort. They needed portals to slip between their own world and Billy's. Maybe this should have been in the middle of the forest, and the two lane rural highway had merely gotten in the way—or been abandoned enough that they decided to use it anyway. The risk of a Trans-Am or a Peterbilt or even a golf cart seemed rather low. Billy wasn't riding so much as a Vespa. He was on foot, as he often was, with only a walking stick to protect himself should the need arise.

He was good with the walking stick, though. He had practiced.

If he called it in—Billy didn't know who he would call or how, unless he dialed the emergency line, but eventually the police and ambulance would contact the proper clandestine governmental shadow agency who would dispatch black helicopters and patrol the perimeter with armed soldiers in black gasmasks and black skintight leather so they could camouflage themselves in the darkness.

But it wasn't dark, and nothing dangerous had threatened to emerge from the hole. Nothing dangerous or, for that matter, helpful. No wish-granting genies, though a hole was nothing like a lamp and Billy knew it. No overflowing pails of gold and jewels. Nothing.

Maybe it was a mine. Would they open up a mine in the middle of a road? Maybe a mile or two in either direction, the road had been closed off weeks ago, and Billy never noticed. But where was the earth-digging equipment? The bulldozers and excavators and pile drivers and trenchers? If they were all below the shadow line down the hole, their sounds should still echo up like a thunderous, cacophonous orchestra. It was weirdly quiet at the edge of the hole. Even the birds and insects seemed silent.

Billy kicked a rock into the hole. It fell and it plummeted, head over toe, if a rock could be said to have such things, and it plunged soundlessly into the darkness. Billy listened for a long time. There might have been a thud, or the sound of other rocks being dislodged in some sort of avalanche, or a splash if there was water at the bottom.

"Hello!" Billy called. His voice echoed back weakly, but for a long time, over and over again as though another version of him called back from every hundred yards until infinity and eternity and forever ended.

Well, it sure was a mystery. Billy liked mysteries, especially the scientific kind. He knew about crystal skulls and mummifying techniques and people who had stepped off their front stoops to find themselves briefly in other centuries. He knew about ghosts and echoes and boogeymen. He didn't know what he believed, but he was open to anything and everything. Whatever waited at the bottom of the hole was one of the greatest mysteries Billy had ever come across in all his thirteen years, and he wasn't about to let this one pass without discovering its secrets. He didn't want to end up like Uncle Joe, mumbling about shock troops and shadowy jazzmen in New Orleans. He didn't want to end up like Gramps, fighting old ladies for the red rocking chair at the nursing home, slapping and popping the strings of an unamplified Fender Precision Bass Guitar, telling all who would listen about ley lines and hypnotists and that one time he'd astral projected to another planet a hundred thousand years in the past. "They're still coming," he would say, if anyone listened. "They're close now, nearly here, only a hundred thousand light years away."

The answer, for Billy, was simple. He would have to jump in. He couldn't climb, he didn't want to risk diving because he didn't want to break his neck when and if he landed. But if he simply stepped off the edge, he might find there was a slight incline to the wall, and ten thousand feet down he might smash his ribs against the wall and find himself bouncing the rest of the way down. So he jumped, and in the middle of the jump realized he could tuck his legs as if doing a cannonball into a pool. There was first that brief upward movement, as if he might fly from here to Kentucky or Copenhagen, a moment of weightlessness as he reached the apex of his arc, then the briefest drop before his father caught him by the scruff of his neck.

"What do you think you're doing?" his father asked. He was so far away. His hand, the hand that dangled Billy over the potentially bottomless pit, was bigger than a hand but also far less substantial.

"Discovering the source of a mystery, sir," he said, the response open, honest, and respectful, just as he'd always been taught.

His father walked closer to the hole, close enough to look over the edge, and said, "Just be home in time for dinner or your momma will have my hide."

Then his father released him, and Billy fell feet first into the mouth of a mystery, and thus into legend.

The Museum of Curiosities

LONG HIGHWAY

The speedometer's been pegged at 120 for a while, but the gas gauge is at fumes and prayers. The road stretches forever in a single direction. It never branches off. There are no intersections. On the side, there are old brick buildings, houses transformed into law or dental offices and later abandoned.

Through it all, since the beginning of time, for weeks on end without even a bathroom break, Tommy drives.

Tommy grips the wheel with both hands. He leans slightly forward in his bucket seat. It's an uncomfortable drive. His right leg cramps against the cracked leather. He stuffs a fist under there sometimes in an attempt to ease, or at least move, the pain. The radio plays like tin through a few broken speakers. The sunlight drowns the road like a sand-blaster.

Tommy's Mercury Cougar doesn't have a rearview mirror. He tore that off years ago. The Cougar doesn't have side view mirrors. He purposefully shattered them by driving too close to a mailbox on one side and an ice cream truck on the other. It hadn't always been his car. The rag top has always been down. The wind has always been in his hair. He tries very hard not to glance over his shoulder. He doesn't want to see the flickers back there. Following him. Pursuing him. Hunting him. Wanting to consume him, body and soul.

The Cougar used to belong to each of them. They can't run, skip, jump, or glide fast enough to catch the Cougar, but they can keep up. If he drops below 70, they can close that gap.

He can't run forever.

He passes a billboard for a gas station. A girl with yellow hair and a red dress smiles prettily like a 1950s dream rendered in four colors. Petrol. Rest. Showers. Eats. His stomach rumbles at the very concept. He looks over his shoulder. They're back there flickering on the edge of the horizon. He's felt their teeth, but now they look distant.

He crests a hill and sees it, an oasis in this verdant desert, the only indication of life on a road that shouldn't exist. He slows down. He hasn't got a choice. The engine's beginning to sputter, draining every last drop out of the fuel line. The Cougar shudders as he eases up on the accelerator. Briefly, he can't even see the flickers behind him.

He pulls into the station.

It's one of those old, forgotten joints where an elderly man in a crisp uniform emerges from the building with a cracked grin and stained rag. "What can I do for you?" he asks as though he has all the time in the world.

"Fill 'er up," Tommy says. He glances back. They blink and titter at the top of that hill. He hasn't got much time.

The old man, his face all yellowed suede, removes the fuel cap and withdraws the delivery snake from the analog machine with dials to indicate the price and quantity. Tommy didn't both to look at the price. It's not like he's got money.

"What about this weather?" the old man asks, casually scratching at his belly as the machine ticks with every dime.

"Yeah, it's hot," Tommy says. He doesn't really want to say anything. He just wants to go. He doesn't care for small talk. There was a rumor, back down the road, in the direction of the flickers, where it was hotter, that this was the only highway, and now he thinks it's true. He's been driving it since before he could remember, ever since those brilliant summer days of lemonade and popsicles came crashing to an end. He stole the car. That makes it rightfully his. He didn't know the flickers came with it. He had laughed at the woman he'd taken it from. She'd looked just like the girl in the sign for the gas station.

"Can't say I care too much about the heat," the old man says. "My bones, they get dry, and my muscles snap when I move."

The price ticks up higher. Fuel pours into the Cougar. It's a thirsty car. But it's fast, and this should have worked.

The flickers have cut the distance in half before the old man reaches the final drops of gas. "I hope you're having a good trip," he says. "I tried myself once, but as you can see, I only got this far."

The flickers chase the car. They're attached to the car. They want the old, rusty Cougar, not the middle-aged man who used to dream about having such a car as a teenager. The doors don't work, so he hops out. It's an effort. It hurts. He's stiff and almost stumbles. "Hey, I've got an idea," he tells the old man. "Why don't you take it?" He dangles the keys in front of him. "It's not like I've got money to pay for the fuel."

The old man eyes the keys. He eyes Tommy. His eyes are arid things, dusty and scarred. He spends two breaths thinking on the offer. Tommy glances down the road at the flickers. "Maybe it's not too late," Tommy adds. "Get out of this Hell."

The old man scratches his unshaven chin, then snatches the keys. He climbs into the car over the unmoving door like a man who's done it every day of his seventy years. When he turns the key, the Cougar roars to life, and the old man laughs.

Tommy leans in to give a word of advice. "Drive fast, old man."

He does. The Cougar spits gravel, launches like a rocket, spins into the road toward the next horizon. A second later, the flickers swarm past Tommy. They're cold and sharp and insubstantial. They're angry and chitter like locusts. They cut his face and arms as they chase the muscle car, but only because of proximity. They go after the old man, and Tommy lets out a sigh. He picks up the rag the old man had dropped and heads into the attendant's shack. He hopes it's air conditioned. He doesn't want to spend the rest of eternity baking in this heat.

When he gets in, there's a woman sitting in the one chair, a blonde wearing a red dress and smiling prettily. Tommy recognizes her immediately, not from the billboard but from the flickers. He nods up the road. "Old man took the car," he says.

"But you took it from me," she tells him. She gets up, sashays straight to Tommy, and says, "You stole my Cougar. That was my means of escape."

"I figure to walk now," Tommy says.

"I figured the same," she says, draping her arms over his shoulders and pressing tight against him. "At least, I once did." She kisses him. She kisses him hard. But it's not a kiss, not at all. She sucks his moisture through his mouth, every drop of blood and sweat and oil, as though the car had become a part of him. She drains Tommy dry, and lets his sack of bones crumble to the pale linoleum floor.

THE MUSEUM OF CURIOSITIES

PEPPER'S CURSES

Through a door under a mushroom, Pepper stepped once again into the self-proclaimed real world. She'd forgotten how big everything could be. It was still nighttime, so under the stars she danced—but even so, she moved in a particular direction.

The big fat moon lit the trail quite well, so she had no trouble following its turns and bends. She pranced along, and sometimes she skipped, until eventually a man on a horse approached.

That was when she remembered how small she was. It wasn't the trees that did it, because they would've dwarfed her anyhow. But the man on the horse was so big, neither rman nor horse even saw her. She hopped into the air, floated a moment, and grabbed the horse's tail as they rode by.

They weren't making any great speed, but each of the horse's steps were a dozen or more of her own, and she never knew when that extra touch of speed would matter.

Anyway, maybe the horseman was who she'd come for.

But he was drunk, or a drunkard, or too sleepy to rightfully observe his surroundings. Even when she climbed the back of the horse and scooted over his hips and knee to grab a chunk of the horse's mane and watch the road ahead of them, he didn't seem to notice. And he never looked down.

Of course. The horse knew the way. The horse always did.

Still, she swung around to the side of the horse's head so he wouldn't accidentally catch sight of her and swat her like a bug. That would be terrible. She hated being swatted. She didn't want to have to kill this man who had been kind enough to offer her a ride—even if he didn't know he'd been so kind.

They rode toward a village. It was merely a collection of houses pressed against each other for warmth and protection and momentum; they only remained standing because they had been standing for so long. One tiny little kick at the right support beam, the whole place might tumble into a ruin.

He was riding through, even at this late—or early—hour, to parts unknown, so she hopped off the horse. He seemed to notice her then, but only briefly, like a man vaguely lucid in the midst of a vapor dream. He turned his head, crouched a little closer to his horse, and whispered protective oaths without realizing he was doing it.

Yes, this was the right place. One of these houses had a small library, some fifty books, but that had already been sufficient. Pepper flitted from window to window, following the scents of leather and parchment and ink, until finally she came upon the place she sought in the very center of the village.

The whole village slept. Fires in the hearths burned low, if at all. But in this one house, a girl of no more than seven, who still towered over Pepper, sat awake in a chair too big for her. She'd perched a book in her lap, but it was closed. Anyway, there was no light to read by.

The window was open to welcome the cool night air. That was practically an invitation. Pepper slipped in and traipsed unseen across the room. The girl alternatively looked at the book and at imagined vistas and murals inside her eyelids.

Pepper scaled the side of the chair. The upholstery made it easy, though she could have simply leapt to its arm and presented herself in the way of acrobats and sideshow hustlers.

"What's your name?" Pepper asked the girl.

Startled, the girl looked at her a moment, then smiled, but said nothing.

"Do you know what I am?" Pepper asked.

"A fairy."

She grinned at that. "Close enough," she said. "I'm here to give you something, but I don't know if you'll like it."

"Why wouldn't I like it?"

"What if I what I give you turns out to be a curse?"

"But you won't," the girl said. "I can see it in your eyes. You're kind. You don't bring curses."

"Tonight, I do," Pepper said, because it was true. She hopped onto the book in the girl's lap so as better to see her eyes. "I'm cursing you with vision, with sight and insight, with a gift for words and language to rival any poet's heart. Indeed, I'm gifting you with poetry, with poetics, and lyricism and rhythm."

The girl smiled at her. "I told you," she said. "Those all sound like gifts."

"They sound like gifts," Pepper told her, spinning as she leapt into the air, floating in front of the girl's face. "But you'll learn, quite soon, the world isn't ready for a girl, a woman, with your gifts. The world might not be ready for anyone like you."

The girl's smile fell away. Solemnly, as if making a vow, the girl said, "But I'll make myself ready for the world."

The talk attracted the girl's father, who came stumbling into the room. He didn't make demands, merely inquired who his daughter might be talking to and why she was up at this wicked hour.

By the time he'd entered the room, Pepper had already left it, slipping through a mouse hole and back into her own world where everything was properly sized. She might want to check back on the girl forty or fifty years later, but she'd never gotten her name.

The Museum of Curiosities

LAST PEACHES
OF THE SEASON

The girl goes to the market in search of peaches. It's a busy, bustling, packed-to-the-gills market selling hand-painted picture frames and fresh corn on the cob and potatoes in multiple colors and sizes, but it's the wrong season for fresh peaches.

The girl is maybe small for ten years old, maybe big for seven, but she's determined, and she's not about to let something so simply as a season deter her.

She says to the man selling tomatoes and broccoli, "But those aren't what I need. Whoever heard of a broccoli pie?"

She says to the woman selling forks twisted into abstract shapes representing horses and stars, "How am I supposed to fill my face with pie using a fork like that?"

To the teenager selling used books and records and antique drinking glasses, she says, "I would buy that lavender glass bowl, but I only have one dollar and I need to spend it on peaches."

The teenager laughs. "You won't find any peaches. But I'll give you the bowl."

So the girl runs through the market with the lavender glass bowl and finds the old man selling carved wood pens to ask him, "Where's your wife?"

The old man looks at her and wrinkles his eyes and says, "What do you want Dolores for?"

Dolores is the old woman who sells peaches. She's from Georgia, and sounds like it, and is always kind to the girl.

"I want peaches," she tells the old man.

"You missed peaches," he says. "It's been two weeks, maybe three, since we got any peaches."

"Your wife will know," the girl insists.

Dolores, of course, would know—she knows all the things worth knowing. She's an old woman, and though her old country is not so far away, she's of old country and therefore has magic in her veins.

Indeed, Dolores comes ambling between sellers of cream and spices and figurines of kings and beauties carrying a basket under her arm. She smiles at the girl, then at her husband, and tells the girl, "I knew you would be here today."

The old man mutters something, rolls his eyes, and walks away to leave his wife and the girl to their mysterious dealings. The girl smiles at the begrudging respect. "How did you know?"

"The goddess of peaches told me."

"There isn't any goddess of peaches," the girl says. "That's silly."

"It's not silly," Dolores tells her, lifting the lid of her basket to reveal it's filled with perfectly ripened peaches not a day too old or young. "Otherwise, I wouldn't have these to sell you."

"I only have one dollar," the girl says. When Dolores frowns, the girl adds, "And this lavender glass bowl."

Dolores makes the trade, but with one caveat. "I know you'll be baking a pie. You must leave a slice out for the goddess of peaches. And maybe a full glass of milk."

The girl giggles. "I'll do that."

She goes home with the last peaches of the season and sets about baking one pie and one cobbler. People think they're the same, but they're not. It takes all day to make the pie; the cobbler doesn't require all that time. The girl lets the pie and cobbler cool together. After dinner, she has a slice of each with dollops of cream. Her mother and father beam proudly and each take seconds.

At the end of the night, before changing into her bedclothes and venturing into the realms of dreams, the girl cuts a slice of peach cobbler for the goddess and pours a generous glass of milk. She even leaves a note, though her writing is nearly an indecipherable scrawl: *Thanks for the peaches.* She leaves the dessert and drink on the kitchen table.

Deep past midnight but long before the first light of dawn, the goddess of peaches slips unseen and unheard into the girl's kitchen. She sits at the table with a proper fork, all smiles for half a minute before realizing the girl did not leave, as requested, a slice of pie.

"*Cobbler,*" the goddess says between clenched teeth. She sighs, leaves the fork on the plate, and drinks the milk. She examines the letter disdainfully. From the fridge, she retrieves all the rest of the pie—and the cobbler—and also takes all the peaches the girl didn't use.

It's a small punishment, but a girl of that age doesn't yet deserve to be transformed into a field mouse. The goddess leaves the slice of cobbler untouched on the table and disappears into the night.

A SLICE OF REFLECTION UNDER A TWILIT SKY

Four people. Watch them walk the deserted highways, amid the dust, the burnt husks of automobiles of a lost era. They taste salt on the air. The wind is stronger here. The trees still green. There's green, still, in other places, but not like this. Here, it's verdant and vivid and blisteringly saturated. It's unreal.

Behind them, they've left their troubles, their worries, their dead, and their struggles. There's nothing left to fight for, nothing to care about, nothing to savor, nothing to hold onto. Except maybe each other. Except maybe hope. The very idea causes short, derisive snorts between them when they eat. Pickings are slim. Dried meats. Tasteless berries from fields overrun by wasps and ants, fields still protected by barbed wire, rust, and rotted wood. Citrus grows wildly, abundantly even, but it's mostly been affected. Turned. Stricken by a white fungus so that the inside, through the rinds, of even the biggest of grapefruits, is powdered and poisonous. No one eats the oranges.

Four people wandering. The last four? Perhaps. They don't know. But they've seen signs. Indications, you might say. Suggestions and hints and innuendos. Messages left on the sides of barns in Alabama. White rocks collected on I-10 in the form of arrows pointing eastward. East, and then south, a series of guide stones. A series of little hopes dotting the road.

A young father who couldn't save his family.

A girl, barely a teenager, talented with a switchblade and quick with her thieving fingers.

A matron, perhaps too young to be a grandmother, too old to be spry, too wise to be ignored.

An old man, a centenarian, as capable as any man one-half his age.

They have names. Had names. When once they knew how to speak, they used names. But their throats are dry now, withered and useless, shrunken things beneath their skin. They persist because they must. What else should they do? Settle in one of the houses, one of the structures that might fall with the next strong gale, in which they would not be safe from coyotes or bears or ravens?

No. They are called by the sea. Guided by the vestiges of hope. Little hope. Little ideas that someone, maybe someone still alive, a fifth person or a whole other tribe of peoples, laid out their path. They follow the source of the rising sun. They cross a long unused bridge from which they can see abandoned sail boats and seafood restaurants and little beaches. Over the Halifax River, there's only a little strip of land separating them from the Atlantic. The endless, fathomless ocean. Already, they hear its quiet roar. They taste the salt water on the air. And sugar.

They taste sugar.

It quickens their steps. They pass abandoned car lots and strip clubs and tourist shops before they reach a concrete gate. Through that, they achieve sand. Ocean. Beach. A place where once upon a time, cars raced up and down the shoreline, turtles crawled into the ocean, college kids drank copious supplies of beer, loves were won and lost and pretended, skin was leathered, sunrise photos were taken with lenses cheap and expensive, teenagers guarded lives from raised wooden thrones, and enormous castles were erected in the sand.

And there, too, just to the north, on the boardwalk, the rides of yesteryear remain upright, including a Ferris wheel, a lighted wheel, blinking and flashing.

Four of them walk, but now at different speeds, each according to their ability and their desire. The girl reaches it first. She climbs aboard, though there's no one to operate the controls. Still, her carriage moves so the next, the matron, can climb alone into her own car. It rocks gently. She sees the girl is no longer alone. The girl is with her mom. The girl has always had her mom, in her head or in her heart or in her soul. And the matron now has her lover, her teenage love lost, the boy next door with the fast car and that haircut and such a heartbreakingly gorgeous smile.

The young father helps the centenarian across the sand. They reach the Ferris wheel, which has moved two carriages, and they know they're each meant to board their own. The centenarian touches the young father's shoulder reassuringly. Pats it. Lowers his head. Cracks his voice for the first time in forever and says, "You did what you could. For them. For us. For yourself. You should be proud." It takes a long time to say, the words all gravel and granules; then the old man climbs into the gondola and pulls the door shut behind him. He doesn't look back, and the young father, alone now on the pier, allows him the privacy of his own memories.

The next car comes. The door opens easily. But the man pauses. He checks his breath. Maybe he no longer needs it, no longer uses it, no longer takes in the air that sustains him. He lets all of it out slowly, a final sigh, and boards the Ferris wheel. To find his wife. His young wife in a yellow bikini, just as she'd worn when they'd come to this beach for Spring Break. Their son, his lips far too red, cotton candy smeared all of his face. The boy's eyes sparkle. His smile, already big, swells, and he throws his arms around his father's legs. To the boy, his father seems impossibly old. Only the boy is young. Only the day. Only the hour.

The operator, unseen and unheard, shuts the cabin door and sets the wheel in motion. A calliope plays. The lights flash. From the apex, even in the long twilight, when the shadow of the wheel stretches far across the horizon, you can see forever.

The Museum of Curiosities

ONE MORE STORY

The storymaster sits in her office twirling a fountain pen around her fingers and staring at the clouds. They're fluffy now, but getting darker on the edges of the horizon. The winds are picking up. A storm is brewing.

Storms brew in her head, too. The storymaster sips her wine—time simply doesn't matter to her anymore—while in her head, pirates sail through warzones, fair maidens transform like phoenixes into heroines, swordsmen are challenged, spies uncovered, marriages shattered, soulmates found, treasures buried, and aliens descend upon an unsuspecting earth intent on—well, nothing good, that's for sure.

The storymaster smiles. She loves a bit of conflict in the morning. It excites the senses. Primes the pumps.

The pen is loaded with an ink called oxblood. The shade of her lipstick matches. She's dressed up this morning, in anticipation of her visitor, and wearing jewelry—or at least a necklace and earrings. It's her best red dress, though she knows her story isn't a romance. That's not always the fate of the storymaster.

She takes the last swallow of wine. As she sets the empty glass on the table, there's a knock at the door.

Hers is a small room with plenty of windows, though it lets in too much of the cold during the season. She says, "It's open." She doesn't bother to get up.

He walks in with authority and purpose—which makes sense, considering his position as overseer of the storymasters. He wears an impeccable suit; she knows he also dresses up to visit her. It's a monthly dance. She almost never sees him, or anyone else, otherwise. Storymasters are frequently ostracized like hermits.

He doesn't shut the door, doesn't take the seat opposite her, just opens his ledger and says, "It's time."

"So soon?"

"It's been..." He scans the paperwork, just to be sure. "A long time."

"I suppose."

"You've done well here."

"I always thought I'd have time for one more."

"You will," he says, snapping the ledger shut. "You're being promoted to editorial."

"I thought I'd have one more story," she says again.

"You'll remain in Story," he tells her.

"Yes, but I won't be creating them anymore."

He raises an eyebrow. It's a trick he probably learned from *Star Trek*. "You'll be assigned an apprentice," he says. "Under your guidance, he'll become a storymaster himself. He will tell his stories with your influence. Through him, your stories will continue to be told, but they'll also be his stories."

"I understand that," she says with a sigh. She sets the fountain pen down on the blank pages on her desk. A single drop of oxblood slips like a tear from its nib and splashes. "Oh, look," she says. "I've stained the paper with ink. Surely, I should at least finish this story."

The overseer bends to look at the blank page with the inkstain. "That's not a beginning."

"Oh, but it is."

He takes a breath. He nods curtly. Once. He says, "Just one more," then walks out.

But the storymaster has more than one story to tell, and she has a month to tell them...

PENPALS

In a hole in the ground, there lived a great, ugly beast with teeth like stalactites and breath like rancid meat. Not a clean, comfortable home with tea kettles and pipes, but a wicked, nasty place filled with creeping crawling insects, vermin defying description, and the bones of those dead, buried, and forgotten. Sometimes, the beast picked its teeth with those discarded human shards. It liked the sounds of Beethoven but also Concrete Blonde, and it could often be found dancing in cemeteries under the moonlight.

Make no mistake: it was a deep hole, easily fifty meter deep, a series of interconnected and mostly natural caves, and the tendrils of caves, snaking into the earth and emerging in unlikely places.

One of those places was Kerri's basement.

But Kerri never told anyone. As a child, she left pints of milk and sometimes cookies for the beast, and when the mood struck, she wrote letters. When she was in kindergarten, her letters were short and poorly spelled and scratched out in crayon; the scent of that wax permeated the basement and drifted through the beast's underworld labyrinth. In middle school, she complained about the other girls; and in high school, she got all sorts of philosophical about the boys in her class.

When she moved away for college and discovered certain truths about herself, she continued writing letters, explaining how she'd grown and what she'd learned. She dropped these into a hole near the lake.

But some holes led to other places. The creature who received these letters licked its reptilian lips and molted, leaving a gossamer-thin rendering of its original form, before slithering from its depths. Near the lake, holes into the underworld were muddy and slimy and slick, filled with the odors of rotten fish.

Unlike the beast, the creature had never danced under the moon, and had never consumed snickerdoodles in a child's basement. Instead, it supplicated its unseen tentacled gods and trawled for flounder and butterfish. It tired of its seafood diet. It desired something from the turf side of the menu.

After intercepting a half dozen letters over the course of a year, the creature emerged and would have howled, but reptilian throats were not meant for howling. It crawled over blacktop and under moonlight which singed its flesh.

The college dorm housed hundreds of delicious morsels, but the creature sought to satisfy a particular taste. No quantity of students would quench its yearning if it couldn't find the woman who wrote about awakenings and mathematics and literature and the women who enraptured her. The edifice was square and brick and tall. The creature couldn't comprehend doors or hallways or elevators, having never navigated such things before, and somehow found itself descending deeper than elevators were meant to go.

When the doors slid open with a tinny bing, its reptilian mouth would have watered. It was ready to consume flesh and meat and bone. No more fish and chips, no more lobster specials, no more crabfests and popcorn shrimp.

Instead of a floor filled with college students, instead of study halls or television lounges or laundry equipment, instead of storage cages filled with the detritus of students decades gone, the creature found the beast.

"You've been stealing my mail," the beast said. Its claws were sharp, its teeth impressive, its anger palpable. Outside of the water, the creature was unable to defend itself.

When the elevator rose again to student levels, it required a thorough cleaning. The scent of crayons and peanut butter cookies lingered beneath the fishy stench that took weeks to dispel.

In her next letter, Kerri complained about the weird smell. The beast sent a response via the post office. Its handwriting was atrocious, and its spelling awkward at best, but the beast advising her to avoid certain lakeside holes and directed her to a hole in her dorm's basement through which her letters would reach it unobstructed.

STONE GODS AND GHOST BRIDES

It sleeps. And as it sleeps, it dreams. In its mind: images of distant worlds, remembrances, dormant desires, the whirling colors and sounds of the darkest abyss, a womb in which galaxies vie for shape. In moments of darkness, of abject terror, it relives its arrival on this planet, then a molten ball of coalescing gas and ice, before life, and it's pulled once again toward the dense core, that rock, that metal, that absurd gravitational fluctuation.

It sleeps, and it dreams, and it likes to dream because nightmares aren't constant and there are other things to remember, but a day will come when the dreams cease and it opens its eyes once again.

It's never truly dark near the city. At night, the city glows, and the stars in the sky glow, and her eyes find and reflect all that light like a cat's. But the car's headlights blaze, and when they cut through the darkness they make everything around them dark by contrast. Made vulnerable in that intrusive beam of light, Elenora, Nora to everyone she knows, kneels in the white gravel on the side of the road. The hum of her engine, a distant nightbird, these are the sounds as she stares at the body.

She almost didn't see it. It's dark. It's a swelling, winding road a good number of miles into the woods outside Richmond. But even on the highway's shoulder, the corpse caught her attention. It's small, a bird, but arranged in a particular way with its broken wings spread and the rocks in a circle around it. There's one drop of blood, one sign the bird struggled. It's not a nighttime creature, so it was brought here, against its will, still alive until possibly moments ago. She feels its warmth, not physically but spiritually, as if something of the bird remains. Holding a hand above it, she says some words to comfort its journey to whatever's next. She doesn't know what happens to a bird's soul. It's not something she's given much thought to. Three more feathers form a triangle around it, but those came from another bird somewhere else, a bird that maybe didn't have to die but probably did.

Nora doesn't believe in omens. This is no omen, merely an indication of activity.

At the car, leaning against the passenger door, invisible behind the headlights, Blake yawns exaggeratedly and asks, "Have you found something important?"

She doesn't immediately answer. She looks out into the dark, as though she might see the trail of footsteps away from the bird, as though she could intuit the make of their shoes or their height from the length of their step. The gravel offers no clues, no evidence, no suggestions whatsoever, yet in the distance, not quite against the horizon but rising above the tree line, she sees an old, old house with a single light in its uppermost tower. Sometimes, it's best to trust her gut.

"Triangles," she says, possibly to Blake but at least aloud. She stands and hurries back to the car.

"This is the edge of one?"

"They're making a sacrifice," she tells him.

"And you want to get in the middle of it?"

"Where's your sense of adventure, Blake?" She hits the gas. The car sprays gravel behind them as she retakes the road.

"Let me at least put on the right music," he says. But he doesn't, of course. He pumps "John the Revelator" through the car stereo, which would maybe be perfect at some other time.

Nora drives through the labyrinthine backroads between abandoned farms and skeletal houses and church graveyards. When the song ends, Blake rolls down his window and leans back in this seat. He thinks everything's a game and always has. Probably why she loves him. She hopes he won't die tonight. She hopes that every time.

She follows the streets past a decrepit schoolhouse and a general store that had briefly, sometime around 1972, been a gas station, and finally finds the road with the house. It's not a nose, just a good, solid sense of direction and an appreciation for the structure of roads. These aren't well kept, filled with holes and grooves. As she nears the house, the asphalt peters out to become hard dirt and dust. A dozen cars are parked outside the house. The party's already under way.

She kills the headlights and gets out of the car to check the moon. It's not really full anymore. It was full half a day ago and it's starting to wane. Blake shuts his door with a little more noise than she'd prefer, but he also shows her his gun as he hides it in the holster under his jacket. He throws her a wink and a smile before they approach the house.

Once, someone or something tried to wake it from its dreams. They did a thing absurd, whatever it was, but couldn't rouse him from the flickerings of the nebulae it once called home. It was old when this world was young, and it wouldn't be aroused for a mere blood offering. No chants, no ancient sigils, nothing on this world would force it from its dreams.

It sits on a throne in a cave deep beneath the surface, where it has sat before the world changed, and before the world changed again. Though creatures have reached through the crevasses to find and know it, they have failed. They have made stories about it, they have made religions over it, they have worshipped and feared and trusted it. They have rut in its shadow and they have prostrated themselves and they have promised the world.

But when it does wake, when it eventually opens its eyes, it won't want this world except perhaps as food. It will consume this and its sister worlds and maybe its sun, and it will return to the expanse, to the darkness between the stars.

Once, someone tried to wake it, and others try to wake it now, and they offer trivial flesh and blood and bone. They call so very loudly he might just rise to extinguish them.

Ellen opens her eyes but there's nothing to see but the inside of a blindfold. The cloth is silk or satin, something smooth and cool, something not entirely uncomfortable, but it's layered and dark and blots out any light.

Her arms are tied by the wrists, her legs by the ankles. She feels exposed. Naked. Vulnerable. She feels as though all her secrets have been stripped away. She pulls, but the tethers are strong, and though they feel like they are lined to keep the metal from cutting into her wrists, they sound like chains.

Ellen tries to speak, but her mouth is gagged. She tries to scream, but can barely pull in a full breath. She hears singing. No, she hears chanting. All around her. As though she's bound to an altar in the middle of a cultist circle. Which, she realizes, as memory floods back to her, is exactly where she is.

She tries to scream and struggle more, but it's no use, and there's no one to help her. She knows who circles around her. Though the words they use are older than any language on earth, she knows the words, and she knows the meaning, and she knows what will happen next.

They will cut her open and expose her blood and organs, the ultimate revelation of her. She isn't ready, she isn't worthy, but she knows what is happening and she knows why her head aches and she knows why her mouth is dry.

They've been preparing her for this.

They've kept her in a cage in a room at the top of the house. There was a window, but she could never throw herself from it because there were always chains. There was a window, but she could never see anyone else in the world because she could only see the sky and the birds and sometimes the moon or the sun, the most apathetic of celestials.

She can name them, the cultists, the men and women in robes. Stan, who would touch her, but she would bite at him and the others would laugh. Damon, who would tell her over and over again how the stone god would take her as its bride and repopulate the earth with all their stone children, and she would be the mother of gods. Nancy, who would bring soup and tell her nothing mattered anyway, especially not these sacks of bone and blood, and it would all be over soon. Deidre, who said nothing, who maybe couldn't speak, who maybe now only mouths the ancient words, who had hoped to be the sacrifice and had slipped poison into Ellen's meals three times, who only ever looked at Ellen through the side of her eyes.

Ellen struggles. She screams. It's useless, and she knows it's useless, but she also knows they are insane and the stone god, the stone thing in their basement, is maybe an old sculpture from an unknown civilization but is not a celestial being waiting for a perfection of galactic alignments to rise.

That doesn't matter, because they will cut her open anyway, they will withdraw each of her organs, her spleen and her liver and her kidneys, her stomach and lungs and heart, and the best she can hope is that her nerves fail and she'll cease to feel pain because she knows, without doubt, without hope, that it will be excruciating. She has seen their scalpels and their knives and their scoops and their saws. They had loved to show her these things.

I don't want to die, I don't want to die, she says over and over inside her head. But the cadence of her mantra falls in step with the rhythm of their chanting, and without even realizing it she is reciting their words instead and just hoping it would end soon. Under the blindfold, she closes her eyes. That way, at least, she's choosing not to see.

The first touch of the scalpel is cold. It's enough to stop her struggling. The world, the universe, becomes the tip of that blade. It cuts smoothly, but not deeply, from the bottom of her throat to the top of her bladder. Her blood is warm. She hopes that will be the last thing she feels. She's not so fortunate.

Nora and Blake climb the porch of the old house. She feels, rather than hears, the rhythmic chanting from inside. The sounds resonates through the floorboards, coming up from the basement rather than down from the tower. It's a big house with a wraparound porch, chairs, a swing, a doorknocker in the shape of an eagle's head. The curtains are drawn. There's no light inside. There's every need for caution.

She doesn't knock. She's not stupid. She tries the door, but it's locked. She walks around one side of the porch, Blake around the other, looking through windows and checking any doors. The porch goes all the way around. They're at the top of a hill. No other houses are in the immediate vicinity, but rooftops can be seen rolling toward and away from the city. The porch obscures some of the moonlight, but otherwise the night is as bright as ever. The Milky Way is rarely this vibrant so close to a city. There's not a single cloud up there.

Around to the back porch, she finds a locked door leading into the kitchen. She sees dishes piled in the sink, skillets on the stove, and a mess of plates and wine glasses still on the countertop, but no one's visible.

She knows it's the right place. This isn't just intuition. She's adept at this sort of thing. She's faced the monsters in the dark before, so she recognizes the subtlest signs, the ozone odor drifting through the cracks under the door, the way the interior shadows fold in on themselves. She'd have to go back to the car to get tools to pick the lock, but there's no need. The back door opens when she turns the knob. She enters.

Inside, the air is still and stagnant. The scents of dinner linger, roasted meat of some sort, red wine, blood. She doesn't bother closing the door. Through the kitchen, she sees the dining room table has been cleared but not cleaned. The lingering smells of a wood fire strike as she enters the living room. There's a big television over the fireplace, two couches and a number of chairs, and a large bookshelf that is all of one wall. She peruses the titles, finding exactly what she expects. A false copy of *The Book of Lost Fates*. A facsimile of *The Necronomicon*, though the faint photocopied pages are illegible in the dark. Non-fiction accounts of vampires in New Orleans and werewolves in London and witches in Prague.

She hears the ghost before she sees it.

The pale ghost drifts near another doorway, her face hidden by a veil, a jilted bride perhaps, whose history will be lost with the house. The ghost doesn't really move except in the way that the ocean moves, in and out, toward and away all at once. This door is closed. It's old. It's wood and unpainted. And it's been opened recently. Nora can practically see the fingerprints on the handle.

"Are you a warning?" Nora asks in a whisper, "or a guide?"

The ghost doesn't look at Nora and doesn't pull back the veil. Nora steps tentatively toward the ghost, but she drifts away entirely, through or into the wood, with the barest echo of a screech like a subway train still a mile away.

With caution and without speed, Nora opens the basement door.

The chanting becomes immediately louder and more distinct, but the door makes not even a whisper of a creak. Nora listens to the words. They're old, they're being mispronounced, and they're utterly unnecessary for whatever it is they think they're doing.

If they were just playing at something, Nora might not care, but she's got an obligation to fulfill, and whether they're right or accurate doesn't matter. They're serious. Intention is vital, integral, the only important element, and their intention pulses through their chant like blood through the veins.

There's also the smell of fresh blood, which Nora cannot abide.

It sleeps and it dreams and it listens with perhaps one ear but it won't open its eyes. They're out there again, insufferable, uninspired, inconsequential little things, offering a bride through her blood, as though such a thing might be of interest when there are pulsars and gas fields and liquid space and globules and starbursts not too different from the first bursts and interstellar clouds and emissions.

It feels lonely, not because of the bride, not in response to the chanting, but because of the things it hasn't seen and the places it hasn't been throughout its slumber. Perhaps a reawakening would be worthwhile. Venture again into the cosmic voids, through the expanse, find the others and spawn a new existence or a new series of existences.

Have they also found rocks to sleep in, planetary tombs to pass the eons and end the monotony? Do they search for others like themselves?

With this sacrifice, these little things call to it, these little things utterly without purpose and without hope and without spirit, but something has changed. There's been a shift of molecules and energy. There's a light, a source of light, a source of heat unlike the others, as though a piece of itself exists within her.

It sleeps, and it dreams, but its dreams are coming to an end.

The first thing Nora sees is the girl with the open chest on the altar and funerary buckets carrying her organs and the masked man withdrawing a kidney. The man wears a golden mask on top of the same crimson robes everyone else wears. He's the leader, the high priest, and when he sees Nora he smiles audibly. "You're too late," he says. "The Stone God rumbles already."

But the stone god, the statue behind him, the ancient and abstract chunk of rock, which maybe a moment before trembled with internal activity, goes quiet and still. One by one, the chanters stop, as if realizing the efforts are in vain. One removes her hood as she looks in Nora's direction. Another shakes his head.

"We've almost purified the body," the high priest says.

Blake shoots him.

Blake, who descended so quietly behind Nora she never heard him, gives the priest a third bloody eye. It's a reaction, of course, to the scene, the girl on the altar, the blood and viscera and surgical apparatuses. The crack of the gunshot rings in Nora's ears, kills any chance of another sound reaching her, and might even be loud enough to wake the dead. Or sleeping stone gods from before humanity.

The high priest is thrown backwards. The kidney in his hands hits the altar, slides, and falls to the floor. The girl on the altar screams. It's the only thing Nora hears over the echoes of the bullet. The other red robes scatter into the shadows of the basement, which is at least as large as the house and probably extends into tunnels that weave through the guts of this hill that might once have been a mountain into tunnels unnatural but not made by human hands.

The stone god, the statue, the abstraction of a thing not of this earth, trembles again. Above, the house shivers, and maybe the whole mountain with it. Dishes fall, pictures leap off the walls, and the books in the bookshelf collapse. The house cracks, here in the basement and stretching all the way to that upper room where the light still burns. Without that light, Nora might not have noticed the house, and might still be wondering about the dead bird on the side of the road. Bricks fall. Supports in the ceiling split and rupture.

From the darkness, one of the cultists rushes forward with a machete. Blake stops him with a single shot. Nora never draws a weapon because she knows it's not necessary. She casts a spell of protection, something meant to save her and Blake from the dying house.

Another gunshot, a different kind of sound, more distant and thunderous, interrupts her spell and kills Blake.

It wakes. It opens its eyes. It sees the supplicants through the darkness, and the bride they offer, and the interlopers, and none matter except the woman, the woman on the steps, the woman with the hint of empyrean expanse at the core of her atomic structure. It inhales, for the first time in a hundred million years, it draws breath into its lungs and reaches for the woman and rises from its throne.

And it crumbles. Even as it moves, the stone, the calcification of its body and spirit, crumbles like chalk and falls away as dust. It scrapes against itself, its ancient self, its celestial self, and the movement of its physical body grinds it into power that drifts, meaningless, insubstantial, into the collapsing house. It reaches for the woman anyway, as though she might save it, as though she might prevent what was impossible but is now inevitable. It opens its mouth to scream. The movement unhinges its jaw. Pieces of it dissipate and drift away until there's nothing but the thought that once there was something, once there was something else, once there was something more but now there's nothing but dust, vulnerable, exposed, and scattered.

After the house collapses, only Ellen still breathes. She breathes because they never reached her lungs. They never took her heart. They left her bound to the altar in the basement, and brisk air from outside scratches at her now because the house itself has fallen away and apart. She's alive because of some spell, some magic, some trick that was never meant to be contrived. She's bound and gagged and blindfolded and still alive though half her insides have been extracted, and her nerves register the sensation of every missing blood vessel, every shorn organ, every drop of blood. And the ghost of the house, the bride, who used to drift into Ellen's room and cry, lies next to her now as soft as breath against her body on fire. The ghost whispers, "It's over now. It's over."

But it's not. For a long time, Ellen will linger, and the pain only intensifies, and even when the medics arrive they can't release her from the altar. It's become a part of her, or she a part of it. When they remove the gag, she has no words to speak, and when they remove the blindfold, there's nothing to see but the eternal expanse.

MOON'S HOLLOW

Constructing new moons wasn't always difficult. It required flat tin and scissors capable of cutting through it. Circles proved tough, but Cade could do it because he'd gotten a lot of practice making hearts when he was young and foolish and romantic. Engraving was the easy part, so faces were never a problem for him. He only had to make two decisions: the shape of the eye, and the shape of the lips. Those were usually easy because he almost always knew who the moon would later belong to. He went through a lot of yellow paint, but today's moon was red, a deep dark red like the wine on special harvest nights.

The town was called Moon's Hollow long before he ever came around. He was born here out of providence. And though he had more or less mastered the art of crafting tin moons and scribbling poetic nonsense in his little black book, he had not yet found his Destiny. The one with the capital D. It waited out there beyond the edges of his peripheral vision. He knew he might have to leave Moon's Hollow to discover it; he understood the shape of stories. The right occasion hadn't yet presented itself. Anyway, Carmen—the girl he'd been in love with since they were children, the woman for whom he'd cast a net to drag down the real moon from the sky, the very impression of his dreams, with her utterly beautiful face and honey bourbon voice and hair like the night itself—was visiting her parents again. She had moved far away to study. This was only the second time she was returning. The last time, she had kissed him under the light of the moon.

He gave this burgundy moon a heart-like shape and heart-like lips. He used the yellow paint to represent the gold in her eyes. He poured his heart into the etching. He worked deep into the night, and in the morning reviewed the work, examining it for blemishes, any indication he had done something wrong. He had included clockworks because they kept the rhythms. He had added images on the inside, sea dragons and lovers on rowboats and shooting stars, in an attempt to recapture memories of stories they used to tell each other. Once upon a time, they had been kids together, running through the forest, dancing and singing with the twilight birds, racing toward their various destinies.

He wrapped the moon in yellow tissue paper and a thin box. He carried it under his arm as he strode through town. He smiled and said good morning to the baker's wife outside the bakery. He greeted the teacher as he passed the school. He even helped Mr. Crane descend his porch; the old man needed support on steps, even when there were only two. Cade practically danced through the street. His heart was light, the sun was bright, and Carmen's car was already outside her parent's home.

He went straight up to the door and knocked.

Carmen herself answered. She looked at Cade's face, then at the box, then back to his eyes, and she smiled sadly when she said his name. "Cade." Not like a curse, but without enthusiasm and without verve. "Cade, you should meet my new husband, Julian. He's from the north."

Cade went through the motions. He was cordial. He shook Julian's hand, and told stories of how he and Carmen had played hide and seek in the wheat fields when they were ten. He stayed for a good long time, but declined when her mother asked him to stay for dinner. He left the burgundy moon, claiming it was a wedding gift, but when he left he walked around the edges of the village, the longest roads possible, before returning home. He didn't feel like smiling, and he didn't feel like talking with any of the other villagers. In fact, he thought it was far past time he should strike out into the world and finally discover his Destiny. The one with the capital D.

He wandered until nightfall. The moon smiled sadly upon him but offered no comfort. He kicked pebbles. He sat on a tree stump and pondered all the great mysteries.

Maybe he fell asleep there, and all the things he experienced after were part of an elaborate dream. The airships, the lightning wranglers, the sky bandits brandishing flintlock pistols—maybe none of that was real. The statues in the graveyard, the widow on her nightly walk, the spirits who sometimes accompanied him on his loneliest walks—maybe they were nothing more than his imagination. Maybe his Destiny, even with a capital D, had never been anything more than making tin moons and pining for lost loves. Carmen was merely the hardest of them to accept—and the most final.

Maybe there had never been an *Iglesia de Maria*, and the *Opéra de Fantôme* never existed, and the *Karlův most* didn't cross the *Vltava*. Who could say? A day came, years later, when Cade found himself back in Moon's Hollow. Older, he was not quite old yet. His house had been taken over by a family of strangers. His shop had been taken down; the foundation had always been weak. He took a room in the Hollow Inn, but Mrs. Gilly had been old when he was young and she didn't remember him, not by face and not by name. She brought wine to his room when he asked for it, and he sat there pondering all the great mysteries. There were so many still to be uncovered.

The next day, he went to the house where Carmen had grown up. Her parents lived there still. They welcomed him into their home and, when they invited him to stay for dinner, he accepted. He regaled them with stories that couldn't possibly be true about his travels through distant and foreign lands. They told him about Carmen, how she and her husband had grown to a family of five, how she taught school in a faraway town. He asked them not to tell him where. He didn't want to disturb her. He was merely pleased she was happy.

Back at the Hollow Inn, he couldn't think, and the wine didn't help him. So instead, he went for a walk, a long walk around the village, taking the least used and longest roads. He found a familiar tree stump, where he had once sat and thought, and seemed still to be sitting there.

And there, the two men talked, Cade of the future and Cade of the past. They talked of rivers of yellow, white, and red. They talked of dusty roads and rainswept plains and, yes, tin moons. "I miss the moons of my youth," the older Cade said.

"I'll make one more, then," the younger Cade promised, "and bring it with me, tomorrow, when I leave."

When the younger Cade left the tree stump, he went to his shop and fashioned one last moon. He cut it, and gave it Carmen's lips but the eye of someone he hadn't yet met. He painted the moon yellow, the usual color, and gave the eye and lips a hint of burgundy. In the morning, later than the last time, he left his home in a rickety old tin lizzie that needed a fresh splash of yellow paint itself. And since the older Cade had gone east, he went west. There he would find deserts and mountains and cities beyond imagination, and perhaps his Destiny, the one with the capital D.

The Museum of Curiosities

BURN BABY BURN

Once upon a time, humankind had a different understanding of science. Physics were entirely the realm of gods, and none of those gods were so great as the sun king. Over centuries and millennia, some such beliefs were lost to myth and legend.

Eric still clung to some of those beliefs. He believed aliens had been visiting his cousins in the middle of the country. He believed mermaids lived under the docks but only came out when no one was around to see them. He believed the sun was a chariot driven by Apollo.

Sometimes, he took pictures of the sun because it was hard to look at directly. He used the best camera equipment he could find, starting with a 110mm camera from a garage sale when he was a kid, later a Polaroid, a 35mm Minolta, and eventually a high resolution digital camera with long, long lenses that allowed him to get real close.

He understood optics, the ways of light waves and mirrors and lenses. And he had a unique grasp of color theory. But as far as Eric and his father and his father before him were concerned, things like astronomy were the purviews of greater beings.

When his mother died, he attended the funeral and cursed the lack of rain. He believed all funerals were meant to be accompanied by rain. He had acquired an umbrella special for the occasion. His father made some off-hand comment, while shading his eyes from the intensity of the sun, about Apollo laughing up there on his chariot.

"Why would he laugh?" Eric wanted to know. "Does he mock us?"

The truth was, Eric never saw Apollo laugh. He never saw Apollo cry, smile, grin, or wink, either. Simply put, Eric never saw Apollo. He and his father went home from the funeral to a house filled with foods other people cooked and flowers like a Biblical plague—and an endless procession of aunts, cousins, and neighbors pointing out how much better off his mother was. No more suffering. No more worrying. With God now, or with the gods, or at least no longer trapped amongst the rest of us on this godforsaken rock hurtling uncontrollably through space to who knows what sort of end.

None of these words brought Eric comfort.

He stayed up through the night with the best of his friends. Jack Daniels. Jim Beam. Evan Williams. Usually, he just drank beer, but tonight felt special. In the morning, when the first thin strip of red slashed the eastern horizon, Eric snuck into his father's gun safe and retrieved a rather formidable high-powered rifle. He climbed the trellis to the roof of his house, and then to the highest point. Since his house sat near the top of the hill, this gave him a good bit of height. He might have been a little unsteady on his feet, but the scope had all the telephoto capability of his longest camera lenses.

The sun peeked over the edge as the chariot left the stables, Apollo with his whip yelling to the celestial steeds. By now, the damn horses knew the route. Was he laughing, this sun king, shining with all the strength of all the stars the morning after Eric's mother had been put in the ground?

The sun rose a little further. Not much. Eric didn't want to give it too much time. Too high, he'd never be able to reach it. He understood, at least in the deepest crevices of his mind, velocity and distance. He propped the rifle on the apex of the rooftop, laid in such a way that he could keep his body still as a gravestone on a windless night. He got the tip of the sun in his sights. He took a breath, brought his finger to the trigger, let the breath out slowly. He didn't take another, not yet, not whilst he aimed. He pulled the trigger.

It was an armor piercing bullet capable of penetrating the skins of tanks. It was a long, powerful jacket of steel. He knew he'd only get the one shot. But he also knew he'd only need one. The bullet tore through the side of that chariot with a sound that thundered across the eastern seaboard. The rifle kicked at his shoulder something fierce and probably bruised him. The gunshot rang in his ears and maybe shattered something inside him. He wanted to pull the trigger again.

But there was no need.

The sun plummeted from the sky. It was way off, on the horizon, probably two or three miles distant. The giant fireball that was the sun crashed into the earth. Its horses scattered. The concussive shockwave rocked Eric on top of his house. The daylights went out, replaced by a sudden inferno in the east.

In fact, the fires were spreading, and would continue to spread, but Eric didn't know this. He looked through the scope, trying to make out details of the flames and the horses, of the shattered chariot, something. He saw mostly ash and soot pluming into the air and a cloud of smoke undulating toward him. The smoke made him nervous. He knew he couldn't inhale that thick gray miasma, but his gas mask was down in the basement. With the speed the smoke was moving, the basement was a lifetime away. He hadn't properly planned for this. He should have anticipated such a consequence. He took three deep breaths: one for practice, a second to see him down the stairs, a third because he didn't think the second had been good enough.

Before he could use that breath, before he could manage a single step down the steep side of his rooftop, Apollo arrived, Apollo in all his glory, orange and yellow and red, angry—no, not merely angry, but furious and enraged.

"What have you done?" Apollo demanded. It was a rhetorical question. The sun king knew damn well what Eric had done, and why—and he was no longer laughing, was he? Not a chuckle. Not a snigger or a snicker.

The sun king burned the house, with Eric and Eric's father and all the leftover funerary foods, to the core, so that only a pile of ash remained, and drifting smoke, and cinders, and the body of Eric, the god hunter, still alive and agonizingly breathing, crisp and suffering though he was.

The Museum of Curiosities

The Life of a Poet

The poet toils.

He works in the deepest of pits with a pickaxe and a shovel and a whip at his back. He expected a life of roses and champagne baths. Though sometimes he's called on for a word or phrase, it's almost always labor, hard labor, and backbreaking ceaseless drudgery.

It's not so bad, what it does to his back—which hurts every day, morning and night, even as he sleeps. And it's not so bad that his eyes strain to see through the darkness, and those few times he's brought into the light he has to squint against its intensity.

It's the layers of his soul they peel away every day. With an apple peeler. Like an onion skin.

He's a poet, though, and he's learned a great many things in his life, which at this point seems to have been much longer than it's been. One of those things: he will always have further, deeper layers to be scraped away.

He doesn't even see the point. What do they do with the rocks he liberates from this mine? They keep him isolated, except for his tormentors, who are regularly changed because they fear his charm and conniving.

But he's lost all touch with concepts of charm.

He's lost contact with the cleverest parts of himself.

He can't even write about sunlight and beaches anymore except as fairy tales and myths.

He can, however, write about rocks: marble and slate, limestone and granite, copper and iron and lead. They don't give him pens, so he scratches the words into his thighs. He's gotten good with the edge of that pickaxe. It doesn't dig too deep. There's not a lot of blood. He keeps the lettering tight. It doesn't hurt as much as the alternative.

Every eight hours, there's someone new to punish him, but the jailors quickly grow bored with him. He can take their whips. He can take their barbs. He's used to extremes of hot and cold, sharp and blunt, even the fingers and ribs they sometimes break just to hear the cracks.

They make him work through those pains. They give him no choice. In a way, his jailors, his tormentors, his guardian angels, are like muses, and the digging has become the new work. He taps out rhythms that make phrases in his mind, and sometimes he thinks he can see the benevolent moon, so thick and bright yellow and brisk.

ΤΗΕ ΜUSEUΜ OF CURIOSITIES

He's taken up an elevator shaft to an underground office to make a word. They need something new, something that's never been written before, something never imagined. He tries to give them something Latin, but he knows that won't work, so instead he reaches through other tongues and comes up with a beautiful sounding phrase in Mandarin. He'll never admit what it really means.

And then he's taken away to return to his digging.

"Wait," the man at the desk says, noticing the way the poet walks, the weight of the twisted muscles on his back, the blood stains on his pants. He calls the poet back and demands that he's stripped to the skin. The man examines the letters, the words, the phrases. They're all across the poet's body now as though they've been tattooed into his tattered soul.

That's the day they put him on display. They contain the poet, cold and naked, behind a glass partition, then parade spectators around him. He's just a carnival exhibit. He can smell the littlest pony and the bearded lady and the sword swallower in adjacent cells. His muscles get soft because he's no longer working the mines. His eyes refuse to adjust to the changing lights as doors open and close between exhibitions. But they make him the star of the show, if only for a little while, and they love him. He hardly notices the irons around his ankles and wrists. They've given him a table and a fountain pen and ink, and they've commanded that he write until his last word is used up.

The audience gawks. They tap the glass sometimes to catch his attention. They point and laugh, and mothers threaten their children that this is how they'll end up if they're not careful. On occasion, on rare occasions only, he sees something through the glass: a spark of light behind the eyes of someone there to witness him. He feels seen, if only for that moment, and knows he isn't alone.

Even if he's alone in the glass cell.

Even if he's alone in the spotlight.

Even if, when they decide the last of his good words have all been taken, they'll drag him back to the mines, to the pit, to the pickaxe and the whips.

BOURBON GOTHIC

She could smell the Mississippi mud from her balcony overlooking Dauphine Street and hear the tourists one block over on Bourbon. But the revelers and the jazz didn't matter. Brigitte had eyes only for the gentleman who had forced his way into her apartment. "Used to be that I owned this place."

"You don't now."

That didn't matter. She'd barred the door. Locked it. Even threatened to call the police. He simply walked right in through the door as if it hadn't been there.

His feet barely touched the ground.

Sure, he dressed the part of a proper gentleman, with his coat and cane and hat, but that didn't excuse certain facts.

He went upstairs to her bedroom, where she had, two minutes ago, been reading a lovely little conjuring book, and to the window looking down on the street.

He looked outside and nodded. "Quick, woman," he said, "I need to know the date." When she didn't immediately answer—she was shocked at the language, the pertinence, the attitude—he turned on her and demanded, "Today's date."

She didn't know what else to do. She told him.

"A parade date," he said, as if that made any sense. He nodded again, then turned his attention to the window. "Have you lived here long?"

"I should call the police," she said, brandishing her mobile phone like a threat. He seemed not to notice or care. She said, "Three months."

"You're new, then," he said. "You'll get used to me."

"I will not."

He shook his head, but still looked outside. "You don't have a choice. You can call for the authorities, but they'll never find me."

"Oh, I can do more than that."

"You might have access to a revolver," he said, "but I suggest you try something simpler first. A knife. A fist. They'll all be useless to you."

"Who are you?" she asked.

"Call me Cézar."

"You lie."

"I didn't answer your question," he admitted, "but gave you a name to use. I am only here to observe."

"To observe what?" she asked. "Me?"

"Oh, my, no," the man calling himself Cézar said. "I am far more interested in the parade."

"What parade?"

"Look."

Outside the window, in the streets, there was indeed a parade, the kind that had likely not been seen on these streets in a hundred years. A group of polka dotted clowns, giant heads that looked like they might be papier-mâché, colorful outfits, children running between the legs of stilt-walkers, masks everywhere, women in costumes that might still be considered risqué, men in fancy threads, musicians with trumpets and sousaphones, baton twirlers, priestesses and houngan, maybe even some actual minor deities.

Brigitte stepped away from the window clutching at her chest in awe and shock and maybe terror. "That wasn't real."

"It was, once," Cézar said, turning to face her. They were mere inches apart now. She had dropped her guard, and he'd gotten close enough to invade her personal space. He lowered his voice as if attempting to seduce her. "I slept in this very room," he said, "in a bed not unlike yours, though I daresay mine was a bit more...stylized."

She gave him half a grin. "Are you criticizing my taste?"

"No, no of course not," he said. "I'm merely admiring our differences. You and I. We are not so alike as one might hope."

"Why are you here?"

"I never miss the parade."

"Why are you here?" she asked again.

He averted his eyes. "I never wanted to leave."

"Why are you *here*?"

"Because this is the place to which I am bound," Cézar said. "And this is the only place I can visit, here and the grave where my dear Marie lies buried, God rest her soul, awaiting me in eternity."

Brigitte gaped. "Marie Leveau?"

"Oh, my, no," Cézar said. "She died before I was born."

Brigitte crossed her arms over her chest. "Tell me about your Marie."

"She was an absolute vision," he said, the focus of his eyes drifting away. "Hair black as the night, skin smooth as silk, the most delicious lips—and the things she could say, the things she knew, would make learnèd men dizzy. She communed with spirits, with guides, with the *orisha* and the saints. She knew things no one should ever have known. And yet she loved *me*, me of all people, with my history, with my past, with the sins stained upon my soul."

His gaze snapped back to the present. He looked straight at Brigitte with eyes that, briefly, she thought might be smoldering—as if he did, indeed, intend to seduce her—but she realized were actually incinerating. She caught a breath in her throat but did not step back. "They buried her outside the cemetery. Unmarked. Not on sacred ground, they said, even then, despite all she did for them."

"Where is she now?"

"Wandering."

"Like you?"

"Not like me," he said. "I keep waiting for her to return to the parade, to the place where I met her, where I first gave her a rose and learned her name, where I first stole a kiss from her lips."

"Marie," Brigitte said.

"Yes."

"Marie," Brigitte said again.

He loomed, growing larger and more foreboding, as if taking up all the space in the room. His voice dropped a full octave. "What do you mean by this?"

Once more, Brigitte said, "Marie."

And the woman, the wandering ghost of the woman, appeared on the balcony. She peered in and knocked on the glass door. She was, as Cézar had said, a vision, possibly the most beautiful woman Brigitte had ever seen, a rival to Gypsy Lee Rose even in the way she wore her hair.

"*Mon amour, mon coeur, mon âme,*" he said, going to the door and holding up his hand on the other side of the glass from hers.

"Open it," Brigitte said.

He couldn't. Of course not. He was insubstantial. Instead, his hand slipped through the glass to touch Marie's hand. Briefly, there was a glow where they touched, and the sound of a jazz piano drifted up from elsewhere on Dauphine Street, and then they were gone.

The silence that followed was thick.

Brigitte stood a moment, looking down on the parade as it faded from view, then sat in her chair beside her lovely little conjuring book, and poured a triple bourbon neat. She barely even tasted it.

Thusly fortified, she went back to her book.

The Museum of Curiosities

ONE COIN, ONE SHOW

It's not a carnival, merely the echoing remains of an amusement park. And even that's too big a concept. It's an old boardwalk, all splinters, nails popping up, and broken boards. There were more rides, once upon a time, but now only the three, and they haven't moved in decades. Ocean mist drifts through the iron skeletons. A few of the old buildings still stand: an empty haunt, a monkey house, the game where you shot water into the clowns' faces and blew up balloons. Only one of the clowns remains. The salt and sun have drained it all of color. The once vibrant reds and yellows and blues are now all dirty shades of white.

It's not a real town, not anymore. It's not a city or a truck stop or anything but a vestige of memory on the side of a New Jersey highway. There must have been postcards, pictures of happy children, balloons and cotton candy and caramel popcorn. If not for the ocean wafting in and out, those scents would linger.

As it is, there's no living memory of this place. No one alive rode an elephant here. It shouldn't be that old, but it is. There hasn't been a highway—and certainly not the Parkway—coming close to this place since happy little families piled into Studebakers to head down the shore.

Yet, when Jackie pulls off the highway on her way from Florida to New York, when she stops in search of food and fuel, she ends up in the empty, abandoned, overgrown lot outside the big glass window of a place whose name has long since faded. She gets out of the car, because this is where the GPS led her, stares at the structure that stands only by sheer inertia, and peers through the dirty, salt-encrusted windows as if there might be something to see inside.

It shouldn't take long to just leave, but Jackie's been on the road almost twenty hours these past two days. She spent the night at a frightful motel in South Carolina that smelled of things best not considered. It's near twilight, and she doesn't relish the idea of hitting the Verrazano in the dark. Another time of year, the days might be longer, the sun might shine more forcefully, she might even want to kick off her shoes and walk through the beach, but that's not going to happen now.

The twilight is stark and quick. She takes a few pictures on her phone. She locks the car and wanders about, shooting the baby Ferris wheel, the carousel occupied now by only three decayed horses, the dark and darkening Atlantic. She tries to post them, but there's no signal.

On the boardwalk, the hundred or so yards of boardwalk that have persisted, she finds a gold token that has somehow survived decades of nor'easters, hurricanes, and rising tides. There's a magician or a devil on the front of it, bent at the waist in an exaggerated bow, the word *Mystik* misspelled on the back, under the words *One Entry*.

Jackie flips it. Palms it. Rolls it over her knuckles. It's got some weight to it, like a real coin instead of a token, like a coin from the days when they were made with silver and had value.

That's when she notices the light.

The rest of the place is dark. It's probably not safe. Any purely sane person would have gotten out of there already. Besides the safety concerns posed by the architecture, this is prime real estate for junkies and rapists and murderers.

But the lights glow around one door. Neon lights. Flashing neon lights. It's not much, not really, but the sign says *Magic*, and Jackie's always been a sucker for a magic show. There can't be anyone here, not anyone performing any real tricks, not even a huckster. But there really shouldn't be any electricity, either, and the letters on that sign are flashing. They're all out of synch, seemingly going at random. But they are going, and their ozone odor rises above the smell of salt and rotting wood. The sign sizzles like at a 1970s diner every time the letters light up.

She pockets the coin. She walks to the door of the magic show. The last vestige of a forgotten age? Or something else entirely? She tries the door, but that's as far as she plans to go. There might be anyone on the inside. But it seems a strange place for a trap. How many people come to this park when the highway obviously usually leads elsewhere most days?

Inside, there's a stool on a stage. There's a man on the stool, but he might not be a man at all. He looks like an automaton. His limbs are hinged at the elbows, the knees, the wrists. His expression is a porcelain mask. His colors, however, remain vibrant. The ocean air doesn't get in here much. There's counter space, like a bar top, alongside the stage. Behind it, there are a half dozen old boxes of magic tricks for sale, a top hat, and some wands. On the counter, there's a coin mechanism like what might operate a gumball machine. The sign says *One Entry, One Show!*

Jackie tries a quarter, but the machine won't take it. Obviously. It wants the magic coin she'd found outside. She considers the possibilities. It might bring the automaton magician to life. She might see a show. Or the gears might have rusted over time, and it might struggle to move until it breaks. If she puts the coin in, she won't get it back, and she really like the idea of keeping the souvenir. If she inserts the coin and turns that crank, a band might erupt from the shadows, or a murderer with a machete, or a demon from one of the shallowest levels of hell.

Jackie realizes she's already been stupider than she usually is. She keeps the coin in her pocket, winks at the automaton, and says, "Maybe next time, sugar."

The automaton's head seems to twist. It should be just a trick of the shadows, but Jackie knows better. Its mouth moves on hinges that squeak. It says, in its own mechanical voice, "Maybe next time, sugar."

She's not an idiot. She never goes anywhere unarmed. Before the echoes of the words have faded, she draws and shoots. She hits the automaton between the eyes. Blows a hole out of its plastic head. The mouth sags like a frown. "Maybe," it says, more slowly this time, "next time, sugarrrrr..." The last word drones on for a bit, struggling to escape. Jackie keeps her souvenir coin, walks up the boardwalk back to her car, and leaves. If she wants another motel, she can drive on to Seaside Heights. Hell, she can go back and try her luck in the casinos of Atlantic City. Or she can get to Brooklyn by midnight and consult a fortune teller she knows and find out what would have happened if she'd paid that coin.

the museum of curiosities

IN SEARCh OF SILENCE

He wanted a place to think.

Thinking was one of those things the world rarely permitted. There was too much noise, too much movement, and few places where you could really get away from all the other people. The slightest word, the whisper sound of a door opening, the distant hum of engines on the highway, the roar of lawn equipment, the incessant beeping of kitchen appliances—it was all a bit much.

He went into the backyard first, and tried the basement, and even arranged a system of pulleys so he could suspend himself from the ceiling in the attic, but none of that cut out the noise.

He drove to the beach. In addition to the people, the seagulls refused to leave him alone, and the ocean drove relentlessly against the shore. It was calming, true, but hardly conducive to thought, unless you wanted to focus on mermaids and dolphins.

He bought a national parks pass and went into the mountains, but he couldn't find a place to sit that wouldn't be interrupted by some random family from who knew where with their kids prancing recklessly about. He saved one from a two hundred foot drop that would've ended with the kid impaled on the tops of pine trees. Despite feeling briefly like a hero, he couldn't make any headway within his head.

Thoughts, good and important thoughts, deep and powerful thoughts, rampaged in the furthest recesses of his mind, but he couldn't reach them. He needed someplace quieter. He looked to the sky, to the stars, to the vast expanse of outer space, and briefly considered all it would take to become one of those most rarified of people: an astronaut. But then there would be constant interruptions from Houston demanding telemetry and observations, and they wouldn't let him go up in a capsule on his own, would they?

Submarines had that same problem: the rest of the crew barking commands, running to and fro, achieving whatever achievements they'd set their minds on. How were you supposed to get time for thinking in such a busy, crowded, confined space as that?

No, he had to consider something more extreme.

A tour of caverns wouldn't work, because there'd always be someone behind him pushing to go farther further faster. A sensory deprivation tank might provide some alone time, but only in short intervals and not without external supervision. No wall in any building would be sufficient to drown out all the sounds of the outside.

So he did the only thing left to him: he dug a hole.

He bought a property in the middle of nowhere, hoping that would be sufficient, and for a while tried to sit on a tree stump and let his mind wander. He even tried an assortment of chemical and organic aides. But no, he had to dig.

He hired a company to dig the well. It seemed the best way. Straight down, deep, but not so deep it actually reached the aquifer. "I don't want water," he told the foreman, who only shook his head and accepted the check.

The well was three feet in diameter, its walls made with natural native materials, the floor rough but comfortable enough. He had them install a ladder. Before the machinery had even been pulled far enough away that he couldn't hear them anymore, he descended into the well.

It was a long climb, but not arduous. Every rung of that ladder brought him to someplace cooler, damper, and more isolated. The quiet buzzed in his head. The silence covered him.

He sat at the bottom of the well, adjusted himself to be more comfortable, pressed his back against the wall, and looked up at the stars—in the middle of the day, no less!—the stars in the sky through the hole at the top of his well. He closed his eyes, listening to the silence, the lack of any noise, the rush of wind only in his ears, the whisperings rising from the chasms inside his mind.

He didn't say anything. He didn't want to interrupt. He listened to the ghosts who had imbedded themselves within him, their complaints, their fears, their hopes for the future. Strange to think that a ghost had hopes for the future, but a few certainly believed they'd have an opportunity to return, to come back maybe as a rock star, an actress, a CEO, a hiker through the Himalayas who didn't have to answer to the demands of modern living.

He listened to the voices, the lost children, the cries of the inconsolable.

In the silence of the well, this hole in the world he'd built, the voices conferred, discussed, and posited. They consulted each other about a great many things that wouldn't matter anymore when he ascended to the real world again. They argued, they jostled, they agreed and disagreed.

Hours or days passed. When he drank the last of his supply of water, he sighed thoroughly, but he didn't move. That single sound, however, was enough to still a great many of the voices, too many of them, so that the silence—something he'd never been graced with before—seemed overwhelming, like the sounds of jet engines on an international runway, like a metal band in Copenhagen, like the demolition of entire cities in an instant.

From that resounding silence rose a single voice, deep and distorted by an imaginary reverb. It was commanding and demanding, and it brought all the other voices in line like legions of soldiers about to be sent to sack an unsuspecting enemy. It was a devil, maybe the devil, at least one of them, and it was the devil who long ago, in an age before humanity had scarred the surface of the earth, been assigned to torment a single man. To drive that man to collect ghosts, to seek unattainable silences, to dig deep into the earth and hide in a well far from civilization.

A moment later, the devil inside him realized there were no competing voices and fell silent. Too late. He grabbed the devil by the throat, thrashed the beast, smashed its head against the hard side of the well until it was broken and bloody, until the devil was dead and the ghosts released and silence—a real, honest, blessed silence—enveloped him.

He remained in the well with the corpse of his devil a long time, until the buzz of tinnitus drove him to seek any external sounds to drown that out.

On the surface, he called the company again and had them return to fill the well. He said it had served its purpose. The foreman didn't know what he meant and didn't care, and was again happy just to deposit the check.

Then he bought a ticket for Copenhagen. There was a metal band there in need of a bassist. He had, after all, developed some skills in his quest for silence. His own private, personal thoughts and ruminations would return over time.

ChE MUSEUM OF CURIOSITIES

BOTTLE CAP POP

The crew on this ship works all day and doesn't spare a thought for me. At meals, half of them don't speak English, so we play cards for bottle caps and count the days. I've got two thousand and nineteen so far.

I gotta tell you about Carmen before I tell you anything else. She was whip sharp, smart, and fast. She could match wits with the best of us and come out on top every time. She was cool, like winter, and her eyes just as blue. I was her guy and she was my girl, as much as we could claim on this ship, and I miss her.

Carmen, she was a light in these caverns, even more than the cargo room with its shaft of sunlight cutting through the hole in the ceiling. I've been in there, basking in the sun, straining to hear sounds of the ocean. There are times, especially below decks—and I'm always below decks—I can't even hear the engines. If I close my eyes and hold my breath and lean against the metal walls, I don't feel the vibrations I think I should feel, but I ain't never been a seafaring man so I could be wrong. Can't count on my clarity. The long corridors, the same on every deck, can confound a guy.

So we play cards, old faded cards with blank backs, the ink all worn off by the oil of our fingers and the environment. The red cards are as gray as the black, the clubs and diamonds barely visible, and a good number of the cards are simply gone. A guy I knew once, seems like ages ago, he took a king of clubs, thinking it might protect him. Protect you from what, I asked, but he never did say. I don't think he knew. But he needed protection, and that king wasn't enough to do the job, so he's dead now and the card is vanished. I asked the old man about that once. The old man looked at me and sucked on his pipe and said something about Cairo and Casablanca and Cancun, and he got that look in his eye like a man who isn't with you anymore and there ain't no telling when he'll come back. Every time I ask about the cards, it's *I remember Kentucky*, it's *storms in Cayo Coco*, it's *I knew a beauty in Bora Bora, you should've seen her lips, God I miss Columbia*. The old man, he'll tell you something important, when the mood strikes, that's what I've heard, but he ain't never got no wisdom for me.

We call it Poker because why not? It's an easy word, even if you speak Cantonese or Basque. We draw a card and ante up a cap, sometimes only a Coca-Cola, those are common enough, but sometimes the stakes get high and you'll see Nehi grape and you'll have to back out unless you've got something worth the risk. I traded one of them once for an hour in the cargo hold. I thought the sun would crack my skin, thought I'd be red like cherry cola when I got out, but I guess an hour don't much matter and I stayed as pale as any of the other ghosts below decks.

The guard that day looked at me and asked who I killed to get me one of them, and I told him I was holding on to something special, a Nesbitt's Root Beer, but he grinned and knew I was lying and told me not to waste my time. I took as much as I could and bathed in that sunlight and it was wonderful, I can tell you that.

There's a lot of ship to explore, and if you ain't careful you'll find someone's stash but they'll find you finding it, and that never ends well. I found an Imitation Orangeade one time just sitting on one of the crossbeams, orange enough that it blended right in with the rust so I almost missed it. Another guy, a stringy guy with bloodshot eyes and not long for this ship, he said it was his and wanted to fight me and even made with the fists, but I'm quick and I ran and I never saw him again. It's a big ship.

Carmen used to take her Coca-Cola caps to the wishing well. It wasn't really a well, but that's what she called it. She had to muscle open the hatch. She would kiss the cap like she loved it and whisper secrets she wouldn't even tell me, then drop the cap and listen. It took a minute. Maybe not a whole minute, but time's a funny thing below decks and even worse when you're waiting for the cap to hit the bottom. Thing is, I never heard it. One time, I thought maybe I heard a splash, but I never believed it. It was in my mind. A sign of the crazy. That can happen down here, The crazy sneaks in and you're done. Happened to my friend Mickey. Mickey found the crazy. He gave me a Kist Cream Soda cap and said the ghosts had caught up to him and there was a stockpile, something spectacular, way deep underneath. Then he went hunting, and I never saw him again, but I heard he got out, he escaped, he earned himself an exit off this boat.

Carmen got off, too. She traded skin for an Old Colony Black Cherry Soda. She told me she drank the drink, then tossed the bottle into the wishing well, and planned to go straight to one of the guards and say she'd bought herself a disembarkment. She said she didn't know if she'd ever be able to kiss another man again, but then she kissed me, and I tasted the Black Cherry, and that was the last time I saw her. One of the guards let her into the big hatch.

The guards are nasty pieces of work. Best to avoid them. I don't know where they come from or go to, I don't know why they control the cargo hold, I don't know what they do with their bottle cap collections, but we all gotta pay when the guardsman calls. They keep the hatch and take whatever they care to take.

I'd told that one I had a special cap. He thought I was lying, but it was mostly true. Mickey's Kist Cream, I'll keep it forever, it's all I've got of anyone so I believe it holds a piece of everyone I ever knew or loved or fought or played cards with. I don't really mean forever, I mean as long as I've got to stay below decks. I don't know what it'll take to get topside. The guard I asked, that one time, only that one time, he damn near beat me to snot, and then he confiscated my caps, all my RC Colas and my Root Beer Crush. I'd been saving that. They don't turn up all that frequently.

All of us, we go spelunking sometimes, down into the darker decks, where there ain't no lights except what you bring, because down there you'll find Orange Cream and Tab and Bubble Up and who knows what else. The rare ones, you trade them for favors—I ain't ashamed to admit I traded a Nehi Red for some affection one night. It gets lonely, since Carmen got out, and sometimes you need someone else's flesh to cry on. She was real nice, too, real understanding, but I can't recall her name. She was no Carmen.

So I was down in the lower decks this one time and I found a stash, a dozen caps in a matchbox. It's all 7-Up and Pink Lemonade, but one's a Lucky Lime Rickey, I swear on my life it was, and I'm thinking this is my ticket out of here. But as I ascend, I'm thinking I need to be better armed, I need to make a play for more, so I hit the poker table and for my first card, a three of hearts, I lay down one of those yellow Lithiated Lemon Sodas to tell them I mean it, I'm betting big, I'm in for the big take. I drop a Dr. Pepper for another card, a second three of hearts, and I'm thinking the card gods are with me and I can't lose. Third and last card, I show my Rickey, and half the table's got to fold. But then I pull a three of cherries.

Oh, it got ugly. I accused the dealer of cheating. Palming cards. Stacking the deck. The table got overturned in the midst of this, so someone stole away with my Rickey and I stayed stuck below decks. I was right, of course. The cards were crooked. I always knew they were, but the dealers, when they do it, they do it so you win just enough to think maybe not, maybe it's all really just a game of chance, but there ain't no such thing down here.

After that, I have to hide, and I'm not welcome to the card table anymore, so I have to find my caps or steal them if I want to buy any more favors. The old man, he tells me this is how it is, there's always a shark in the waters, but then he's back to the Tortugas. He still smells the salt, he says. We're at sea, I says, but he just looks at me and we both know he ain't seeing me anymore.

Carmen, she told me once, she says love is like a tidal wave hitting the shore, but she won't tell me what she means. I gave her an A&W Root Beer once for no reason at all. She tells me she'll cherish it, that she'll always remember me, that she wishes for dreams and moonlight and butterflies. I can't remember what butterflies are supposed to look like. Orange like Crush, like Sunkist? Blue like Strawberry Squeeze? I saw a cap once, it was somebody else's, I didn't have a shank to take it, with a moon on its underside, a quarter moon with eyes and a nose and a mouth, and I don't think I've ever seen one rarer than that.

And now I find a thing I didn't think existed, a case, a six pack really, a cardboard six pack with five empty bottles and no caps, but one dusty old bottle full of liquid gold. It sits in the middle of the floor in a room way below decks, amidst Mickey's treasures. I still got his Kist Cream hidden deep in my cabin, not with my stack of caps but alone and by itself and in a place I hope no one will look because I don't care if they steal my Pepsi, but I couldn't cope with losing everyone and everything. But here, even rarer, and still doing its job, is an Old Colony Creme de Cocoa, something I ain't never even heard whisper about.

No time for dealers this time, no cards, no risk, this is my token off this damn ship. I go to my cabin first. It's been ransacked. Happens from time to time. They took my stash, the caps that don't matter to me no more, because on the islands you don't need bottle caps, you drink straight out of the coconuts, you swim with eels and octopuses and rays, you've got rum in a hundred flavors, more flavors than there are fizzy drinks. No mere Mr. Cola is gonna get you there. Mickey's Kist Cream is safe, or was safe, because I take it and hit the corridors and seek out Carmen's wishing well. When I get there, I tell her I'm on my way, I'll find her again, there's no more days for me to count below decks. I'm aiming for sunlight and ocean and island and love and everything it comes with. I kiss the Kist Cream cap just like Carmen kissing her

Coca-Cola, and I close my eyes and make a wish shaped like Carmen, and I drop the cap into the hatch. I listen, and it land in a pile of wishes.

Then I find a guard, not the one at the cargo hold with that thin shaft of sunlight, and I show him the unopened bottle and say it's time for me to get off this ship. The guard shakes his head and smiles and says something about pity. He radios to someone, but I've never been able to understand voices over those things, and the hatch—the big hatch, the one that swallows the guards and regurgitates them and that no one else has ever been beyond except those who have already escaped—the big hatch opens and the guard gestures me through.

One of the other guards calls to me as I leave. He says I ought to head west, that's my best chance, to follow the setting sun, and I want to thank him but I'm too excited. This corridor looks like all the others, but there's stairs going up, up higher than any stairs I remember, above decks, and I can already feel the sunshine and the wind. I forgot all about wind, didn't remember such a thing even existed, wind caressing my back under the big blue sky, bluer than Nehi Grape Soda, blue like Pepsi-Cola, so much blue I can't see anything else until finally I do.

The desert. Stark, scorched sand stretches to the horizon, where it kisses the blue sky, and I can't remember any horizon looking so barren or so wonderful. Now I know why I never feel the engines.

There's a steel ladder bolted haphazardly to the side of the ship. It doesn't stretch all the way down to the sand, so I've got to jump and that makes it a one-way journey. I follow the sun west like a young man. I walk until the sun disappears, and I walk again when the sun rises behind me, and repeat until I find Carmen.

She's all bones now, blanched clean by the sun. I know it's her because I recognize the shape of her, because I made a wish, and because she's still clutching that Old Colony Black Cherry Soda bottle cap in her bony fingers and I can still taste traces of it on her lips.

There ain't nobody else about. I'm alone in the desert, no guards, no crew, not even the ghost of Carmen on my shoulder, so I sit and crack into my bottle of Old Colony Creme de Cocoa. I mean, I pop that bottle cap and take a good whiff of what's inside, and it smells fresh and clean like the white sands of an island paradise. I take a swig. It's disgusting, terrible and flat, separated into parts, and tortured by decades, but it tastes like freedom and I drink every last drop.

Acknowledgments

It's impossible to thank everyone who should be. This collection of stories spans decades, but the majority of them were first published on my Patreon account: so thank you to everyone who has supported and continues to support me there.

First and most importantly, I must thank Morgan for being the kind of friend I needed when I most needed one, for walking (and dancing) with me through the darkness, and without whom none of this would have been possible.

The following people have definitely helped along the way: The Four Horsemen (Brian, Coop, Mike, and Mikey), Mary, Gina, Momo, my Mom, Jeneine, Linda, Jezzy, Becky, Lindsey, Karen, Jane, Ahsley, Martel, Tina, Jenna, Sean (and all the Madrid Writer's Club), Kristen, Rich, Brent, Henry, Jay, Veenu, Jackie, Eygló, Deena and Dave, everyone who hosted me during my cross-country drive, Ana, Cristina, all my various translators, and countless others who have provided refuge, friendship, first reads, and sounding boards. You're invaluable to me, and a greater treasure than has ever been housed in a museum.

As always, a special thanks to Sabine and the Rose Fairy.

John Urbancik has visited museums in New York, Sydney, Madrid, Paris, Richmond, Los Angeles, Orlando, Pittsburgh, and a hundred other places. Some museums are huge and beyond comprehension, while others were small enough to fit in a single room. Museums dedicated to art, natural history, whaling, cars, clowns, artists, and writers. Public and private collections. He keeps his own Museum of Curiosities.

In addition to books of poetry and a nonfiction book based on his podcast *Inkstains*, Urbancik (pronounced Urban as in City, Sick as in Puppy) has written books like the *DarkWalker* series, *Stale Reality* (also available in Russian), *Choose Your Doom*, and *The Night Carnival*.

Born on a small island in the northeast United States called Manhattan, he is currently sequestered in an undisclosed location in the woods of Pennsylvania near the Susquehanna River.

ALSO BY JOHN URBANCIK

NOVELS
Sins of Blood and Stone
Breath of the Moon
Once Upon a Time in Midnight
Stale Reality
The Corpse and the Girl from Miami
DarkWalker 1: Hunting Grounds
DarkWalker 2: Inferno
DarkWalker 3: The Deep City
DarkWalker 4: Armageddon
DarkWalker 5: Ghost Stories
DarkWalker 6: Other Realms

NOVELLAS
A Game of Colors
The Rise and Fall of Babylon (with Brian Keene)
Wings of the Butterfly
House of Shadow and Ash
Necropolis
Quicksilver
Beneath Midnight
Zombies vs. Aliens vs. Robots vs. Cowboys vs.
Ninja vs. Investment Bankers vs. Green Berets
Colette and the Tiger
The Night Carnival

COLLECTIONS
Shadows, Legends & Secrets
Sound and Vision
Tales of the Fantastic and the Phantasmagoric

POETRY
John the Revelator
Odyssey

NONFICTION
InkStained: On Creativity, Writing, and Art

INKSTAINS
Multiple volumes

www.ingramcontent.com/pod-product-compliance
Lightning Source LLC
Chambersburg PA
CBHW052032240626
47153CB00006B/2042